the Vampire Slayer™

S+AKE Y⊕UR DES+INY

NIGHT TERRORS

Buffy the Vampire Slayer™

Buffy the Vampire Slayer
(movie tie-in)
The Harvest
Halloween Rain
Coyote Moon
Night of the Living Rerun
Blooded
Visitors
Unnatural Selection
The Power of Persuasion
Deep Water
Here Be Monsters
Ghoul Trouble
Doomsday Deck
Sweet Sixteen
Crossings
Little Things

The Angel Chronicles, Vol. 1
The Angel Chronicles, Vol. 2
The Angel Chronicles, Vol. 3
The Xander Years, Vol. 1
The Xander Years, Vol. 2
The Willow Files, Vol. 1
The Willow Files, Vol. 2
How I Survived My Summer Vacation,
Vol. 1
The Cordelia Collection, Vol. 1
The Faith Trials, Vol. 1
The Journals of Rupert Giles, Vol. 1
Tales of the Slayer, Vol. 1
Tales of the Slayer, Vol. 2
Tales of the Slayer, Vol. 3
Tales of the Slayer, Vol. 4

The Postcards
The Essential Angel Posterbook
The Sunnydale High Yearbook
Pop Quiz: Buffy the Vampire Slayer
The Monster Book
The Script Book, Season One, Vol. 1
The Script Book, Season One, Vol. 2
The Script Book, Season Two, Vol. 1
The Script Book, Season Two, Vol. 2
The Script Book, Season Two, Vol. 3
The Script Book, Season Two, Vol. 4
The Script Book, Season Three, Vol. 1
The Script Book, Season Three, Vol. 2
The Musical Script Book: Once More, With Feeling
The Watcher's Guide, Vol. 1: The Official Companion to the Hit Show
The Watcher's Guide, Vol. 2: The Official Companion to the Hit Show
The Watcher's Guide, Vol. 3: The Official Companion to the Hit Show

The Lost Slayer serial novel
Part 1: Prophecies
Part 2: Dark Times
Part 3: King of the Dead
Part 4: Original Sins
Omnibus Edition

Child of the Hunt
Return to Chaos
The Gatekeeper Trilogy
Book 1: Out of the Madhouse
Book 2: Ghost Roads
Book 3: Sons of Entropy
Obsidian Fate
Immortal
Sins of the Father
Resurrecting Ravana
Prime Evil
The Evil That Men Do
Paleo
Spike and Dru: Pretty Maids
All in a Row
Revenant
The Book of Fours
Tempted Champions
Oz: Into the Wild
The Wisdom of War
These Our Actors
Blood and Fog
Chosen
Chaos Bleeds
Mortal Fear
Apocalypse Memories
Wicked Willow Trilogy
The Darkening
Shattered Twilight
Broken Sunrise
Stake Your Destiny
The Suicide King
Keep Me in Mind
Colony
Night Terrors
Queen of the Slayers
Spark and Burn

Available from POCKET BOOKS

STAKE YOUR DESTINY

NIGHT TERRORS

Alice Henderson

**An original novel based on the hit television series
created by Joss Whedon**

POCKET
BOOKS

LONDON • SYDNEY • NEW YORK • TORONTO

POCKET BOOKS
An imprint of Simon & Schuster Ltd
Africa House, 64-78 Kingsway, London WC2B 6AH
™ & © 2005 Twentieth Century Fox Film Corporation. All rights reserved.
All rights reserved, including the right of reproduction in whole or in part in any form.
POCKET BOOKS and related logo are
trademarks of Simon & Schuster, Ltd.
Printed and bound in Great Britain
First Edition 10 9 8 7 6 5 4 3 2 1
A CIP catalogue record for this book is available from the British Library
ISBN: 1-4165-1146-6

Acknowledgments

My deepest thanks to my fantastic editor, Patrick Price, for giving me this opportunity to contribute to the Buffyverse and being wonderful to work with; thanks to Debbie Olshan at Fox, Joss Whedon, and all the talented writers, cast, and crew who have brought Buffy to life on the page and screen, and my most grateful thanks to Norma and Jason for their endless encouragement.

Buffy
the vampire slayer™

STAKE YOUR DESTINY

NIGHT TERRORS

Prologue

You can't believe your mother signed you up for this. How does she talk you into these things? As hordes of squealing, crying, shouting voices swell around you into a cacophony of near hysteria, you vow that this is the last fashion show you'll ever agree to do. Even if it *is* for charity. You breathe in deeply and relent, concentrating on the children's home this will benefit. But even that doesn't completely detract from the sheer bunchy discomfort of the ridiculously poofy blue dress you're in. If it were any bigger, Dorothy could have used this very dress as a balloon and flown home without needing to find the wizard at all. You try to shift it around on your shoulders, but its stiffness and the utter volume make you feel like you're contending with a punching bag on each shoulder.

Here, behind the large stage at the mall, a frenzied mass of Sunnydale High students dash chaotically around you, donning dresses and suits, attempting to tie bow ties and affix silver lamé bustles and strange scarflike accoutrements. New York designers donated the clothes to this cause, but since the designers themselves did not attend the benefit, no one had any idea how to actually *wear* the avant-garde clothing. Case in point, you see Simone, a friend of Cordelia's, struggling in one corner with a sash that could be worn on either the head or the hips. She sets it down forlornly and slumps into a chair.

Your best friend, Willow, approaches you shyly, wearing a slinky yellow evening dress over a purple long-sleeved cotton shirt. The shirt's teddy bear design peeks out coyly from under the dress's neckline.

"Will," you say, "I don't think you're supposed to wear the dress over your regular clothes."

"But," she says, in a conspiratorial whisper, "it's all spaghetti strappy. I can't wear spaghetti strappy."

"Sure you can," you say encouragingly, attempting to place a comforting hand on her shoulder. Instead the puffy blue sleeve locks your arm to your side like a medieval torture device. With no peripheral vision and restricted mobility, you hope no vamps come looking for tasty morsels tonight. Just in case, earlier you slipped a stake into the waistband of the dress. It's not like anyone will see it amongst all that fabric.

Willow grasps at her shoulders self-consciously and looks around. A sudden voice to your right startles you, making you jump. You hadn't seen Cordelia walk up. In fact, in this dress you wouldn't see a charging rhino approach.

Draped in a scarlet evening gown, she looks perfectly stunning. How come she gets the cool dress? "Willow," Cordelia quips in a snide tone, "only you could make a twelve-hundred-dollar designer dress look like the latest in fall fashion for the nerd squad."

As Willow's face falls, you see Xander making his way through the masses, looking quite sharp in a black tuxedo and gray vest. "Xander!" you call, wanting to distract Willow from Cordy's scathing words. He spots you over the heads of several students puzzling over their attire and glides around them.

"Whoa, Buffy, you in there somewhere?" Xander asks, leaning to the side to spy you through the two puffy sleeves.

"I think so," you respond. "Either that, or I've been transported into a world consisting purely of taffeta." You pause, taking in his tux. He looks great. This is beginning to be very unfair. "Looking good, Xander."

He gives you a suave smile. "That's Harris. Xander Harris."

Cordy cuts in. "More like Dork, Unbelievable Dork."

He glares at her.

"Anyway," Cordelia goes on. "I'm not over here to

actually talk with you guys. I came to tell Buffy that something's up with Simone."

You look over at Simone, who still sits in one corner dejectedly. She turns in the chair to face a mirror and begins haphazardly applying makeup. You've definitely noticed that she's let herself go in the last couple of weeks. As she applies foundation, you know that no amount will ever cover the deep gray circles under her eyes, or even conceal the unhealthy, grayish tint of her skin. You've seen her dragging through the halls at school, barely awake.

"She has seemed really tired lately," you comment.

"Not that," Cordy says. "I mean she's been acting really weird. And I know that weird is your thing."

You blow off the insult and ask, "How weird?"

"Well, just now? She didn't know who Michael Garavelli was."

Xander puts a hand to his head in mock panic. "No! It can't be! Call the newspapers! Get her to the hospital!"

You've never heard of the name before either.

"Is he a student?" asks Willow.

Cordy rolls her eyes. "Well, I wouldn't expect dweebs like you to know who he is. But he happens to be the hottest clothing designer in Milan right now. Everybody knows who he is. Everybody with taste anyway," she sneers pointedly, taking in your tremendous sleeves and Willow's shirt bunched under her dress.

"I feel so ashamed at my ignorance," Xander laments.

"Anyway, Michael Garavelli has always been Simone's favorite designer. In fact, I let her be my friend because she knew who he was and even owned one of his designs."

"And I bet she's been ruing the day ever since," Xander says.

"Shut up, Harris. I'm trying to get a point across here." She turns toward you. "So just now, I was talking with her, and she didn't even know who he was! It's like she's not even herself."

Glancing back at the makeup table, you watch as Simone ineptly applies eye shadow to her sunken, dark eyelids. Her hair looks like it hasn't been combed in days, and the dark circles under her eyes seem to have deepened even in the last few minutes. As you study her, she leans forward in the chair, her chest rising and falling rapidly, as if struggling for breath.

"Maybe she's just stressed out," Willow offers. "Maybe her mother doesn't take a personal interest in her life, and Simone's just expected to be this amazing superstudent, like she's sort of an academic genius or something. And it's always like, 'Hey we need to hack into the computer. She can do that,' or 'Hey, who wants to stay at the library and search through books for hours? She will.' Like she doesn't even need a social life."

"Uh, Will?" Xander asks. "Are we still talking about Simone here?"

"Sorry," Willow responds, cheeks burning red as she glances away.

Still studying Simone, you see that now she really

is leaning over, obviously unable to breathe well. Staggering, she rises to her feet and grips the wall. "Go get help," you tell the others as you squeeze your way through the crowd, heading quickly toward Simone.

Someone's elbow catches you in the back, and another person bumps into you while putting on a pair of shoes. You lose sight of Simone. When you finally reach the other end of the room, she is no longer standing by the wall. Glancing around, your eyes fall on a nearby maintenance corridor that leads away from the stage to the back part of the mall. Breaking through the edge of the crowd, you reach the open corridor entrance and look down the hall. At the end of the gray cinderblock corridor, you see Simone stumbling as if in a daze.

As quickly as you can manage in the stiff dress, you hurry down the hall. Simone reaches a T intersection and turns right. Just as you approach the intersection yourself, you hear heavy footsteps coming from the left.

You press against the wall around the corner as two men in jeans and black leather jackets dash by, unaware of your presence. Trailing Simone, their faces transform, browridges and cheekbones standing out against pallid skin. Vampires. You quickly follow them, hoping no one will see you dust them. A few hundred feet down, the corridor ends abruptly at a dented metal door.

Simone tries the knob, but it is locked. She turns around, still in an exhausted daze, and starts when the two vamps race up behind her. "Do you know where the bathroom is?" she asks reluctantly, her face contorting in fear.

"Well, well," one says in that overconfident, condescending tone vamps master the moment they crawl out of their graves. He straightens his eighties metal jacket, which sports a venom-dripping cobra affectionately squeezing a blue Camaro. "Looks like it's easy pickin's tonight."

"I'll say," the other one chimes in. His jacket features a fanged skull vomiting up an array of flaming electric guitars.

Simone's eyes fill with wild panic.

You've seen enough. As you prepare to fight, the dress once again pins your arms to your sides like the latest in evening boa constrictor fashion. Reaching down, you rip holes in the sleeve stitching along both sides of the bodice, allowing you welcome freedom of movement. Then you rip the skirt along both seams.

"I don't think your meal's as ready-to-eat as you thought," you say, announcing your presence.

Cobra Vamp spins quickly, right into your fist, which catches him in the throat. Coughing, he bends over, grabbing at his neck, and you smash into him with a knee to the face. Reeling back, he slams against the wall. His hunting buddy moves in, a much bigger vamp with a nose as crooked as the prom queen voting process.

You realize that you can't keep an eye on both with the ridiculous sleeves, which still bounce around, blocking your eyesight. Quickly you tear them off the dress, flinging them aside. Crooked Nose narrows in on you, a rank stench wafting out from him. He probably hasn't bathed in several years, if ever.

"Just because you're dead," you quip, "is no reason to completely let yourself go."

He grunts at the insult and tries to dive-tackle you, but you move deftly to one side. Off balance, he careens into the cinderblock wall.

Cobra Vamp shakes his head and comes at you for round two. Growling, with fingers flexing like claws, the vamp makes a grab for you, but you clench his wrist and bring an elbow up, snapping his arm audibly. As he reels from the pain, you whip the stake out from your waistband and drive it hard into his chest. With a sigh, dust billows up and rains on the floor.

Crooked Nose suddenly grabs you from behind, and you bend and throw him to the floor. He lands with a grunt, and in an instant you're on top of him, driving the stake into his chest. More dust blooms out around you, covering your already ruined dress.

You stand, brushing yourself off, and make your way to Simone. She stands shaking against the locked door, her eyes no longer showing terror, but instead a sort of gleaming triumph, her mouth spreading into a maniacal grin.

"Simone?" you ask, thrown off by the strange facial expression.

She wavers on her feet, then collapses to the floor in a cry of pain. Footsteps thunder in the corridor behind you, and you look over your shoulder, afraid you'll see more vamps. Instead, Xander and Willow appear at the T intersection with two paramedics. "Hurry!" you call to them.

Quickly you kneel down at Simone's side and grip her hand. "It's going to be okay," you tell her.

Her body writhes in pain, thrashing on the floor.

Then she suddenly falls still, fixing you with an intense gaze. "Slayer," she says in a coarse growl, "I'm coming for you next."

With a final convulsion, she falls into unconsciousness, blood trickling from her ear and mouth.

SLAYER ACTION:
Turn to page 10.

You're having the dream again, for the third night this week. It doesn't feel prophetic, just disturbing. Unusually disturbing, and it takes a lot to disturb you. Every time you dream it, you remember a little bit more. You're walking along the beach, sandals off, bare feet sinking into the warm sand. The sun dips low in the western sky, hanging above the horizon, huge and red. A wavering line of light gleams out over the vast stretch of waves, the ocean growing darker beneath the fading sun.

A warm breeze lifts your hair, and you raise your face to the sky. For a moment, you close your eyes, breathing in the fresh air.

But a dark feeling, like someone tailing behind you, makes you snap your eyes open and whirl around. Expecting to see an attacker, you find only empty beach behind you. In the distance, a few families pack up picnic baskets and large beach umbrellas. Two little girls chase a rainbow-colored inflatable ball in the shallows of the rolling surf, giggling and splashing each other.

You turn back, continuing to walk, trying to recapture the feeling of solace the beach often brings you. But as soon as you begin to drift away, listening to the cry of seagulls and the pleasant rolling thunder of the surf, the ominous feeling creeps up your spine, like fuzzy tarantula feet creeping delicately up your skin, and you spin around again, certain this time that you will find a creature lying in wait to attack you.

But you see only your footprints in the sand,

stretching far away, and the same families, now walking to their cars, and a lifeguard stand with a bored-looking lifeguard resting his chin on his hands and peering out over the waves.

You can no longer enjoy the sun's warmth or the soft feel of the sand under your bare feet. The feeling of being stalked grows too strong, and you just want to get off the beach and go home. Hurrying now, you turn away from the rolling water and start heading toward the parking lot and concession stands.

You've taken only a dozen or so steps when a searing pain erupts in your back, like burning claws raking down your spine. You spin, eyes wide, and see a thick, powerful shadow with raised reptilian wings bearing down on you. Though translucent, the shadow strikes with considerable force and weight, knocking you over on your back. You hit the sand hard, sinking into it, unable to wriggle free. The shadow draws ever nearer . . . a mouth opens to reveal rows of white fangs in the black . . .

You start awake suddenly, your heart racing. Eyes wide in the dark, you feel terror sweeping over your body, pure and blinding.

You're in your room, at home in Sunnydale.

But you are not alone in the room.

You can sense something there with you, malevolent and purposeful, though you don't see anything in the dark.

Panic builds inside you, and you try to leap up out of bed. But instead of sending the covers flying, you find you can't move at all. As the terror snakes into your throat, you feel every limb in your body heavy and paralyzed, unable to move or even flinch.

You sense the malevolent force moving in closer, feel its eyes on you, its evil intent. All of the air suddenly rushes out of your lungs as a terrible weight crushes down on your chest. You can't breathe.

As your lungs burn for air, you try to move your hand slightly, just a finger, and find it achingly difficult. As panic threatens to sweep over you, you feel your index finger move a few millimeters. You force it to move more, then your thumb.

Tears of effort stream down your unmoving face as you finally manage to curl all of your fingers into a fist.

You can't see the thing on top of you, and your mind has no time to wonder what it could be. Every ounce of concentration in you focuses on the movement of your hand, trying to raise your fist above the bed.

Slowly you feel your skin part with the sheets, cool night air rushing in under your hand, and your arm begins to lift up—

—and the pressure suddenly releases. Immediately you sense the departure of the terrible presence.

You sit up in bed, leaning over quickly to turn on the bedside lamp. Light floods the room, illuminating corners and dispelling shadows. Throwing covers aside, you leap up, as if staying in the bed might make the thing return.

Deeply drawing in sweet, welcome air, you search the room for any hint of a disturbance. Nothing looks remotely out of place.

What was that thing? you wonder, bringing your hand up to your chest where it had pressed down, nearly crushing you.

Finally catching your breath, you think of the sheer terror of the incident—unable to move, something evil in the room. It was one of the more unsettling experiences you've had, and you've had more unsettling experiences than a werewolf with a perpetual bad hair day.

Spooked, the last thing you want to do is lie down again, and with the hammering in your heart, it would be a long time before you could go to sleep anyway.

You glance at the digital clock next to your bed, which glows back 3:12 a.m.

If you got up now and changed, you could get in a couple of good hours of patrolling before sunrise. Hey, maybe you could even distract a few vamps long enough to use the sun itself as a weapon. Lead a whole nest of them outdoors to fight you where they'll be more sunny-side up than the two-dollar breakfast special at the Sunnydale Diner.

Or maybe you could swing by Angel's and see if he's home. He's always good for picking up talk on the street. Maybe your waking nightmare has terrified other people, too, and he knows about it.

As you think of changing into your clothes, your eyes fall on the textbooks sitting forlornly on your desk. *Western Civilization* sulks on top, not cracked open all week. You are several chapters behind on your reading. With your heart still slowing from the frightening experience, you wonder if you should stay in and catch up on your homework. You have a quiz on ancient Greece in two days that you are in no way prepared for. Even the SS *Minnow* was more prepared than you.

Either way, you can talk to Giles first thing at the school library and tell him about the nightmares.

SLAYER CHOICE:

Do you decide to . . .

❚ put aside sleep and homework to fulfill the duties of the Chosen One? *If yes, turn to page 15.*

❚ find Angel to see if he's heard of similar occurrences around town? *If yes, turn to page 20.*

❚ take advantage of this rare, still hour to catch up on your homework? *If yes, turn to page 24.*

Stealthily, careful not to make too much noise and wake your mother, you pull on jeans and a black, long-sleeved shirt. You can always change again before you go to school, saving your clothes that are more vamp-rippable for nonpatrolling activities.

After listening at the door, now positive your mother is still sleeping, you move to the window and open it. You climb out and in seconds are down on the soft grass below, heading toward the cemetery. It's always a good place to start. No hint of dawn has yet arrived in the east, but you know that you have only an hour for some vamp slayage before they all go crawling back to their crypts or sewers, or tuck themselves into their little vamp nests. So cozy. You smile at the thought of shattering that image, of preventing the bed-time snack of the undead.

As you walk down quiet streets, with only the distant murmur of cars on the more main roads, the gates of Sunnydale Cemetery rise into view. Not for the first time, you wonder why vamps always hang out in the cemetery. Do they ever go to their graves and stare down in wonder, or feel somehow lost? Then you remember how cruel the demons are inside vampire bodies, and how they only imitate humanity. They'd probably celebrate the scene of their body's grave.

A rustle from behind snaps you to the present moment. Two vamps, both dressed in hideous 1970s prom suits, complete with ruffled tuxedo shirts, stroll together about fifty feet away. The juxtaposition of the yellow and powder blue suits in the dark of the cemetery jars your fashion sense. You duck down behind a tomb-stone, hoping to move from monument to monument and surprise them.

"Who, Angelus?" Yellow Suit is saying.

Angelus? you wonder. *They're talking about Angel.* Shortly after you discovered that Angel was a vampire, Giles found Watcher journals that described Angel's violent past, when he went by the name Angelus.

"Yeah, what happened to that guy?" wonders Blue Suit. "Thought he was some badass from a long time ago."

"Long time ago is right. That guy ain't tasted human blood as long as I've been around, and that's more than thirty years."

Blue Suit nods. "It's like he's been defanged or something. I saw him the other day when I was hunting behind the Bronze, and he looked real tired."

"Maybe that jerk's finally going to keel over. He's been messing up our hunting ever since we came to this damn town."

"It's what he gets for not eatin' right," Blue Suit says in what you now place as a Southern accent. Georgia, maybe.

This guy came all the way from Georgia? you wonder. The Hellmouth, that seething portal of evil energy that lies beneath Sunnydale, never ceases to attract huge numbers of vampires and other things that go bump in the night. Or when you have your way, things that go ouch in the night.

You sneak to the next large tombstone, then to the

next, gripping the cool, rough stone with your fingers as you peer around the side at your quarry. Normally you'd just attack them outright, but tonight you want to conserve your strength. You've been really tired lately.

"Hey, that reminds me!" Blue Suit suddenly exclaims. "You see that thing slinking around over by Willie's the other night? What the hell was that?"

Yellow Suit nods emphatically. "If I was crazy, I'd say it was a mummy or something. One of them Egyptian ones."

Ooooh . . . they know their ancient cultures. You are almost upon them. Pulling a stake from your inside jacket pocket, you lunge forward, nailing Blue Suit right in the back. You push the stake in all the way, where it connects with his heart. Ash spirals up, pluming around you. Yellow Suit looks at you, afraid. He backs up slowly, bumping into a tall angel statue and clumsily stumbling to one side.

"Now there's no need to get all riled up like a gator. Just when I got all my finery on."

You lower your body, move forward, and throw a kick that knocks him off his feet. As he grabs for you, fangs bared, you leap on top of him and drive the stake in through all those shirt ruffles. The spray of ash rains upward, spilling over the grass and your jeans. You brush off, grateful that vamp clothes disappear simultaneously. You don't think you could take the sheer horror of having to slay those pastel tuxedos. They would have proved far too formidable enemies.

A sharp snap behind you causes you to whirl

around. Another vampire stands only feet from you, clad in a black leather coat, black shirt, and black jeans. You exhale in relief. You actually like this vamp. It's Angel.

"Hey," you say, playing it cool, though your heart refuses to do the same and starts pounding away nervously.

"Hey," Angel answers back.

You study his drawn face, the dark circles under his eyes. The vamps were right. He does look really tired.

"You're out late," he says.

"Early, actually."

"Couldn't sleep?"

"Bad dreams," you tell him.

You take a few steps closer to him, surreptitiously stealing a look around the cemetery to be sure no other vamps lurk nearby. Then you return your full attention to Angel.

"Portentous?" he asks, referring to your ability to have charming, prophetic dreams in which you usually witness the rise of evil new foes, or, if you're really lucky, the destructive end of the world.

"I'm not sure. Mostly they just felt like regular nightmares."

He raises his eyebrows. "Mine are still there when I wake up."

Your mouth falls open a little in surprise, but you quickly catch yourself and shut it. *Not too attractive, Buffy of the Hanging-Open Mouth,* you chide yourself.

You want flies with that? "You're kidding," you say. "They're not all unable to move, evil-thing-in-the-room, are they?"

His eyes widen in surprise. "Yeah. Exactly."

You've got to tell Giles about this. Happening to you is creepy, but happening to Angel, too, is more . . . well, you hope it's not an epidemic.

Over Angel's shoulder to the east, the sky is still deep black. But you know the sun will be rising within the hour. "You'd better get home," you tell him.

"Yeah." But instead he just stands there, then takes a step closer. He takes your hands, his skin cool on yours, then pulls you closer and wraps his arms around you. "I'll go in a minute," he says, leaning down to kiss you.

You can smell him then, the sheer alluring scent of him, and lean in closer, slipping your arms in under his leather jacket and feeling the muscles of his back. "Me too," you say, thoughts of leaving to get dressed for school and talk with Giles evaporating.

You can do all that soon enough. Right now it's still night, and you're with Angel.

SLAYER ACTION:
Turn to page 29.

After debating for a full microsecond, you change from your pajamas into black jeans, a dark red long-sleeved top, and your black leather jacket. It'll still be chilly out there in the predawn.

Quietly sliding open the window, you glance back to be sure the door to your room is fully closed and then carefully climb out onto the sloping roof. You jump down, landing solidly on the grass below.

Stealing another furtive glance at the house, you find your mom's light still off. *Made it.* You pick up the pace, moving through the quiet streets of Sunnydale. Only the hiss and chatter of sprinkler systems punctuate the silence as you move through the suburban neighborhood. Watching for vamps, you almost hope you'll run into a few. Taking out vengeance on them for your earlier nightmare attack, even though they had nothing to do with it, would still be mildly rewarding.

However, no outdated dressers with pointy teeth emerge from either garbage-strewn alleys or even the cemetery as you cut through it. It's a real shame. You had this whole technique worked out in your head where you could kick a Dumpster and send it flying, pinning three vamps at once against a wall. Then you'd be on them in a second, brandishing a stake. Of course, their hearts would be shielded behind the thick metal of the Dumpster, so you'd have to roll it out again, and anyway, ewwww, garbage.

Not what you want to smell like if you run into Angel.

A few minutes later, as dawn begins to glow in the east, you descend the stairs to find yourself standing by Angel's door. He must be home by now. You don't enjoy the thought of him as a crispy tater tot. You rap gently on the door. "Angel?" you say quietly, letting him know it's you and not his old evil vampire chums Dru or Spike or someone even worse, if that was possible. Spike was practically blinding with his peroxide blond hair, and Dru seldom, if ever, made any sense whatsoever to you. You can't even understand how Angel could have stood their evil company. Of course, you know back then he was an evil vampire himself. Now he's a good vampire, with a freshly restored soul and a keen fashion sense. You say, "Angel?" again very quietly, but he doesn't open the door.

As worry creeps into you at the thought of him caught aboveground after sunrise, you suddenly hear him screaming on the other side of the door. Sheer terror fills that scream, like nothing you've ever heard come out of him.

"Angel!" you shout.

The screaming continues and you grab the doorknob, breaking the lock with a single, sharp turn of your wrist. You bang the door open and see Angel lying face up on his bed, covers strewn, face twisted in fear. His arms lie pinned to his side, his entire body unmoving. The frightful scream comes again, expelled from his unmoving lips, his eyes wide in terror.

No one else is in the room. It is all too familiar.

You dash to his side, placing your hands on his

bare shoulders. "Angel!" you say, shaking him gently, trying to rouse him.

Suddenly he can move again. He sits up straight, seizes you into his arms, and clutches you so tightly that for a moment you can't even breathe. You wrap your arms around him, holding him. "It's okay now. What happened?"

After a minute, still recovering and reluctant to let go, he pulls away from you and his dark, intense brown eyes meet yours. "Never felt anything like that. Like this force weighing down on me. An evil presence in the room. I couldn't move." His eyes focus on something far away, and he runs one strong hand through his short brown hair and flops back onto the pillow. Then he looks at you out of the corner of his eye. "Hey, what are you doing here, anyway?"

"Couldn't sleep."

"Bad dreams?"

"And bad awakes."

Angel sits up again, and you try not to blatantly stare at his bare, muscular chest. He raises his eyebrows. "Same thing?"

You nod.

"What is it?"

"Not sure. Going to ask Giles this morning. I'll tell him you had the same." A bad thought suddenly sweeps over you. What if it's a town epidemic? What if things are crushing everyone, even your mom at this very instant? What if only you and Angel were able to throw it off because of your Slayer strength and his vampire strength?

"I'd better go," you say suddenly, getting up.

Angel looks disappointed. "But you just got here . . . are you sure?"

"Yeah, I want to check on my mom."

Angel nods, no longer disappointed. He understands you, understands your responsibilities. You love that about him.

Smiling in farewell, you turn and hurry out, then remember the broken lock. "Sorry. You need a new lock."

"Again?" you hear him ask as you close the door behind you.

Running now, you close the distance to your house in no time. Your mom's light is still off. You climb up the tree next to your window, step onto the slanting roof outside your bedroom, and climb in. Quickly you cross to the door, wasting no time in reaching your mom's room.

In the soft, filtered light from the street lamps outside, you see she is sleeping soundly on her back. Relieved, you return to your room and slump on your bed. Your muscles ache with fatigue. When was the last time you really slept soundly?

As your lids begin to droop, you catch yourself and sit up abruptly. No more nightmares tonight.

Western Civ still lurks on the nearby stack of rarely opened books. Looks like it will see some action after all.

SLAYER ACTION:
Turn to page 29.

You sit down at your desk, opening the spiral-bound notebook in which you've taken only five pages of cumulative notes since the start of the semester. You pull *Western Civ* down from the top of the stack, then glance at the most recent assignment in your folder, figuring the quiz will most likely cover that.

"Read pages 142–154."

Twelve pages? And this is dense stuff. Don't teachers realize that you have a life outside of school? That you have the Bronze to go to, friends to hang out with, clothes to try on, demons to track down, and vampires to slay? Okay, you know they don't actually know about the last two. Even your mom doesn't know about those.

You open the book to page 142 and dig in. The chapter, it touts, is a "fascinating study of the Mycenaean civilization." *It better be*, you think, already feeling your eyelids getting heavy again. You take sparse notes and read about the lost city of Troy and its rediscovery in 1873 by Heinrich Schliemann. It's not too bad, actually. All this talk of lost civilizations is kind of cool.

A quiet rap on your door interrupts your reading. You look up. "Come in?"

Your mother, Joyce, pokes her head in through the opening door. "Honey, you okay? I saw your light on."

"Yeah, I'm okay, Mom," you answer.

She sees you're doing homework and comes fully into the room, tying the white sash of her silk robe. "You're doing your homework." It's a statement, not a question. Disbelief. She strides over to you hurriedly and feels your forehead. "Honey, why are you doing your homework?"

"Jeez, Mom, I'm not *that* bad," you tell her. "Okay, maybe I am. But you're not supposed to say it out loud like that."

Joyce shakes her head. "Oh, honey, I'm sorry. I just meant, why are you doing your homework at four in the morning?"

"Couldn't sleep," you say, looking back at the book. Though between your loss of sleep and lengthy passages about Heinrich Schliemann, you suspect you'll soon be slumped over *Western Civ* and wake up later with the imprint of the book on your forehead. Attractive.

Joyce studies your face with concern for a moment, but at last relents, turning to leave. "Okay. But be sure to get plenty of rest. High school can be very stressful, and you really need your sleep when you're this age."

"Thanks, Mom," you say, knowing she has no clue how stressful high school is for you. Between too many classes, staying after school to train with Giles, then going out at night to patrol, you barely have any time for sleep on a good day. Let alone time to read about the lost city of Troy.

She smiles and closes the door behind her. You go back to reading about the Mycenaean culture.

A little later you start awake. You find yourself slumped over your textbook, your pen digging into your cheek. Your heart pounds, and for a second you wonder if you're under attack again.

But you're not. You're able to move, to breathe. *Forget this.*

You close the book, recap the pen, and throw on some clothes. You're going to see Giles. You glance at your clock, which glows 4:18 a.m. You don't care if you wake him up. He's your Watcher, right? Isn't he supposed to watch over you?

You listen for a moment at your door, making sure your mom is asleep. After detecting no movement in the hallway, you creep to your window and slip outside.

Dropping down onto the lawn below, you start toward Giles's apartment.

When you reach it, you stride across his patio, starting to feel a little guilty about waking him up. You're so exhausted that you can appreciate letting people sleep. Still, you want to know what's going on.

Just as you raise your fist to knock on the door, you hear a rustle in the potted plants on his patio.

Whirling around, you spot Ethan Rayne tripping on a garden hose as he tries to dart out of view. In a second you're on top of him, tackling him to the ground.

"Don't hurt me! Don't hurt me!" he pleads as you sit on his back, giving the crown of his head a good biff.

"Why not?" you ask plainly. "First we're nice enough to let you just leave town. But you don't know when you've got a good deal, and you show up again, kidnapping me so some demon will kill me in your place! Do you know how much it cost me to have that Eygon tattoo removed?" You grab him roughly by the collar of his jacket, slamming him back onto the cement. "Do you realize how many shoes and designer bags I could have bought with that?"

"Please, please!" he continues to plead. "I came here for your help. Yours and Rupert's."

"And I'm supposed to buy that?" you ask incredulously.

He manages to lift one hand from the cement in a placating manner. "Sunnydale could be in grave danger if you don't listen to me."

"I think Sunnydale will be in grave danger if I don't smash your face into this cement," you growl.

A familiar voice calls to you from the street. "Buffy? Is that you?"

It's Angel.

Your heart starts hammering. Damn. You try not to be obvious as he appears around the corner, stepping onto Giles's patio.

"I heard scuffling," he says, then sees Ethan Rayne. "Oh. Now I understand why."

"Please don't let her kill me!" Ethan pleads to Angel.

"Why not?" Angel asks.

"That's what I asked," you say. "But he can't give a good reason." You can't help but notice that Angel looks exhausted, as if he hasn't slept in days.

"I told you!" Ethan whines desperately. "Sunnydale is in great danger! You must listen to me."

"And your heart just bleeds for Sunnydale. Why, all you've done since you arrived has been spawned from your brimming sense of civic pride. Oh, no, wait—that was you trying to get all of us killed. I can see how I'd confuse the two."

"Listen. There's an evil force in town, and I don't want anyone else wreaking havoc here. That's my job."

Sounds like a fair enough Ethan Rayne reason for you. Reluctantly, and resisting the temptation to biff him one more time across the back of the head, you get off him. Still holding on to his neck, you steer him toward Giles's front door.

"Knock," you order him.

SLAYER ACTION:
Turn to page 183.

Freshly arrived at school and feeling worn out from lack of sleep, you walk into the library. You expect to see only Giles, milling about in the back shelves, pulling out books and examining their spines. But you're surprised to greet Willow, sitting at the large table that has hosted so many Scooby meetings.

"Hey, Will," you say, approaching her. You glance around for Giles, and find him milling around by the back shelves pulling out books and examining their spines. "What's up?" Then with concern, "Couldn't sleep? Bad dreams?"

She looks up at you, holding her stomach. "Bad fish cakes." She shakes her head, gesturing toward a book on Linux. Even the yellow rabbit on her blue and red knit sweater looks downcast. "I was up half the night, groaning and tossing. And because this was the last thing I'd read, I kept obsessing about operating systems and servers. And the little mascot penguin? Pretty soon it took on a life of its own, toddling around in its little Linux way, with its little beady eyes and seemingly innocent expressions. Before long it had self-replicated, and there were dozens of them with rope, tying me down to the floor like evil little Antarctic Lilliputians." She imitates their toddling/roping action with her arms, just to be sure you get it.

"Uh, Will? Are you sure the bad fish cakes have left the building?"

She frowns, rubbing her belly. "I think so. But I wouldn't trust them for a second. I'm sure even if the stomach bouncers have thrown them out, they're skulking around the side of the building, trying to find a way back in."

"Evil," you say, shaking your head.

"Tell me about it," she answers, looking back down at the book.

"And you're still reading that stuff?" you ask, amazed.

"I'm trying to reclaim my original good feelings about it."

You nod, humoring her, raising your eyebrows. "Reclaiming Linux penguins. Got it."

Giles stirs from the upper book loft and looks down at you. "Ah, Buffy. I'm glad you're here," he says, holding six thick volumes precariously balanced between his left hand and chin. He clutches three more in his other hand.

"Really?" you say, curious. "Demons to slay? Evil midnight rituals to interrupt? Minions to pummel?"

"No," he says. "Just needed some help with the dusting back here. I don't think the librarian before me ever touched a feather duster, much less fulfilled his duties to these delicate volumes."

"Giles," you say in a threatening tone, "I dust vampires, not books."

"Well, it's always good to broaden your horizons. The feather duster awaits in my office."

You look down at Will for support.

She waves you off. "Go. Dust. Be happy."

"Yeah," you growl, walking into Giles's office.

The feather duster in question is of the synthetic kind, and bright pink. Day-Glo beacon-in-the-night pink. You grab it and head up the stairs, grateful at least to talk to Giles privately in the back shelves about the nightmares. You don't want to alarm Willow unnecessarily, and there's still a chance, though you gravely doubt it, that the nightmares are just basic bad dreams.

"Giles," you whisper, pulling him back into the stacks.

He pushes his wire-framed glasses up on his nose and meets your eyes. "Yes?"

"So Angel and I had the exact same nightmare."

"Prophetic?"

You shake your head. "No. Nothing like that. This is different. I wake up, and I'm paralyzed, unable to move at all. And Giles, there's something in the room with me, crushing my chest. Something evil."

He takes his glasses off, squints in concentration, and absently puts one stem between his teeth. "And you say Angel has had the same experience."

"Yes. Both of us more than once. Last night was the third time for me."

He nods thoughtfully, replacing his glasses. "You know, I think I've read something about this."

You look around at the dusty volumes with black covers and fine leather bindings. You're positive that Sunnydale High has the best demonology section of any North American high school. "In one of the demony books you've got here?"

He shakes his head, moving past you, already in Giles-on-a-Mission mode, his brow creased with concern. "No, in a journal on sleep research."

You raise your eyebrows in surprise. "You mean this happens to other people? Regular people?"

"Yes," Giles says, climbing down the stairs and attracting Willow's attention. She turns to face the two of you. "It's called sleep paralysis, or sometimes night terrors." He enters his office. "I'm almost sure I've still got that issue here somewhere." He begins thumbing through stacks of scientific journals. He stops suddenly, turning, his hand still on top of one stack. "And I'm almost sure there's some kind of folklore surrounding the phenomenon. I'll have to do some digging."

Willow appears at the office door. "Ooooh, can I help?"

Giles frowns at her. "But what about your, uh, stomach bug?"

"Nothing cures a stomachache like good old-fashioned research," she says, grinning now.

"Gee," you say. "And I would have thought Tums and a lie down."

They begin digging animatedly through the magazines in Giles's office. "You need help, or should I dust?" you ask. Your question goes unanswered.

The doors to the library swing open and Xander enters. He grins. "Buffster!" His striped shirt and light brown corduroys make you think back to the fashion show, and how good he actually looked in his tux. Was that only a week ago? You can't believe it. This whole loss of sleep thing is throwing off your week.

"Hey, Xand. What brings you to the land of knowledge at this unmentionably early hour?"

"Actually," he says, craning his neck to see around you. "I was hoping there might be doughnuts."

You shake your head. "Nope. No doughnutage. Just two wild and crazy academics and one currently useless Slayer."

"Oh, Will's here?" He walks to the office door and gives a little wave. Giles continues to plow through the journals, but Willow looks up and smiles.

"Hi, Xander."

"Well, I guess I'll get going then," he says, backing out of the door.

"Wait," Giles says, finally looking up.

Xander snaps his fingers in disappointment, then slumps his shoulders down in resignation.

"We're going to need your help later going through some books."

Xander winces. "Now how did I know you were going to say that?"

The doors swing open again and your very favorite person enters, glowering, his jaw set in consternation. You feel your heart sink.

"Principal Snyder," Xander says in mock politeness.

"Don't Principal Snyder me," the grumpy administrator growls. "I don't know what you people are doing here before school in the library, but I'm sure it can't be good."

"Reading books?" you offer, pointing to Willow's open textbook on the table.

Snyder crosses his arms, the morning sunlight glinting off his bald pate. "I'll just bet."

You notice that Willow isn't coming out to offer support, instead staying in Giles's office. Even Giles isn't coming out. Some friends. Sure, they help fight off the apocalypse, but throw in a malicious school administrator, and where are they?

"Since you're all just standing around doing nothing—," he starts.

Snyder really is evil.

"Well, actually—," you cut in, trying to make up something you could be doing in addition to just standing around.

Snyder ignores you. "The gym needs to be decorated for the Importance of Eating Breakfast assembly this morning. And I expect you both to be in attendance."

Disbelief sweeps over Xander's face. "They actually give assemblies on eating breakfast?" He pauses. "Are they actually going to *serve* breakfast?"

"Not in my gym, mister. So get to it. There's crepe paper, balloons, and signs on the table outside the gym."

"Signs?" Xander says incredulously. "What do they say? 'Know the Fruit Loop'? 'Never Trust a Marshmallow-Bearing Leprechaun'?"

"Don't be smart with me, Harris. I'm so far ahead of you, you haven't dreamed of where I am. I want that gym decorated from the floor to the rafters. And I don't care if you have to skip breakfast to do it." He turns away and walks back to the door. Before he disappears, he says, "And I expect it to look festive."

When he's out of earshot, Xander gestures rudely in his direction. "Am I the only one who sees the irony in that last remark? Man, I *hate* that guy."

"He does seem to have no end of tedious school activities for us to do," you agree.

"How come he never gets eaten?" Xander wonders. "He could get eaten."

You walk to the office door. "How's it going?" Your stomach emits a loud, long rumble.

"I think we're getting closer," Giles answers distractedly.

Willow looks up. "At least we've narrowed it down to the right year. So are you and Xander going to go decorate the gym?"

Xander pipes up from the other room. "So! You *did* hear. And left us to our misery."

"Naturally," Willow says, smiling amiably, and returns to the current stack she's digging through.

"We can manage without you," Giles says, leafing through an issue of the *Journal of Sleep Disorders*. Your stomach continues to growl, and you realize how hungry you are. You forgot to eat breakfast. Maybe you could grab something to eat before class? But still, what with being so tired and behind on your homework, the last thing you need is to have Snyder on your case.

SLAYER CHOICE:

Do you decide to . . .

❚ decorate the gym with Xander? *If yes, turn to page 80.*

❚ duck out to eat, go to classes, and then return at lunch to see if Willow and Giles found any reference to night terrors? *If yes, turn to page 73.*

When Angel is out of vampire earshot, which is clear down the block, you climb out of the window onto the tree beyond and drop down. Careful not to lose him, you follow at a distance, aware of every little scuff sound your boots make. But Angel doesn't turn around, and you follow him downtown, near the Bronze.

He saunters down an alley between two old brick buildings. One is an abandoned factory, and the other a group of new artists' lofts, which you suspect is really just another way of charging exorbitant rent to poor struggling artists who want the prestige and inspiration of living among their peers. You round the corner of the abandoned factory and enter the narrow corridor. Angel strides nearly to the end of the alley, which will put him out onto a main street again. But suddenly he turns back, forcing you to retreat around the edge of the building, out of sight.

You're not sure whether he saw you, and you don't want to peek around the corner. He'd certainly see you then. You wait for a few breathless seconds, then realize you need to hide in case he emerges from the mouth of the alley. Glancing around, you see a Dumpster and head for it. Ducking down behind it, you wrinkle your nose at the overwhelming stench of rancid milk, rotting fruit, and some horrible scent that is reminiscent of radioactive goat cheese.

After several minutes, you realize that Angel is not going to reappear. Stealthily, trying to breathe through your sleeve, you emerge from behind the Dumpster and head for the alley.

When you surreptitiously look around the corner, you take in a sharp breath of surprise. Angel is standing halfway down the alley and has backed a young, attractive girl against the wall. He strokes her face languidly, and she looks up at him with adoring eyes. A hard lump moves into your throat, and you feel like you've been sucker punched in the gut.

SLAYER CHOICE:

Do you decide to . . .

❚ walk away dejectedly without saying anything? *If yes, turn to page 44.*

❚ stay and watch to be sure that what you're seeing is really what you think you're seeing? *If yes, turn to page 45.*

Giles puts down the Pendant of Kamrusepas and its incantations lovingly, stroking the medallion as he lifts his hand as if it were a child he'll never see again. Then he holds the orb aloft.

"Once I say the proper incantation, the orb will be activated. I'll immediately return to my body, and the Night Terror will presumably be ousted, returning here."

"Presumably?"

Giles nods. "Yes, I should think so."

"Reassuring."

"Then if we want to send it back to its native body, presuming it has one, it'll have to then touch the orb."

"There's a lot of presuming going on with this plan," you point out.

"What I'm saying," Giles says, sounding irritated, "is that you'll have to stay behind after I leave and make sure it touches this."

"Gotcha. Guess I'll need to think up an excuse for it to touch the orb. Any guess on how fast it'll show up? Because I'm sort of sleeping in a tree right now."

"I imagine it will be instantaneous. The trouble is *where* will it appear, and will you be able to find it before it takes another host?"

"Or before I fall out of the tree."

"Exactly."

"Sounds like fun," you say, ready for the challenge. "I am Dream Slayer."

Giles looks at you disconcertedly, as usual, then holds out the orb before him. On second thought, he leans over and grabs a silk scarf draped over a small silver crown. "Oh, and get ready to catch it in this. Don't touch it with your bare hands, or you'll be sent to your body too. I imagine it will fall when I disappear."

"Right." You take the scarf from him.

Giles speaks an involved incantation in some unknown dialect, which you're pretty impressed he knows off the top of his head, even if this is his dream world. The orb sparks and begins to glow, giving off an ethereal blue light. Lightning forms inside it, forking out toward Giles's fingers. Giles then vanishes, and you leap out to catch the orb in the little scarf as it plummets. Grasping it gently, you raise it up to eye level. It still glows, casting shadows around it.

A little nervousness tugs at you as you think of meeting the Night Terror in person. You've fought countless demons before, but the dream world will be a rather strange battleground. And where will you find it? You turn to leave, thinking up reasons for the Night Terror to touch the orb. You could tell the creature that it's a magical healing orb, or that it will allow him to escape to any dimension he chooses.

Just as you're really making some mental progress, a huge, winged creature winks into existence before you. Standing nearly seven feet tall, with four horns jutting from its massive skull, it flutters its wings in surprise. Three rows of teeth glisten with viscous saliva, and silver eyes with no pupils widen in surprise. You're not sure exactly what the Night Terror was doing before it transported here, but it's in a sort of golf-swing pose. It lowers its arms, which bristle with spurs, and looks at you.

"Catch!" you yell, tossing him the orb.

Instinctively it reaches up and catches the orb in its hands, then winks out of view once again, transported back to its body. You dive, scooping the orb up in the scarf before it lands on the marble floor.

Inspired, you don't see why you should stop here. You decide to journey out into the dream world and find the other disembodied spirits. Everyone can go home!

Emerging from Giles's Parthenon, you call out for those who have been stranded, shouting that the Night Terror has been vanquished. Vanquished. You like that word. It sounds so . . . heroic.

As you walk through the streets of your dreamscape, calling out the news, you feel rather like you're in Oz, announcing the death of the Wicked Witch.

Soon people draw closer to you, and you're amazed at the wealth of time periods represented. Roman centurions, medieval archers, women dressed in corsets and multilayered skirts, men sporting Napoleonic fashions with long coats and shiny buttons, flappers, hippies, punk rockers . . . the Night Terror's victims across the ages. Some of them aren't human, but creatures with wings, horns, hooves, skin of gold, green, red, and bright blues and violets, reptilian, furred, and feathered.

You know many of these people will merely return

to bodies long dead and go on to their afterlives, whatever those may be. But some of them, at least twenty of them, look to be roughly from your time period. They may still have living bodies, though many may already be in comas. You imagine how surprised and delighted their families will be when they wake up from such long sleeps.

Holding out the orb in the scarf, you tell everyone to touch it, and the disembodied spirits shout and cry out in amazement as one after another disappears, returning home. It finally comes down to just you and another girl your age, dressed in a purple velvet turtleneck and a long black skirt.

"I'm Meg," she says. "Thank you. I've been trapped here for ten years. I've had to witness the nightmares of my family, struggling with the dilemma of whether to end my life support. My body is almost dead, you see." Her eyes brim with tears. "Maybe, maybe with my spirit back, my body can make it, and I can be with my family again."

You hold out the orb for her, and tentatively, filled with so much hope you can feel it emanating from her, she touches it. Instantly she vanishes, and you now stand alone on your own street, your dream street.

Then, so the orb doesn't get lost, you retrace your steps back to Giles's Parthenon, which isn't easy, because suddenly there's a whitewater river where there wasn't one before, and after you ford that, you have to plow your way through some kind of strange

Tour de France–style bike race where the racers are actually flamingos with chef hats.

At last you arrive on the marble steps and climb them. Placing the orb and scarf down gently beside the rest of Giles's dream loot, you give it all one last look— the gleaming gold and silver, the sparkling gems.

Then you touch the orb yourself and awake with a start in the tree. Catching yourself just before you teeter off the branch, you gaze out over sun-drenched Sunnydale.

You don't think you've ever had such a good night's sleep.

THE END

You turn away, sadness consuming you. You really thought Angel loved you. He may not have ever actually said that to you, but you distinctly remember Darla mentioning it just before she tried to fill you full of bullets.

You stride sadly through the darkened streets of Sunnydale, a thick, painful stone in your heart. You think of finding Willow, but you are just too devastated for company.

The only thing to help you now is ice cream, and lots of it.

SLAYER ACTION:
Turn to page 144.

You press yourself into the shadows at the mouth of the alley, listening to the hollow buzzing of the street-lights as your heart pounds in your chest.

Could Angel really be seeing someone behind your back? Why would he do that? You thought you were magical together. . . . Would he really lie to you? Was he no better than Ford, your L.A. friend who lied to you and endangered your life in his misguided quest for immortality?

Placing a hand against the cold brick, you watch Angel and the girl. *At least she could be unattractive,* you think. She could have a big, warty face or bad hair or no fashion sense. But this woman is tall, willowy, some-where in her twenties, you think, and impeccably dressed.

As you watch, Angel bends down and starts to kiss her neck! You can't believe it. The woman leans her head back in ecstasy as Angel brings her closer to him, enveloping her in his arms.

SLAYER CHOICE:

Do you decide to . . .

\ cry out, "Hey! What's going on, Angel?" *If yes, turn to page 95.*

\ run up and pummel Angel? *If yes, turn to page 97.*

\ leave silently and go home and eat way too much ice cream? *If yes, turn to page 100.*

Needing to load up on coffee on the way home from school, you and Willow go by the espresso shop and find a table near the window. The sun is now just over the horizon, and you think of the upcoming night, of sleep, of nightmares, of the *mare*. Determined to stay awake, you swig down your third triple espresso, gritting your teeth and curling back your lips at the horrible bitterness.

"You should try Turkish coffee," Willow says, "if you think that stuff is strong."

"Where can we get some?" you ask seriously.

"Buffy, don't you think you should cut back a little until you're actually feeling sleepy? You don't want to be so jittery you jump around and knock yourself unconscious on a lamppost."

"Which is very likely to happen, Will," you say, humoring her.

"Well, you know what I mean."

Just then a cute guy with short, spiky hair walks by, sipping a frothy cappuccino. He slows when he sees Willow and gives her a warm smile before continuing on to his table. You know his name is Oz and that he's the guitarist for the band Dingoes Ate My Baby, but you know little else about him.

Willow smiles back, entering an extreme state of shy, and then quickly brings her hands together in her lap, twisting them and looking down. Smoothing out her skirt suddenly becomes a high priority.

"Have you asked Oz out yet?" you say, knowing Willow's been far too shy. "He's cute."

Willow looks up at you and says, almost impercep-
tibly, "I know."

"And he likes you."

She fidgets nervously, stealing a look at him. "You
really think so?"

"It's obvious, Will. Go for it."

She instantly blushes and looks back into her lap.

You sigh. It's a shame Willow is so shy. She's so
intelligent and attractive—if only she'd notice the second
part of that equation, it would probably lessen the falling
apart of Willow around guys of the cute persuasion.

"So what about you and Angel?" she asks, deftly
changing the subject. She sips innocently at her own
mug of hot cocoa with whipped cream on top.

You hate it when she does this, because it's a trap
you can't help but fall into. You do love the occasional
Angel chat. "Things are . . . good," you say, playing it
low-key. In truth, you've never felt so powerfully drawn
to someone. Even if he is a vampire and you are sworn
to slay vampires, the fact that he has a soul makes
him an exception. And it's such a good soul. An attractive soul. You feel that something larger than the two of
you has brought you together here in Sunnydale. It
almost feels, well, *magical* when you are together, like
there is some kind of brilliant energy burning inside
you. Yes, *burning*. That's an apt description. Sometimes
you feel like you're on fire for Angel, that your desire
to be near him is the most powerful thing you've
ever felt. And what's even more amazing is that Angel
seems to feel the same way about you—just as drawn

toward you, just as compelled to be with you.

"Just . . . good. I see," Willow says, with a hint of a sly smile. "So do you think you'll be able to stay up all night?"

Suddenly you have a pretty good idea about what would make it easier: Angel. You could spend the night with him. Stroll around some graveyards. Kiss. Slay a vamp or two. Kiss. "I think so," you say.

"Mmmm-hmmm," Willow says suspiciously. "Well, if it turns out you need me to do jumping jacks with you or something, let me know."

"I'll be sure to do that," you tell her with mock solemnity.

She looks at her watch and gasps. "Oh! I need to go. There's a paper I have to write on the history of cultures in Mesopotamia."

Panic seizes your heart. "What? Is that due tomorrow? I thought we had till next month."

"We do," Willow says simply. "I just think the whole thing is fascinating. I mean, Akkadians, Hittites— they brought in the wheeled chariot, you know—and Babylonians."

"Oh," you say, knowing that somewhere in some academia dimension, an ivory tower is one Willow short.

You pack up your things and bid farewell to your friend. Looking forward to a night spent in Angel's arms, or rather, that is, slaying vamps, yes, slaying vamps, you start walking toward home.

It's dark by the time you arrive, and a message waiting on your answering machine from your mom lets you know she won't be home for dinner. She's staying late unpacking a new shipment at the gallery. You reheat some pizza and chew it distractedly in the kitchen, wondering if Angel is up yet.

A half hour later, you've donned your black leather jacket and hit the merry streets of Sunnydale in search of vampires. But while you search the shadowed tombstones and alleyways, staking a vamp here and there and even decapitating one with a Dumpster lid, you don't run into Angel. He isn't at home, either.

Disheartened, you continue patrolling, running across a four-armed demon carrying a cat spleen and a deck of playing cards. You dispatch him with the metal stake from a yard sale sign. You don't even want to know what he was up to.

Though you were already suffering from lack of sleep to begin with, and your muscles ache and eyes burn by the end of the night, you nevertheless think you'll manage to stay up all night. But so far, no Angel. You suppose he's just up to something mysterious that probably involves brooding.

After a while you go home and pretend you've been tucked away in bed all night with a good book, which your mom finds immensely suspicious when she returns from the gallery. You sit in front of the mirror, brushing your hair. Ugh. You hope Giles comes up with something in the morning, because you don't think you can take another night of staying up. You feel seriously exhausted, and your tongue, no matter how many times you brush your teeth, feels like it is wearing a terry-cloth robe and furry slippers. Your eyes burn; the rims are red, the whites lined with small veins. Dark circles under your eyes are beginning to outgrow their territory and spread into your cheeks, giving you a slightly sunken look. Very attractive. In a corpse kind of way.

At last your mom retires and you are ready to sneak out the window to continue patrolling.

But as you cautiously slide up the window, glancing over your shoulder to be sure your mother isn't going to check on you again, you suddenly sense a presence. A cold hand closes on your shoulder. You spin to find Angel standing on the other side of the window.

Breathing a sigh of relief, you step back. "Angel! You startled me."

"Did I?" he says, more of a statement than a question. There's something strange about him. He climbs gracefully through the window and straightens up, looking down at you.

"I, uh, looked for you earlier," you say, suddenly feeling shy now in his presence.

"I was looking for you."

He continues to stand there, regarding you curiously, almost scientifically, as if he's never really studied your features before. "I had to come be with you, truly, to try and understand."

"Understand?" You raise your eyebrows.

"To see what all the fuss is about." He touches your face, but his cool fingers feel particularly chilly. There is no emotional warmth in them. "He couldn't stay away from you . . . and I have to know why."

"Who couldn't?" you ask, beginning to feel really uncomfortable now. You back up slightly, moving away from his hand.

Suddenly Angel grabs his head violently, buckling over at the waist. "Buffy . . . ," he mutters. You go to him quickly, place a hand on his back comfortingly.

"What is it?"

Then he straightens up just as fast, grabbing your hand. "Nothing, I—" Just as quickly he lets go, bending over again, letting out a moan of pain. Not sure what to do, you continue to stand there, wondering what's wrong with him. He clasps his hands to his face, and for a moment you see the vampire emerge, brow ridges growing, fangs descending, and then just as quickly they vanish, leaving the angelic face behind. Angel cries out in pain, falling to his knees.

"Angel!" You kneel beside him. "What can I do?"

"Nothing." He grits his teeth, then looks up, lowering his hands. "Oh, Buffy . . ." Trembling, he gets to his feet. "I'm okay now. Not sure what's happening." You stand up alongside him, and he caresses your face. "You look so beautiful tonight."

"What's going on?" you ask, puzzled.

"Oh, I've just been . . . having these headaches," Angel explains lamely, and you know that he's lying.

"Really?" you press.

"Yeah. I think—I think I'm just going to go home and get some sleep." You suspect now that the *mare* is causing Angel's strange behavior. Maybe it is sucking his energy dry or something. . . . Man, you hope Giles comes up with something tomorrow.

"Maybe you should try to stay up," you suggest.

"Because of the whole nightmare thing?"

You nod.

"Oh, no. Those went away. Not sure what was causing them."

"That doesn't mean they're gone for good," you caution.

Angel gazes absently out the window at the tree swaying in the night air.

"In fact, as this is Sunnydale, they're very likely *not* gone for good. Nothing's gone for good here until something has reached up out of a pit in hell, usually with tentacles, destroying a wealth of linoleum in the process. And don't forget the stench of sulfur," you add, "and sticky, gelatinous demon goo that takes a week to get out of your best jacket."

Angel doesn't crack a smile. Not even the barely perceptible one that seems reserved just for you. "Well, I'd better get going, Buffy," he says, almost robotically. Something is definitely up.

"Okay," you tell him. He gives you a strange, cursory kiss on your lips and then moves toward the window. "Let me know if you get one of those . . . headaches again," you say.

"I will," he says absently, his brow furrowed as if he's trying to figure something out.

As he drops to the lawn below, you wonder what's

going on with him, and if you should follow him. On the other hand, you look at your watch. Eleven p.m. It's not too late, and Giles is likely still up. Maybe he knows more about what's happening.

SLAYER CHOICE:

Do you decide to . . .

❘ follow Angel to see if you can figure out what's wrong? *If yes, turn to page 37.*

❘ go see Giles to see if he's found out anything yet? *If yes, turn to page 54.*

You start off toward Giles's place. What is wrong with Angel? You think over the host of strange things you've seen in Sunnydale. Possession? Madness? Migraine brought on by too much shopping? Brain tumor? Do vampires even get brain tumors? You doubt it.

It's either that he's more moody than usual, or it's possession. Perhaps the *mare*'s objective is to take people over, not suck the life out of them.

Giles may know, and you're almost at his house when a furtive shape darting between two buildings catches your eye.

You step into the shadows and creep to the mouth of the narrow alley. The quick movement, the predatory stance—it's definitely a vamp.

You hear a woman scream, the scuffle of shoes on asphalt, and the next second you're in the alley, stake in hand.

You see the vampire clearly now, pressing a woman against one wall of the alley. He drinks deeply, and her neck and shirt stream with red. You tell your feet to move forward, command your arm to react, to stake, but you remain immobile, staring.

The vampire is Angel.

Finally you compel your body to rush forward. You grab Angel's shoulder and he turns to you angrily, yellow vampire eyes flashing, forehead ridges severe in the shadows of the alley. He is all vampire, with none of the kindness of Angel surviving in those eyes.

He shoves you aside harshly and continues to feed. You tumble backward, regain your balance, and raise the stake. You can see that the woman is now dead. You know she has been since the scream—the wound is too savage. "I will kill you," you warn.

Angel drops the body and looks at you, wiping some excess blood from his mouth. "But darling, why would you do that? After all, I *love* you." No sincerity marks his words—they fall cruel and hollow on your ears.

"Things like you can't love."

"Things? Things! Oh, Buffy, your words cut." He places a hand over his heart in mock pain and then lowers his head, a malevolent grin spreading across his blood-stained mouth.

"See you around," he says, then turns and sprints out of the alley with a flourish of his black coat.

You turn and speed after him, boots slapping hard on the asphalt. But as you reach the other end of the alley, Angel leaps into the air, clear to the top of a neighboring building. You stop, staring up, searching for a fire escape to climb. Then you spot him leaping to the next building over, and then the next, moving with more speed than you've ever witnessed before— true vampire speed.

You've lost him.

And he's a killer.

You see the woman's body lying in the alley and know the police will find it tomorrow, another victim of the strange blood loss epidemic that plagues Sunnydale.

For now, you want to get to Giles's house.

SLAYER ACTION:
Turn to page 141.

You awaken, startled to find yourself no longer in the Sunnydale High Library, and no longer even in the twentieth century. The sound of horse hooves on cobblestone echoes down thick, fog-laden streets. Flickering candles held in glass boxes atop poles do little to illuminate the gathering darkness, lighting up more of the fog than the shadows. The people brushing by you on the street wear seventeenth-century dress: long, elaborate coats over buttoned vests; knee-high socks and black, buckled shoes; multilayered dresses overly wide at the hips; corseted tops. Some men wear powdered wigs, others wear their hair long, tied back in dark ribbons. Many women wear elaborate wigs, piled high on their heads and adorned with pearls and ribbons. Around their feet scuttle dirty children, begging for change or liberating a watch or two from an unsuspecting man's pocket. You smell a delicious aroma and spot a nearby food cart, steaming in the chilly evening, the vendor calling out to the passing crowd to buy hot candied nuts. The sharp scent of horse manure greets your nose as a passing carriage churns through some freshly laid horse leavings.

For a moment you are so taken in by the vividness of the scene before you that you forget how you came to be here. None of the passersby take the slightest notice of you. You look down at your own clothes and see you're wearing a short red dress, black knee-high boots, and your black leather jacket. Not exactly from the set of *Amadeus*. Something squirms in your pocket and you reach in and pluck it out, casting the wriggling thing to the ground. It's your stake; it writhes there, whipping around, one great eye opening in the wood. It stares up at you, then winks and slinks along in the gutter, moving toward the food cart. You don't blame it. You can't think of the last time you fed it.

You turn away, hoping to find a place where you can buy one of those fantastic dresses. A familiar figure darts out of an alley up ahead, stalking after a young woman. Her clothes are plain, and she carries a basket full of fruit, wine, and cheese. As the dark figure grows closer, you realize it's Angel. The woman passes you by, walking quickly and nervously, glancing behind her. Angel pursues. When he draws near, he turns to you and says in a hopeless voice, "Buffy! Please stop me. I can't do this again," then continues after the woman, face turning vampiric, fangs extending, brow ridges growing.

It's a dream. You're dreaming. With lucid clarity, you remember falling asleep in the library, with evil Angelus and the Night Terror in possession of your love's body. But you're not in your dreamscape, you're in Angel's. You've successfully entered his nightmares.

You reach into your pocket, then remember the stake crawling away. That's okay. You only need it in the most dire of situations. And this is a dream. You chase after Angel, catching up to him as he darts down a side street after the woman. She stops to knock on a small, battered door and waits for a response, glancing repeatedly at Angel. He approaches slowly, playing with her, eyes glowing yellow in the dark. She pounds again on the door, desperately this time. "Let me in!" she shouts as Angel closes the distance. "Please, please let me in!"

"I don't want to do this," Angel tells her, "but I have to."

And then you're on top of him, spinning him around. The door opens and the woman slips inside. You hear it locking behind her.

"Buffy! Stop me. I can't kill them over and over again."

"You don't have to, Angel. This isn't real. It's a nightmare."

"A living nightmare. I deserve to witness these terrible crimes. I did them."

You shake your head. How can you convince Angel he's dreaming? "I know you feel responsible for the people Angelus tortured and killed. But that wasn't you back then. Your soul wasn't in your body. You're innocent. And you feel guilty enough when you're awake. You don't have to torture yourself in your sleep, too."

He covers his face, his back slumping against the wall. When he looks up into the sky, you see tears in the corners of his eyes, slowly trickling down his face. "Buffy, this is worse than usual. I'm used to reliving past crimes at night. But usually I can wake up before it gets bad. I can sometimes save myself from the look on my family's . . ."

His voice trails off.

You take his hand.

"I can't wake up, Buffy. I've tried. I'm trapped here. Forever. It's my punishment."

"Listen, Angel. You're not trapped here because you're evil. A demon has taken over your body. Remember those terrifying dreams we were having? Waking up, paralyzed?"

He nods.

"Well, something crossed over from the dream-world and traded places with your soul. Now you're trapped here, and it's walking around in your body. And it's not alone."

"Angelus." Angel's eyes widen, his voice haunted.

"Yes. He sensed the loss of your soul and has been slowly gaining dominance over the *mare*. Unless you can follow me, let me lead you back to your body, Angelus will completely take over."

Angel looks at you, blinking away the tears, understanding. "So I'm not trapped?"

"You don't have to be." Still holding his hand, you lead him out of the alley into the path of foot traffic. "This is the spot where I entered your dream." You squeeze his hand. "Think about Sunnydale. Think about your life there." You kiss him lightly on the mouth. "Think about coming back to me." You close your eyes, willing yourself awake. "Don't let go of my hand. Don't lose sight of me."

"Okay."

Feeling only the coolness of Angel's fingers entwined in yours, you concentrate on returning to Sunnydale, to the library, to the hard wood where you're sleeping. You grip Angel's hand tighter and tighter, feeling your body grow light.

Then you snap awake, jerking your head up off the table. You're in the library.

You stand up, rushing to the cage imprisoning Angel's body.

"Buffy!" Willow says as you dash by her. You have to know if it worked.

"Angel?" you ask, stopping two feet from the cage.

His body lies on the floor, stirring groggily. He lifts his head up, then gets to his knees. "Buffy?"

"I'm here. Is it you?"

Xander joins you, shaking his head. "You can't trust him."

"Just wait a minute, Xander," you snap, a little too harshly.

Angel slowly gets to his feet, then laces his fingers through the wire of the cage. "Buffy," he says again, groggy and barely cognizant.

"Did you let go of my hand?" you ask.

"No." He blinks, then opens his eyes wider, focusing on you.

Giles enters the library, arms laden with books, and draws near as well. "Be careful, Buffy. Remember how clever Angelus can be." He sets the tomes on the table.

"I'm not Angelus," Angel says from the cage, waking up more.

"If that's true," you ask, "then where were we just now, and what did I tell you?"

He shuts his eyes, hanging his head low, then says, almost in a whisper, "In 1760. London. I was . . . going to kill the maid as she returned from her errands . . . again. You appeared. Talked to me in the alley. You told me I wasn't trapped. You told me to come back here."

"It's him," you say, happiness swelling inside you. "Unlock the cage."

"Buffy, are you sure?" Giles asks, understandably cautious.

Xander grips your shoulder. "It could be a trick."

"Xander, I'm positive."

Your Watcher moves to the cage and unlocks it. Angel steps out, walking with some difficulty in the heavy chains, and you move to him, wrapping your arms around him.

"Thank you," he whispers into your hair.

"Any time."

"Oooh, Buffy," Willow cuts into your moment. "We found something while you were asleep. A German protection spell against the *mare*."

"What are we waiting for?" you ask.

While Giles and Willow prepare and execute the spell, you remove the shackles, then remain in Angel's arms, grateful to have saved him from his unending nightmare and to have him with you once again.

THE END

"**M**arch!" you tell Ethan, forcing him out of the magic shop.

Angel falls in beside you. "Can we really trust him to take us to the right spot?"

Ethan nods vigorously. "Of course you can. And I'm sure you'll find there's nothing to see there, and I can just go on my way."

Angel regards him suspiciously. "Maybe we should get Giles," he says to you.

"There's no need to do that," Ethan says quickly. "No need at all!" He is a little *too* insistent. As you walk along, Ethan grows increasingly nervous. "You're not going to call Rupert, are you? I wouldn't want to wake my old chum at this hour."

You don't know if he's pulling a Brer Rabbit and the Briar Patch or not, but the more nervous he gets, the more you think you *should* get Giles. No one knows Ethan better than he does, and he sure as hell brought Ethan's chaotic Halloween plans to an abrupt halt.

"No," you tell Ethan, "I'm not going to call him. We're going to go by his house and we'll all go by your hotel room."

"Oh, gods," Ethan breathes in apprehension.

In a few minutes you stand outside Giles's door.

"Knock!" you order him.

SLAYER ACTION:
Turn to page 183.

Cautiously, you approach the gym door. Your Spidey Sense tingles. Pressing your ear against the cold metal, you listen for any clue that could tell you what to expect.

But all you hear is that dull roar of whispers, and the strange dragging noises. It's possible a team is here early, practicing. But why would Snyder want you to decorate a gym that was full of active athletes? It went against his almost supernatural Snyder sense of efficiency.

Next to the doors stands a table full of crepe paper, balloons, markers, and blank card stock for creating signs. The words "Don't waste my time, Summers" are written in all capital letters on one of the signs in Snyder's crisp block print.

"Jeez, this guy doesn't let up," Xander says.

"Not to mention he's either psychic or telekinetic. I mean, he either wrote this before he found his gym-decorating victims or after, but he couldn't have beaten us here."

"Creepy."

You nod. But it's not as creepy as the increased roar of harsh whispers now filtering through the cracks in the twin gym doors.

Tentatively, you press on the horizontal metal bar that opens the doors. Leaning against the door, you swing it open, with Xander following closely. The door shuts behind you with a click.

Before you stands the basketball team. Or rather, before you *staggers* the basketball team. Ten boys

NIGHT TERRORS   65

dressed in the Sunnydale team jerseys and white shorts mill around aimlessly in the center of the room, a cluster of students moving like a single confused mind. They bump into each other, grunt, whisper, groan, all staring mindlessly at the walls and gym floor.

"What the—," Xander says, and his voice brings the players' attention to their presence.

Immediately one of them points, grunting more forcibly now, and begins stiffly walking toward you, drool dripping from his mouth.

And now you clearly see the horror of their faces. Eyes dark and sunken, dried blood caked on their necks and chins, fresh blood dripping from some of their mouths.

Slowly they shuffle toward you, a single-minded mass, groaning and now eerily ecstatic at the sight of you.

With their bloody mouths and skin-and-hair-coated broken fingernails, it doesn't take long for you to realize what they are.

"Xander, run!" you cry.

He freezes next to you.

"Xander!" you shout again.

He springs to life, spinning and pulling at the door. "It won't open!" he says in exasperation.

"What?"

Straining at it as the horde draws ever nearer, he shouts, "It's locked!"

Vaguely you remember that the entrance into the main school from the gym is locked up until the start of school in order to prevent vandalism.

You give the door a swift kick. But instead of breaking the lock, the door crumples and dents under your foot, bending and jamming the lock mechanism. You tug at the door in vain with Xander, but the metal only groans and distorts more. Now you've trapped yourself inside.

You see two fire exits across the room, but the mass of shuffling, muttering, and drooling ghouls stands in the way.

"We're going to have to barrel through them!" you say.

"What?!" Xander says, almost hysterical. He points at the staggering mass. "Those are zombies, Buff. Ever seen a Romero film? You can't run into a group of zombies. One bite and you're dead. Or rather, undead."

You nod. "Okay, then . . . we'll run around them. It's not like they're decathlon runners." You point to the right. "You run on that side. I'll attract their attention and run to the left."

Xander nods and dashes away in that direction.

You shout and whistle, attracting the mass over by you, watching as Xander rounds the gym, heading toward the fire exit on that side.

He's almost there, and you move more slowly, now with all ten players in tow.

You hear Xander cry out in surprise and look quickly across the gym. The equipment room door now stands open, and two more zombies have emerged from it, each grabbing one of Xander's arms. As he screams, you watch in terror as one of the zombies bites down on his arm.

Heart hammering, you take off, skirting around the mindless center mass of zombies, and reach Xander. Grabbing one zombie by the shoulder, you toss him aside. Xander sobs and punches the other zombie as you shove it aside, knocking it to the ground.

"Buffy—," Xander says hopelessly.

"You're going to be okay," you tell him. "We just need to get out of here."

But now more zombies emerge from the equipment room. One of them, you notice, isn't a student, but a parent. Is this how it spread? A parent bit his child, who then went to basketball practice while the infection spread through his body?

Supporting Xander, you kick zombies aside as they emerge from the equipment room. But even as you do, the center mass disperses, closing up on all sides of you.

Moaning and staggering, they come forward, frantic arms reaching for fresh food. You kick them aside, punch them, but there are too many. One of them grabs your leg as you kick out at him and bites painfully into your heel.

You're stunned. You can't believe it. Both of you have been bitten. You're going to become zombies.

But maybe there's hope. Maybe you can both get out of there, get to a hospital, find a cure. Maybe Giles will know of a spell or something.

You start to feel dizzy but continue to lash out at

the quickly closing horde. You punch one of their
throats as hands close on your shoulders, wrenching
Xander from your grasp.

You're the Slayer! a voice inside you yells in disbelief. *It can't go down like this!*

As a dozen sets of teeth bite down on your arms,
legs, and sides, you thrash violently, still fighting them
off. You see Xander lying a few feet away, one shoe
off, zombies swarming over him.

As the pack pulls you down to the ground, your
soul cries out in anguish as they begin to eat you.

THE END

Slowly you approach the closed doors to the chemistry lab. You stand on tiptoes and peek through the small window in one of the doors.

The lab looks empty—equipment all packed away from the day before. Xander peers over your head, rocking from foot to foot to get a better look into the room.

"Anything?" you ask.

He shakes his head.

Then a shuddering sob reverberates through the door. Taking a deep breath, you push the door open. You're not usually one to interfere in people's personal affairs, unless those personal affairs have to do with vampire bites, sacrificial rites, or zombie boyfriends.

But you find none of the three in the lab. Instead, on a stool at the far end of the lab sits a student about your age, with dusty brown hair, glasses, and a crumpled jacket and pants that look like he's slept in them.

His face rests in his hands, and you can see tears dripping through his fingers.

"Hey," you say softly, walking forward into the room. "Are you okay?"

The student doesn't answer, just keeps sitting there, sobbing. His chest heaves with each shuddering intake of breath, the kind of breathing that comes when someone's been crying a long, long time.

You look to Xander, who shrugs. Both of you approach the student.

"Are you okay?" you ask, feeling lame the minute

the question leaves your mouth. *Obviously not.* But you've got to start somewhere.

Still the student doesn't even look up. You begin to wonder if he's so despondent that he's not even aware of your presence.

You stop just a foot away, watching as he gasps and sobs profusely. You see now that mucus clings to his hands. Ewwww.

Xander notices this too, grimaces, and walks back to the front of the room where a tissue box sits on the teacher's desk.

You tentatively reach out one hand, not sure if touching the student's shoulder and possibly startling him is the best thing to do.

Before you can decide, the boy throws his arms down on the lab table in front of him and bows his head as he really lets loose with the crying.

"Hey," you say again. "Is there anything I can do?"

Without warning, the student's hand snakes out, closing sharply around your forearm. Instantly he stops crying. "Such a bleeding heart . . . I was right. You're so easily lured," he hisses, fixing narrow, red-rimmed eyes on you. "You may have thwarted me since the mall, but you can't stay awake forever, Slayer." The grip grows painful, and you twist out of it, backing away.

The student steps away from the stool, head low, stalking. "If you don't go to sleep soon, I will be forced to take over someone else. And next time I'll make sure it's not a stranger to you."

You furrow your brow, breath coming unevenly, continuing to back away. Just as the student gets a little too close for your comfort, he falls down abruptly on the floor, collapsing as if all of his bones suddenly went limp.

"What the hell?" you hear Xander exclaim.

"I don't know," you say, shaking your head. Quickly you bend down. "He's breathing. I think he just fainted or passed out."

"I'll go see if the nurse is in yet," Xander says, leaving quickly.

You are tempted to ask him to switch, that you should run to the nurse. You'd get there faster, and besides, you don't relish the thought of being stuck in the room with someone who mysteriously has knowledge of your secret identity.

The student, sprawled on the floor, continues to breathe evenly, his eyes fluttering behind closed lids. Dreaming, you wonder? So soon after collapsing? It doesn't make much sense, though you don't know too much about sleep patterns.

Soon the school nurse arrives and checks out the student's vitals, then calls an ambulance just in case. She reassures you that he'll be just fine and says that you should go on to class. You ask her to keep you posted on his condition, and then you and Xander clear out of the room as the paramedics arrive.

Students have arrived now for school, and the halls are filled with loud shouts, the rustling of papers, and the slamming of locker doors. Some of your classmates stop and stare as the boy is wheeled out on a stretcher.

You feel unsettled, and as the first bell rings for class you find yourself eager to get back to the library to see what Giles and Willow have dug up. You know now that your nightmares and the strange incident at the fashion show are related. But first, the quiz in Western Civ awaits. Xander says he'll meet you at the library for lunch, that he's starving and in need of sustenance in the name of Doublemeat Palace.

SLAYER ACTION:
Turn to page 73.

As the bell rings for lunch, you quickly gather up all your books and notebooks and hurriedly head out of the classroom. Outside, the hallway is filled with the usual level of chaos associated with lunchtime. Some students pull wrinkled brown paper bags out of their lockers, while others round up friends, generally by shouting down corridors at them, to go off-campus for food.

Locker doors slam, papers flutter, and most students descend en masse to the stylish and ever-tasty cafeteria. You head in the opposite direction, quickly covering the distance to the library.

Pushing through the swinging doors, you find Willow and Giles seated at the wooden center table, a pile of books and papers before them. Willow's Apple laptop sits open before her, her face bathed in its glow. You understand that Giles never seems to leave the library, but how did Will get here so quickly after class? Then you remember she has a free study period. At least you think she does. Maybe she is just becoming a mini-Giles and will soon be a permanent fixture in the library.

"Hi, all," you say, slinging your pack onto the table.

"Hi, Buffy!" Willow responds cheerfully.

Giles hisses a sharp *tut-tut-tut* noise as your pack barely brushes one of his old leatherbound books from the Mesozoic Era.

"Sorry," you say, rolling your eyes and removing the pack. You set it on the floor next to the table leg, then sit down on the edge of the table, eliciting another nervous *tut-tut* from Giles as the breeze you create slightly ruffles one of his papers. You ignore his fussiness and say, "So what'd you find?"

"A lot," Willow says.

"It's really quite fascinating," Giles adds, not looking up from his current book, which appears to be in some ancient dialect of—well, you have no idea.

You stand there for a moment longer as they continue reading, engrossed. You realize they aren't going to continue without a little prompting. "Hey, Slayer here? Give of the information?"

"Oh, yes, of course," Giles says, taking his glasses off and rubbing his eyes. "It's really quite fascinating."

"I got that," you say, nodding.

"It's actually more than just a physiological experience."

"We learned the bare bones pretty fast from that article. Once we found it," Willow cuts in.

Giles looks at her with his Don't Interrupt Me, I'm Imparting Wisdom face.

"Go on," she encourages.

Giles leans back in his wooden chair. "The underlying physiological problem is that the brain secretes a chemical that paralyzes us in our sleep."

"So we don't act out our dreams," you put in, picturing yourself leaping about in the hallway of your house and staking your mom during a nightmare about the Master.

"Exactly," Giles continues. He puts one stem of his

glasses in his mouth, creasing his brow thoughtfully. He removes the stem. "In some rare instances, however, sleepers are actually able to awake while their bodies are still under the influence of this chemical."

"So the brain is conscious," Willow says excitedly, "but the body is paralyzed."

"Wow," you breathe, thinking of your experiences this week. That was definitely what was happening.

"After a while, the chemical wears off," Giles says, "and the sleeper is able to move his body again." He leans forward, tapping the long-sought journal on sleep disorders, which lies among the piles of books on the table. "Now this is a well-documented phenomenon, the subject of sleep researchers who seek to assist people in achieving healthier sleep."

"But wait till you hear what we found in Giles's *other* collection."

He nods, a grin appearing. You know he can't help it. He loves the research. "Yes, there's an entire folk phenomenon surrounding sleep paralysis, only there is another factor in these accounts."

He pauses dramatically.

You raise your eyebrows. "Which is?"

"When sleepers wake up in this state of temporary paralysis, they are convinced there's something in the room with them. Something malevolent."

In spite of the warmth of the library, a chill travels up your arms. "Totally the same thing I felt!" you say, "and Angel too."

"It's what thousands of people have described all

through the ages, in a vast array of cultures, each one giving it a different name."

You get off the table and pull up the chair next to Willow.

"The first record I found of the folk tradition surrounding this phenomenon was in Newfoundland."

"People up there call it the Old Hag," Willow puts in, tag teaming with Giles. "They picture this old, shriveled woman with long white hair kneeling on their chests, crushing the air out of them."

Giles nods. "But it's far older than that. In fact, the very word 'nightmare' comes from the old Anglo-Saxon word literally meaning "night crusher," something that crushes one during the night."

This is majorly starting to creep you out. The vivid memory of that *thing* on you last night, pressing down on your chest, your lungs burning for a breath, unable to move or cry out . . .

"The Anglo-Saxons believed that a horrible creature, called a *mare*, sat on the chests of sleepers, paralyzing them, pressing down on their lungs so they couldn't breathe. This translated into the later lore of Denmark and Norway, who also told tales of *mare*, or *mareridt*."

"Mare rides," Willow explains, hooking her fingers at you as if she herself were a *mare*.

"In fact," Giles goes on, ignoring her, "the well-known twelfth-century writer Snorri Sturleson described the hideous death of the Swedish king Vanlandi, who was smothered by a *mare* while he slept."

"Yeah, good old Snorri," you say, having no idea who Giles is talking about.

"The Germans have a tradition about it too," Willow says—definitely, you realize, digging all this research as much as Giles. "They call it the *alp*—a creature that presses down on sleeping people's chests, exerting what they call *alpdruck*. Literally, alp-pressure. Eerie, huh?"

"Too eerie."

You can tell they've wound things down on the research front, as both of them sit silently steeping in their revelations.

You lean forward. "So this *thing* sits on sleepers' chests, trying to crush the air out of them. But what is it? Where does it come from? What does it want? And most of all, how do I kill it?"

Giles and Willow look at each other, obviously feeling a little deflated. Willow's cheeks start to burn in embarrassment.

Giles immediately begins cleaning his glasses with a soft handkerchief, staring at them in great concentration.

"So you don't know."

"Well, not in so many words," Giles says, stammering a bit. "But we're relatively certain that it means harm and that it may gain some sort of sustenance from its victims. Or perhaps it is trying to enter our waking world by crossing over a veil or some kind of dimensional portal, or maybe it merely delights in killing people."

"That specific, eh?" you quip.

"I'm afraid so," Giles says lamely.

"What about taking over the body of a sleeper?" you ask.

Giles looks up, intrigued. "What do you mean?"

"Well, after Simone collapsed at the fashion show, she talked to me in a voice that wasn't hers. In fact, she knew things she couldn't possibly know."

"Like what?" Willow asked.

"Like that I was the Slayer."

Giles lowers his head and looks at you gravely. "And that surprises you? Slayers are supposed to work alone, with the exception of their Watcher, yet you have assembled an entire legion of helpers during just the two years I've known you."

"Well . . . I wouldn't call it a whole legion," you say defensively. "More like . . . a small posse?"

"Legion, posse, regardless, she could even have overheard you and Willow talking one day and just picked up the term."

"I don't think so, Giles. It wasn't her. And she threatened me. She said, 'Next time I'm coming for you, Slayer.'"

"Hmmm . . . ," Giles mumbles, returning his glasses to his face. "And you think she was taken over by this *mare*?"

"Maybe," you offer. "It's a lead, right?"

"Definitely." He slides over one of his books. "I'll see what I can find. In the meantime, let's determine what course of action you're going to take. If this thing has targeted you and Angel, it could likely attack again, and soon. You need to decide how you're going to fight it."

"Well," you say, "it can't get me if I don't fall asleep. But then I wouldn't be able to fight it at all."

"There's something to be said for both approaches," Giles counsels. "If you fought it, you might be able to defeat it without further research. If nothing else, you could begin to test its weaknesses, see what you can learn about it."

As good as that sounds, you have no idea how to fight an intangible creature while you're paralyzed anyway. On the other hand, maybe you could try lashing out at it with your mind.

"Still, perhaps staying awake so you're not vulnerable to it might be the best course of action until we learn more."

Both options sound good to you.

SLAYER CHOICE:

Do you decide to . . .

❙ stay up tonight so the Night Terror can't attack you? *If yes, turn to page 46.*

❙ fall asleep tonight and try to fight the Night Terror? *If yes, turn to page 85.*

Reluctantly, you depart with Xander for the gym. The school is eerily still and silent this early. The first bell won't ring for another half hour, and no one except crazily ambitious students (and seemingly you and Xander) are even present yet.

On your way to the gym, you pass Lola Heffmeyer, a student you've heard lives a good hour's drive from Sunnydale, on her family's historic ranch. She sits on the floor, leaning against a wall, reading Sherlock Holmes.

"Hi," you say. "You're here early," then chide yourself for such a silly, obvious comment. It's right up there with, "Hey, you got your hair cut." As if people didn't notice when their own hair was cut.

"My dad dropped me off early to see to some business in town."

"Bummer," Xander says. "As if we don't have to toil away enough hours in this place. Now you have to do it in your free time."

"What about you guys?" she asks.

"Doughnuts," Xander says.

She looks at you expectantly, and you find yourself struggling for words. "Uhhhhh . . . mothballs?" you say, almost posing a question to her. *Mothballs? Smooth. Very smooth.*

Xander raises his eyebrows.

Lola looks a bit confused but quickly recovers. "Well, have a good day, you two. I'm going back to Dr. Watson."

"Oh, are you sick?" Xander asks, immediately

realizes his error, and fumbles to recover. "'Cause, uh, you look a little peaked."

Lola raises an eyebrow. "Peaked?"

You raise an eyebrow. "Peaked?"

Xander looks away. "Okay, so maybe I'm spending too much time with Giles."

Lola shrugs and says, "No, I'm fine. But I don't know about everyone else. . . . I thought I heard someone crying in the chemistry lab earlier, but the door was locked."

"Snyder probably got to them in a vulnerable moment." Xander claps his hands together, rubbing them a little. "Shall we go, Buff?"

You nod and begin to walk away, then stop and turn back to Lola. "Hey, how come Snyder didn't rope you into decorating the gym for the assembly?"

"I hid," she says simply, and goes back to reading.

As you walk away, Xander says, "Great googly moogly. You'd think I'd have done that. But no, I just stand there like a goob while Mr. Crabby McTweety Pants hands me yet another 'voluntary' assignment."

"Well, what about me? I have enough ghoulies to deal with without having to see Snyder this early in the morning."

A sudden voice behind you makes you start. You and Xander spin around to see Snyder behind you.

"Well, I hope you ate your Wheaties this morning, Summers," he says through a sneer, "because that's a big gym, and I expect to see a lot of mirthful crepe paper all over it."

How the hell does he do that? Sneak up on you when you're at your most vulnerable? When you're suffering from lack of sleep and doughnuts?

"And balloons, Summers. I expect it to be a regular balloon extravaganza in there."

"Extravaganza." You nod. "Got it."

You and Xander turn around and hurry away, suddenly eager to get to the gym, if only to escape Snyder's probing eye. You suspect he could kill someone with his forehead alone.

You hurriedly turn the corner, leaving the overzealous administrator behind.

"Yeech, that man gives me the creeps," Xander whispers, looking over his shoulder. "I wouldn't be the least bit surprised if he was some kind of creepy crawly."

"What do you mean 'if'?"

You near the gym, passing by the chemistry lab doors. From inside the gym, you can hear a dull roaring sound, like a chorus of moaning voices all growling in unison.

"What the heck—," Xander starts to say.

With the gym doors shut, you can't see inside, but when you strain your ears you can also hear strange shuffling noises, as if a group of people are sliding things around on the gym floor.

You move closer, tentatively reaching for the metal bar that will admit you into the gym.

Xander hangs back, disquieted, and as you glance over at him, you hear a sudden sob from the chemistry lab.

Xander whirls, facing that door now.

Another sob echoes down the hallway, and the muffled sound of sharp breathing and crying ensues from beyond the lab doors. You can't tell if it's male or female, but it's definitely full of fear.

You look to Xander, who shrugs, putting his hands up deferentially.

As the multitude of strange, whispery voices builds beyond the gym doors, you wonder which sound you should investigate first.

SLAYER CHOICE:

Do you decide to . . .

❘ enter the chemistry lab to investigate the crying? *If yes, turn to page 69.*

❘ push open the gym doors to check out the dull roar of voices? *If yes, turn to page 64.*

You dive to the side as a deafening boom shatters the tranquility of the night.

Giles curses as you roll away behind some bushes, and you see him raise the revolver again, cocking it and getting another bead on you.

"Buffy!" Angel shouts from the door. You don't have time to see what he's doing. You have to keep moving, and fast. If you can wait until he's fired, you can tackle him while he's thumbing back the hammer again.

Giles walks closer to the bushes. He doesn't want to miss this time.

You dive to the next set of bushes, these discouragingly smaller as another boom resounds through the night. Immediately, you emerge from the shrubbery, racing toward Giles.

But you've underestimated his speed. He cocks the hammer back and aims at your heart, and you hear a thundering roar as something pounds painfully into your chest, ripping through muscle and tissue, hot and burning inside you. You stumble, landing facefirst on the sidewalk, your eyes fluttering shut. You don't hear your heart. Blackness swims into your brain. Air leaks out of your chest, your lungs refusing to work any longer.

The last thing you hear is Angel's agonized wail of grief.

THE END

After school, you wear yourself out training with Giles, then patrol for several hours. Your already exhausted body is ready to fall over and sleep on a tombstone. It's still a decent hour by the time you get home, and you actually use the front door. Quiet and peaceful, the house is empty except for you. You're glad; too tired to eat, you don't know if you could have thought up a good enough excuse if your mom asked you to eat dinner with her or wanted to know why you look so tired. Sometimes you think the slaying gig would be a lot easier if she just knew. You find a note on your bed: She's at the gallery, cataloging a new shipment, and won't be back until later. There's cold pizza in the fridge.

You decide you can at least get that down to keep up your strength, so you grab a slice, munching it on your way upstairs. After brushing your teeth and putting on your PJs, you crawl into bed, the mattress like heaven on your aching back. You doze off before you even have the chance to turn out the light.

Drifting into dreams, you find yourself on the beach again, bare feet in the warm, soft sand, feeling it push between your toes with each step. You walk closer to the waves, the sand now cooler and wet, watching two seagulls combing the surf-washed shore for bits of sea creatures brought in by the tide. The strange feeling of déjà vu, that you've dreamed this very thing before, creeps over you, and you spin around, seeing a dark shape vanish just beyond the periphery of your vision. The ominous feeling of being watched intensifies and you search the shore for threats.

The only other creatures besides the seagulls are a young couple walking in hand in hand, the woman leaning on the man's shoulder.

Then you feel a sudden crushing weight as a blackness surrounds you, constricting your air supply. You throw your arms out, trying to strike anything solid. But your hands flail in empty air, and the vision of the ocean before you and the sun on the water, the sound of the seagulls' cries, all dim and mute out as darkness swims into your vision.

You jerk awake, finding yourself lying on your back in your bed in Sunnydale, with an invisible force still crushing down on your chest. You try to lash out but find yourself paralyzed, and terror sweeps over you. You can't get a breath.

Though you're staring only at your ceiling, a mental image suddenly fills your head: a beast with reptilian wings folded across its back, pointed chin sloping up to high cheekbones, narrowed silver eyes with no pupils gazing down hungrily at you; and teeth—small and pointed, growing in three rows inside the parted mouth. Four horns arc up from the back of its head, long and curving, brown and white and hollow, translucent in the illumination from your bedside table lamp. You know this is the true face of a thing that calls itself the Night Terror.

As your lungs continue to strain and burn for air, you feel something reach down *inside* your chest, an intangible tentacle of energy wrapping around your heart. Pain erupts in your ribcage, a terrible piercing agony that opens your mouth in a breathless, silent scream.

Then the tentacle starts filling up your chest, dark energy pouring into you, and you can feel your soul pushed aside, straining against the confines of your body. And with the dark energy comes the knowledge that if you let it fill you, if you let it drive your soul out, you'll be able to breathe again. Your spirit will be able to move and live and breathe. All it needs to do is leave your body.

With your lungs on fire now and your head starting to swim from lack of oxygen, the temptation is overwhelming. For the briefest instant, you feel your mind meet with the Night Terror's, and a flood of images washes over you.

. . . *the Night Terror, imprisoned in the dream world, longing for escape*

. . . *flashes of bodies worn down and even comatose, past victims of the Night Terror's possession, its demonic spirit too strong to be contained in a normal human body for long*

. . . *frustration and rage filling the Night Terror as host body after host body breaks down, forcing the demon to leave it*

. . . *then the Night Terror learning of the existence of the Slayer, a human with supernatural body strength, and wanting to claim a Slayer as a host*

. . . *taking over the body of a Slayer in 52 C.E., a warrior Celt Slayer fighting during the Roman occupation of Britain, the Night Terror rejoicing as he takes over the body and learns it does not wear down*

. . . then rage again when the Slayer body is killed by a nest of vampires—though the Night Terror possessed the body of a Slayer, he did not know how to fight, and that ignorance caused the Slayer's death

. . . then searching through the centuries for another Slayer to possess, until at last it found you. That fight in the mall, slaying those vamps in front of Simone . . . the creature knew you were the Slayer and longed to possess you

You try to latch on to these images, to learn all you can, searching for a weakness, but even as you struggle to do so, your body aches desperately for a breath. Again you feel the tantalizing suggestion that your body can breathe if you just leave it and free your spirit from this torment. Without even consciously willing it, your spirit, gasping, erupts from your body and floats up near the ceiling. For a few terrifying moments, you are able to turn and look down on your prone body lying on the bed. Now that you are disembodied, seeing not with your eyes but with your spirit, you can see the Night Terror's haunting visage, and it is just how you had imagined it. A great, hulking demon, bristling with spurs and horns, crawling inside your skin, folding its leathery wings flat against its back and nestling down inside your body like some kind of alien cockroach burrowing into soft flesh.

You watch the thing merge with your body. Its arms disappear inside yours, its legs inside your legs. Finally the horned head lowers down into your head and the union is complete. Your body's eyes jerk wide

open, staring, and for a second they flash silver, pupil-
less and demonic. Then they blink rapidly, becoming
your familiar eyes once again, staring up at you.

You try to reach down, try to grab your body and
rejoin it, but you are floating up, up, up through the
ceiling and then through the roof, up into the cold night
sky, into the clouds, and then it gets hazy and warped
and you feel nauseous and disoriented.

And then you open your eyes and find yourself
lying facedown on the floor of your room. Propping
yourself up with your elbows, you pick a piece of carpet fuzz off your tongue. In your chest your heart ham-
mers steadily, your body full of adrenaline.

Suddenly the nightmare attack floods back into
your memory—the winged thing, all leathery skin and
horns and spurs, climbing into your skin as you watched
from the ceiling, terrified. But now here you are, back in
your body.

With a great sigh of relief, you press your hands to
your face. What a nightmare! You can't remember one
so vivid. It felt positively *real*—no oxygen, your soul
tearing out of your body to breathe.

Legs trembling, you rise to your feet. If that
nightmare about the Night Terror was real, then the
demon came for you, and you were able to drive it
away and keep your body. *Round one goes to the
Slayer,* you think. But that doesn't make you any
closer to figuring out how to stop it for good. And you
can't keep doing this night after night. Though you
feel pretty refreshed right now, you remember the

way your body ached earlier tonight while patrolling.

You need to find a way to stop the Night Terror altogether.

You wonder if you should go to sleep again, tempting it into another confrontation. You learned quite a lot about it during that strange merging of the minds. If you could do that again, you might be able to find a weakness.

But first, you need to get a drink of water. You walk groggily to your closet to grab your robe, and open the door. But instead of your clothes hanging up in there, all the dresses belong to your grandmother. You see her familiar old red woolen suit—the one she always wore on Christmas Eve. You can't figure out why her clothes are in your closet. Did your mom store them in here? And where are your own clothes?

A scurry of movement attracts your gaze to the floor of the closet. A small mouse stands there, holding a tiny microphone and adjusting a small amplifier. You kneel down and meet its eyes.

"Excuse me," the mouse says through the microphone.

"Yes?" you answer.

"I am looking for the cure for cancer," it tells you. "Do you know where it is?"

You consider this a moment. "Disneyland, I think."

"Thank you!" it gushes, then packs up the microphone and amplifier into a little rolling suitcase and wheels it out of the closet and across your floor, and it disappears into the hall.

You stand up again, still trying to figure out why your grandmother's clothes are in your closet. Only now some of them aren't your grandmother's clothes. Her robe is now Willow's fuzzy teddy bear sweater, and her pair of shoes seem to have become Brazil.

Shrugging, you shut the door.

You still need to find a weakness to defeat the Night Terror. Maybe your robe is in your mom's room. You walk out of your bedroom into the hall, except that the hall leads to Giles's kitchen. You walk by the counter, where you see a bottle of scotch and an empty glass, and steal a chocolate chip cookie off a baking tray cooling on the stove.

Giles sits at his desk in the living room, bent over a stack of books. You approach him, placing your hand on his shoulder.

"Oh, Buffy, I'm glad you're here. You won't believe what I've found!" He holds the current book up for your inspection. It's a pop-up book, with the gingerbread house from *Hansel and Gretel* protruding from its pages. You see a tiny griffin, the size of a thimble, warbling and wandering around outside the house.

"Do you think it could be the geese?" you ask him.

He nods, then considers and changes his mind. "Not this time. You have to be careful, Buffy. The Night Terror—if you face it . . ." His voice trails off and the gingerbread house in the book sprouts wings, which flap dully against the cardboard backing of the book. He puts it down. "I must concentrate . . . ," he whispers to himself.

Then he stands up and takes your hands firmly. "Buffy, it's possible that if the Night Terror is successful in taking someone over, their soul is then transported to the dream world."

"Whoa!" you say.

"And Buffy," he continues earnestly, "it can become trapped there."

Grateful for the concern, you squeeze Giles's hands, then let go. "I'll be careful, Giles. But I fought it tonight and drove it off." A faint squeaking noise pulls your attention toward the desk. The griffin in the book is now looking up plaintively at you and Giles, waving its arms to get your attention.

"What is it?" Giles asks it irritably.

"I just wanted to know about the bats," it squeaks.

"They come out after dark," Giles informs it impatiently.

"Okay," the griffin says, and continues circling the paper gingerbread house, peering into its windows.

"Giles," you reassure him, "I'm not going to get transported to the dream world."

"Just be careful," he pleads.

"I will." You sit down on the edge of his desk. "So what have you found?"

He turns back toward his desk. "From what I can tell from my research," he says, pulling a book on gardening off the stack, "the Night Terror seeks to exchange places with a human body in order to escape its imprisonment in the dream dimension."

"Imprisonment by who?"

"That wasn't clear. Something from long ago." He flips to a page about tulips and points to a particularly striking gold and red one, next to a photograph of a wilted one. "See? He can't stay in a body for long before it starts to break down, eventually falling into a coma. There could be a myriad of displaced souls out there, Buffy."

"Okay. You try to figure out how it got to the dream dimension in the first place. I'll find Willow. Maybe we can figure out a way to reach these disembodied spirits. They might know of a weakness." You remember the mind merge. "Also, when it tried to take over my body, I could read its thoughts."

"Really?" Giles looks up from his book, intrigued. "What did you see?"

"Images, mainly. I wonder if the same thing happened when it attacked Angel? Maybe he knows something."

The small griffin on the book clears its throat. "I can take you to the Night Terror itself," it squeaks.

You raise your eyebrows in surprise. You're pretty sure griffins know about scratching their backs on trees and that's about it. "Can you show me?" you ask it.

It nods.

"I don't think this is such a good idea," Giles warns you.

"Why not?"

"Griffins?" he says, expecting you to follow his logic.

You don't.

He opens his hands to reveal a baby bluebird nestled among some twigs. "Birds are better in the hand."

You see his point, but the griffin may yet have a clue.

SLAYER CHOICE:

Do you decide to . . .

\ follow the griffin in the hope that it can lead you to the Night Terror? *If yes, turn to page 224.*

\ see if Willow can find a way to communicate with the disembodied spirits trapped in the dream world? *If yes, turn to page 226.*

\ find Angel to see if he gleaned information during his Night Terror attack? *If yes, turn to page 230.*

Y̲ou step into the light and cry, "Hey! What's going on, Angel?" Tears brim in your eyes, but you force them back.

He snaps his head up, yellow eyes fixing on you. It isn't the sweet face of Angel that greets you, but instead the face of the vampire, sunken, ridged, fangs protruding. And dripping from those fangs is fresh blood.

With a barely perceptible exhale, the woman collapses onto Angel's shoulder and he pushes her carelessly to the side, where she slumps onto the ground. Blood pools out of her throat, but not in pulses. She is dead.

Hatred brims in Angel's eyes and he approaches you, licking the blood from the corner of his mouth.

Your mind reels. What is going on? Angel never kills people. You know this. Has he gone evil? Like he was in the Watcher accounts Giles read to you?

"Slayer," he growls, drawing nearer. "Where is your precious Angel now? Do you know how sickened I've been, trapped in this body, while he actually felt *love* for you?"

Your heart sings and sinks simultaneously. Angel *loves* you. It really is true. Then you shake that thought aside as your mind takes in the turn of events. Why is Angel talking about himself in third person?

Has he been possessed by a *mare*?

As he stalks toward you, you see little of the person you have come to love. The face so changed, the demeanor so threatening, the utter contempt in the eyes . . .

"Oh, Diary," he mocks in falsetto, "how I love my sweet Angel." He presses the imagined book lovingly to his chest. "How we flit about the city fighting evil and saving innocent lives and rescuing abandoned puppies and kittens from trees." He turns then, sneering, as you stand on in silence, mouth dry, heart heavy, unable to believe his cruelty. He continues relentlessly, his voice low again, menacing. "How I've thought of killing you . . . how I've fantasized about drinking the blood of a Slayer." He smiles contemptuously and raises an eyebrow. "Especially yours. How sweet it must be . . ."

As he advances on you, you back out of the alley, unsure of what to do.

SLAYER CHOICE:

Do you decide to . . .

\ brace yourself to fight Angel? *If yes, turn to page 101.*

\ try to question him to see what's wrong? *If yes, turn to page 104.*

\ hightail it to Giles's place before hurting Angel so you can figure out what's going on? *If yes, turn to page 106.*

You dash up to him with the full intent to pound your fists into his face. You know it's an immature reaction, but you can't help it. You're furious that he could pretend you are his only love and then go cavorting around with this woman behind your back.

Gripping your fists at your side, you stop a foot away. Startled by the sound of your feet on the pavement, Angel and the woman turn and face you. The woman wobbles a bit, moaning, and then brings her hand up to her neck. Instantly you see the blood seeping through her fingers. Eyes wide with terror, she spins and flees down the alley, pushing Angel away.

"What the—," you breathe, looking from the woman to Angel.

"Hi there, sweetie!" he says melodramatically.

"Angel—"

As the woman disappears around a corner, he shakes his head, putting his hands on his hips and clucking his tongue in disappointment. "Now why'd you have to go and ruin my dinner?"

You don't know what to say.

"I mean, do I come into *your* house and eat all your Wheaties? Do I steal your pizza with extra anchovies or abscond with Belgian waffles?" He raises his eyebrows, waiting. "No. I don't. So why," he goes on in an angrier voice, "do you have to ruin *my* dinner?" At this, he lunges forward, startling you.

You back away, unsure of what to do. What's happened to him? Has he turned evil? Has the *mare* taken him over?

"Now I'm going to have to scare up a new dinner," he continues, lowering his face so he is eye level with you. In those dark brown eyes, where you'd seen so much affection before, lies only a dark void. He thrusts his hand out and grabs you by the neck, lifting you bodily off the ground. With a sudden jerk, you bring your knee up into his solar plexus and he grunts, dropping you.

Jumping to your feet, you yell, "What the hell is wrong with you?" Tears burn at the corners of your eyes, but you refuse to let them fall.

"Nothing a little Slayer blood won't fix," he answers, closing in. You dart out of the way as he makes a grab for you, but you don't see the kick until it sweeps out, connecting painfully with your calf and knocking you over.

In an instant Angel is on top of you, his weight crushing down on your ribcage.

"Angel, why are you doing this?" you cry out in surprise, throwing him off you with a twist of your back.

He falls to the side, catching himself with one hand, and then kicks you so hard in the face that for a moment you lie there stunned, bright stars winking out behind your eyes, your brain dazed. Slowly the world comes back into focus, and you taste a warm stream of blood coming from your nose. As you struggle to your feet, before you have the chance to even get your bearings, Angel grabs you from behind, sinking his teeth into your neck.

You cry out in agony as you feel his teeth rip through muscle and tendons to get to your artery. You buck violently to one side, throwing him over your shoulder. But he grabs onto you as he flips, wrenching your arm down painfully, pulling it out of the socket. You stumble, off balance, and he brings one leg up to kick you as he lands, sprawling onto the pavement.

You duck just in time, but he anticipates this, grabbing your leg to throw you over. You twist and kick, landing solid blows to his stomach, groin, and throat. He relinquishes his hold. You stagger back, exhausted, unable to breathe through your nose.

So many times you've fought side by side. Angel knows your moves.

And he's using that to his advantage.

In a flash he leaps up to his feet, grinning with the thrill of the fight.

"Angel, I know you're in there somewhere," you plead, not wanting to take this fight to a lethal end. You don't want to stake Angel. And you don't want Angel to finish you off. The only hope is to make a hasty retreat now and then figure out some way to capture and question him.

SLAYER ACTION:
Turn to page 303.

You walk away dejectedly. You can't believe it. Angel? Your true love? You really had something magical. At least you thought you did.

Maybe it was all you. Your stupid imagination carrying you away. What did you think? He may have a soul, but he's still a vampire, right? And that means he's evil. Yeah. Totally evil. The jerk. You love him so much. It is you. You know it. You did something wrong.

You slump along through the dark, empty streets of Sunnydale, hoping you don't run into a vamp. You're too depressed to even enjoy a fight.

Then it hits you—you're *out* of ice cream at home. You're going to have to swing by the mini-mart.

SLAYER ACTION:
Turn to page 144.

Bracing yourself, you prepare to fight Angel, still reeling in disbelief. You don't relish the thought of pummeling your true love. Plus, you two have sparred before, and you know that you will walk away from this with a body full of broken bones. You've seen Angel fight when he has no mercy, and he can be brutal.

Stalking toward you, he stops abruptly, then cries out in pain. He drops to one knee, clutching his head. "No!"

Then he springs up, all fangs and maniacal grin, and resumes his approach. You start moving around, making yourself a harder target to hit. Just as he gets close enough to engage in battle with you, the smug smile vanishes, and his face contorts in pain. "No, damn you!" Angel cries out, spinning away from you and stumbling. Unable to right himself in time, he topples to the ground. "I won't let you do this!"

For a moment he lies there motionless, and then, staggering to his feet, he turns toward you. His furrowed brow smooths out and he says in a low voice, "Sorry to keep you waiting, Buffy. I'm having . . . technical difficulties."

You'd swear that two personalities are vying for dominance inside his body. Resuming the onslaught, Angel rushes toward you, vampire quick. You dodge out of the way just in time, sweeping one leg out as he goes by and tripping him. He gazes up at you full of disgust and hatred. "Angel, tell me what's going on!" you demand.

He stands up, wiping a small trickle of blood from

the corner of his mouth. The woman's blood, not his. "Well, first off, you ruined my dinner. That's a bit rude, don't you think?"

He lashes out suddenly with one fist, catching you unexpectedly. It strikes you painfully on one cheek, and face burning, you stare back at him with anger. Why is he doing this?

Holding your hands up to block blows, you dart around to one side of him, landing a powerful kick to his solar plexus that makes him grunt and double over. You follow it with a kick to the face that sends him back into a mound of festering garbage, where he stumbles and hits his head on the corner of a Dumpster.

Heart racing, you wait for him to get up, considering your options. You could run away now and get Giles and the Scoobies and then you could all capture Angel and tie him up until you figure out what's wrong with him.

With a low growl, Angel stands up in the garbage, picking a long spaghetti noodle off the sleeve of his black leather coat. "I *like* this coat, Slayer. Now I'm tempted to do this the quick way!" He suddenly leaps up, arcing high in the air and landing almost on top of you. You maneuver to one side but can't completely dodge a fist that meets your nose. Momentarily stunned, you reel back, the now out-of-focus world spinning. Eyes tearing up with the pain, you struggle to stay out of Angel's reach, retreating into the darkness of the alley.

He advances, then falls to his knees, cursing. Rising

up again, he stumbles a few more feet, then falls. He lies still then, one hand in a murky puddle of water and oil. You remain where you are, suspecting a trick. A moment later, Angel lifts his head to look at you, predatory eyes focusing on his prey. He rises agilely to his feet. "At last!" he growls, stalking toward you. "I got rid of that damn—"

As if something invisible yet visceral punches him in the head, Angel cries out in surprise and staggers backward. He hits the alley wall violently and gives a final scream of pain and frustration. Then he stands there, very still, head lowered. Seconds pass by, each one stretching into oblivion. Still braced for a fight, you watch him closely. If only the others were here, you could figure out a way to overpower him and tie him up.

As if in a trance, he continues to stand there, leaning against the brick wall.

SLAYER CHOICE:

Do you decide to . . .

\ take advantage of his out-of-it state to dash off and bring the Scoobies in the hopes of binding Angel? *If yes, turn to page 149.*

\ continue to stand there, eyeing him closely to see if anything changes? *If yes, turn to page 152.*

" **A**ngel?" you ask softly, in disbelief that you've just seen him kill a person and that now he is advancing on you.

"Not home," Angel answers, continuing to approach.

You keep backing up, wanting to keep distance between the two of you. Angel sees this and instead of coming closer, stops and leans a hand casually against the wall of the old factory. "What's wrong, darling?" he asks, filling the last word with contempt.

"You stole the words right out of my mouth."

"Well, gee, I just don't know what's wrong, muffin. Could it be that I'm about to kill you?"

The sting of hearing those words out of your beloved's mouth takes you momentarily off guard, but you recover quickly.

"What happened to you? You were fine last time I saw you, but then you show up at my house and go all *One Flew Over the Cuckoo's Nest* on me." You decide to follow his lead and adopt a casual stance as well. "I don't want to have to dust you."

Angel suddenly doubles over, falling to his knees, clutching his head. He shakes it gently, trying to rise. Looking over at the body of the young woman, blood seeping out over the asphalt, he wails, "No! What have I done?" and then clutches his head once more, screaming in pain.

Thrown off by his behavior, you aren't sure what to do. He slumps over on his side, hands pressed against his temples.

SLAYER CHOICE:

Do you decide to . . .

❚ go to Angel's side and try to help him? *If yes, turn to page 107.*

❚ be extra cautious and remain where you are? *If yes, turn to page 109.*

Pivoting away from him, you take off at full speed into the night. You don't want to fight with Angel. The thought of hurting him makes you feel sick. If only you can get to Giles's place, you can tell him that Angel isn't himself. The two of you can figure it out. Angel hasn't gone evil. You can fix this. Right?

Biting your lower lip, you run on, chest heaving in pain at the thought of what you've just witnessed.

SLAYER ACTION:
Turn to page 141.

Cautiously you approach Angel, who remains on his knees, groaning in pain. You stoop down, trying to see his face, which is still buried in his hands.

"Angel?" you ask quietly.

He doesn't answer, but instead grunts in pain.

Tentatively you reach a hand out and touch his shoulder. "What's going on?"

He removes his hands from his head, and says haltingly, "Nothing . . . I'm—I'm fine. Sorry about earlier. . . . I'm not sure what's gotten into me."

"Gotten *into* you?" you retort in disbelief. "Angel, you *killed* that woman."

Angel shakes his head, turning his gaze to the woman's body, sprawled in the alleyway in a pool of blood. "I know, I know!" he cries out in exasperation. "I didn't want it to happen! If I could just get this under control!"

You frown. "What, Angelus?"

He nods.

Confused, you say, "But before it hasn't been this much of a struggle . . . right?" You hope he hasn't killed a whole slew of victims and simply hidden it from you.

"Things are . . . different now," he manages. Slowly, he struggles to stand. "I just need to get home and rest."

"But, Angel," you insist, "you just killed that woman!"

"Please, Buffy," he says, bringing one hand to his

temples again. "Can't we just forget about this for right now? I need rest."

You are incredulous. "Forget about it? How am I supposed to 'forget' about it? You killed someone and even started to come after me!"

SLAYER CH⊖ICE:

Do you decide to . . .

\ say, "I'm the Slayer. I kill vampires because they hurt people. I can't just forget about this"? *If yes, turn to page 112.*

\ let Angel leave? *If yes, turn to page 114.*

Keeping a safe distance, you watch Angel doubled over, groaning in pain. "Angel?" He looks up at you, dark eyes pleading for help. But something in you tells you to stay put. Just when you think he is about to cry out again, clasping his hands feverishly to his head, he calmly rises to his feet and regards you with a strange mixture of curiosity and contempt.

"My darling Buffy," he sneers, walking toward you.

The voice is Angel's, but the tone is that of a stranger.

"What's gotten into you?" you ask.

"An interesting question. But it's more what's gotten *out* of me that's relevant here."

"What are you talking about?"

"'What are you talking about?'" Angel mocks. "Heh. Well, I'd have thought your little Slayerettes might have some ideas about that. Hasn't stuffy Giles come up with a theory yet? Or what about bookish Willow? She hangs on your every word. Surely she's been slaving around the clock to figure things out for you."

"Night terrors?" you venture, wondering if this extreme change in behavior could be explained by a sleep disorder. Of course, if a *mare* had taken him over, who knows how much his behavior would change? Was Angel still in there somewhere, struggling to reach the surface? Is that the war you are witnessing? A war for control over Angel's body between his sweet soul and the *mare*'s hateful spirit?

"The Night Terror." Angel laughs. "I'd say he's the

least of your worries, Buffy." He practically spits your name out, his voice is so filled with disgust.

"The Night Terror? It's a thing? Like a creature? Is it tangible?"

"Tangible, no. Though if it were, I'd be the first to point you in its direction to destroy it. I have much more"—he glances at the dead woman in the alley, eyeing the seeping blood hungrily—"*wet* endeavors to partake in."

"So it has control of you?" you ask, wondering how much more information he'll volunteer.

"Presently, no, my dear. Quite the opposite. And as I said before, the Night Terror is the least of your worries."

Suddenly Angel lunges forward, lashing out at you. You barely have time to dodge out of the way. You've seen him move fast before, but this is unreal.

As he closes in again, he catches you with a surprisingly painful kick to the gut that robs you of the wind in your lungs. For a moment you are stunned, trying to draw in a breath, and he takes this moment to strike you in the throat with the palm of his hand. Unable to breathe at all now, you reel backward, eyes swimming with the lack of air, and prepare to defend yourself.

He kicks out at you and you duck, swallowing painfully, your Slayer healing abilities pushed as you struggle for breath. As Angel recovers from the kick, you strike out with your foot, connecting painfully with his knee. You hear an audible *pop* and he cries out in surprise.

Finally you are able to take the smallest of breaths through your bruised windpipe. You suck in the fresh air, your lungs still burning. He throws a punch, which you block and counter, landing a solid blow to his solar plexus. Immediately your hand slips inside your jacket pocket, and your deft fingers close around a freshly sharpened stake.

You brandish it threateningly, and Angel laughs. "You're really going to use that on me?" he says over-confidently.

You don't know what to do. It's clear to you that he means business. Somehow he's gone evil, and you may have to stake him. But stake your true love? How can you?

SLAYER CHOICE:

Do you decide to . . .

\ try to stake Angel? *If yes, turn to page 116.*

\ continue to fight him with nonlethal blows? *If yes, turn to page 118.*

\ run away and find Giles so you can figure out what's wrong with your beloved? *If yes, turn to page 106.*

You shake your head, incredulous at the suggestion that you just walk away. "I'm the Slayer!" you remind him. "It's my job to kill vampires that hurt people. I can't just forget about this, Angel!" You watch him standing there, unsteady on his feet. "Angel," you plead. "Please tell me what's going on—what's different."

"It's too complicated to explain." He begins to stagger away, one hand holding his head.

"I can't just let you go. What if you do this again?" You watch his receding figure, which passes into a plane of shadows. "Come with me to Giles's. We'll be able to figure this out. Does it have to do with the night terrors?"

Suddenly Angel spins around, locking you in his gaze. "What? What do you know about that?"

Your brow furrows. "Me? You? Having them? We just talked about this. Giles found out a whole bunch of stuff on them and—"

Without warning, Angel breaks into a run, heading straight for you. You barely have time to dodge out of the way, and he narrowly misses you. He stops a few feet away and turns on you. "You're always going to be there, aren't you? Always watching, ready to stake me if I make the slightest misstep."

"Misstep? You *killed* someone, Angel. I'd say that qualifies as more than a *misstep*."

"I can't have you hounding me! Don't you see I need this?"

"You need what?" you ask, confused.

Angel takes another dash at you, but his fighting

style is slow and sloppy, not at all the quick vampire whose moves you know so well. You use his momentum and grab his arm, whirling him away, where he smacks into the alley wall. His head meets the brick with a sickening thud. For a moment you think he's going to slump over unconscious. But instead he continues to stand there, unmoving. A great sigh leaves him. Unsure of what to expect, you remain where you are, watching.

Then, as if in a trance, he moves away from the wall and begins walking away. You tell him to stop, but he doesn't seem to even hear you. You follow at a safe distance. At least this way, if he tries to kill someone, you will be there to stop him.

SLAYER ACTION:
Turn to page 137.

Against your better judgment, but wanting to have faith in Angel, you walk away from the incident, your mind a tangle of thoughts.

Has a *mare* taken him over? You can't believe you just watched him *kill* someone. But you couldn't have just staked him. Could you? Your true love? Just the thought of it makes you sick inside. Yet you don't know what to do.

The Slayer side of you demands the defense of human life, whispering to you that Angel has turned evil and that you should have staked him.

But the Buffy side of you, your heart, your soul, wants to believe in him. Surely he's not responsible for this turn of events. He must be possessed by the *mare*.

You decide that answers lie with Willow and Giles. You look at your watch. One fifteen a.m.

Giles will likely still be up, probably poring over some arcane text at his place.

Willow is probably already in her jammies, snuggled up with her laptop.

Of the two of them, Giles, with his endless resources, has probably uncovered more information, but the thought of having some comforting friend talk after all you've seen tonight is an appealing one.

SLAYER CHOICE:

Do you decide to . . .

❙ hurry over to Giles's place to see what he's found? *If yes, turn to page 141.*

❙ go throw rocks at Willow's window for some information and reassuring friend talk? *If yes, turn to page 132.*

You reel back and say, "Don't test me." The usual quips you pride yourself on when staking vamps are all gone. This situation just makes you sick. You never thought you'd have to stake Angel, at least not since last year, when you learned he was good.

With a swift kick to the chest, you knock Angel flat on his back. In moments you are straddling him, sitting on his stomach, bringing the stake down hard.

His eyes widen in those final seconds, and then he abruptly bucks you off. You careen backward, landing hard on the asphalt.

But instead of Angel leaping to his feet, as you expect, he curls into a fetal position on his side, clasping his head in his hands. "Please, no . . . ," he whimpers. "This will not work. . . ." After a moment, he uncurls and looks over at you, terror in his eyes. You rise to your feet, stake at the ready.

Then, on unsteady legs, he gets up too, never taking his eyes off you. "Please . . . no . . . ," he repeats, then turns and sprints away from you.

You follow, close on his heels. You don't trust for a second that he won't lose it and kill another human. But when he reaches the building next to the abandoned factory and spies you close on his trail, he stops and springs to the top of the three-story brick structure, leaving you behind.

You turn back down the alley, past the murdered woman, trying to track his progress on the rooftop. He leaps from building to building, far outpacing you with his vampire speed.

You can still see him in the distance. He may be headed back to his place, though he'd know how easy it would be for you to find him there.

You could also head over to Giles's place. Maybe he's dug up something that might explain Angel's radical change in character.

SLAYER CHOICE:

Do you decide to . . .

\ find Giles and see what he's learned? *If yes, turn to page 114.*

\ see if Angel returns to his place? *If yes, turn to page 137.*

Not truly wanting to stake Angel, you continue to dart from one foot to the other, staying out of his reach. If only you could somehow subdue him, you could get him to the Scoobies and together you could figure out what is wrong.

Angel is fast, though, vampire fast, as he lashes out at you again with a powerful kick. You dodge, but his foot lands a glancing blow on your kidney, and a bloom of pain erupts in your back. Off balance, you stagger briefly and then recover, just in time to turn and see Angel too close, in trapping distance. He lands a fierce head butt to your face, your already throbbing nose exploding again in a rain of blood. With bright, popping stars in your eyes, you strike him several times in the throat and sides, to no avail.

You feel the wet of his tongue as his mouth closes painfully on your neck. He tears and rips at your flesh there, drinking deeply as your blood pumps into his mouth. Starting to feel dizzy, you try to knee him in the groin. But he's so close, you can't lift your knee. He slams you against one wall of the alley, his teeth clamped onto you like a pneumatic vise. Your head swims as you struggle to stay conscious, feeling the very life ebb out of you in pulses—feeding Angel, making him ever stronger while you grow weaker and weaker.

So tired.

You feel so tired.

You try to push against the cold leather of his jacket, try to punch a finger through his eyes, but he continues to drink deeply. He fights you to the ground, crushing you with his weight as more and more blood pumps out of your body from your carotid artery.

The pain subsides. You can no longer really feel the hard asphalt beneath you, or Angel's weight pushing down on you. The throbbing in your neck dies away, and all you want to do is sleep.

But you know it isn't sleep that lulls you now into oblivion.

It is death. Death at the hands of your love.

But grasp as you might, you can't hold on to the last, fleeting strains of life in your body. Your heart tries to pump, but finds little blood to move. You feel it flutter irregularly in your chest, then stop completely. Your life slips away against your will, into Angel's terrible hunger, and at last you close your eyes to the darkness, and it consumes you.

THE END

"**O**kay," you say to Ethan. "Spill. What's this great threat to Sunnydale?"

Ethan has led you, Giles, and Angel to a seedy hotel on the outskirts of Sunnydale. But now he won't get out of Giles's car.

"A mummy," Ethan explains. "It's in my motel room. At least it was when I left."

"How did you get a mummy in your motel room?" you prompt.

"Well," he continues, glancing at you nervously. "I more or less reanimated it after stealing it from the Sunnydale Museum."

"More or less?" You're really getting cranky now.

"Okay. I reanimated it by restoring its soul. I wanted it to do my bidding."

"Oh, how cliché," Giles breathes.

"There were a few little trinkets here and about Sunnydale that I wanted to use for a little experiment."

"In chaos?" Giles hazards.

Ethan shrugs. "Well, chaos and power. The usual."

You're growing impatient. "Go on."

"Yes. What 'trinkets'?" demands Giles.

"The Gem of Ehktat. It's an enchanted crystal that allows the user to see exactly when they are going to die—"

"Like right now?" you threaten him.

"—and how to prevent it," Ethan finishes, throwing a worried glance in your direction. "I stole it from a private collector."

"You mean the mummy stole it," Angel corrects him.

"Yes."

"And the other so-called trinkets?" Giles prompts.

"Just one more. The Dagger of Draknar."

Giles sighs. "I've heard of this one. It *was* on display in the archaeology department of UC Sunnydale. It can mystically cut away the memories of its victims."

Ethan clasps his hands together in delight. "Oh, together they would have made a wonderful weapon to cause great inconvenience."

You shake your head. Is this guy for real? Turning people into their Halloween costumes? Weapons of great inconvenience? He must have missed the whole world domination lecture of Villainy 101.

"It was all going swimmingly. But then the mummy starting having these night terrors. It would awake, paralyzed, screaming in terror, convinced something else was in the room with it, though I couldn't see anything."

That certainly sounds familiar.

"It happened three nights running, and tonight, when I got back to my room, it had simply stopped obeying my commands. Its behavior changed drastically. I asked around, did a little research, and learned about a creature called the Night Terror that takes over the bodies of sleeping people. It's trapped in the dream world, you see, and longs for permanent escape. And it's successfully taken over my mummy. It won't do anything now. It's like it's on vacation. Go on, see for yourselves." He gestures toward the hotel room.

You all climb out of the car, and Ethan unlocks the door to room number 15. You can hear the television blaring inside.

An Egyptian mummy sits propped up on the bed, watching *Stargate SG-1* and eating spoonfuls of chocolate brownie swirl ice cream straight from the carton.

It sees you and shakes its head. "Slayer," it rattles in a voice like crackling dry leaves. "You're too late now. You and Angel stay up so I can't have your bodies. Well, it doesn't matter now, because I've found one, and I don't even need to *try* to blend in in this thing."

It goes back to shoveling spoonfuls of ice cream into its mouth. You can see the chocolate dribbling out through the bandages near its stomach. You wonder what chocolate ice cream would taste like to thousand-year-old taste buds. Pretty much like dust, you imagine.

"It'll be watching *Oprah* next," Ethan says. "It loves that show."

"This is the great evil threat to Sunnydale?" you ask Ethan as the mummy opens a box of Ding Dongs and digs in.

"Got an extra one?" Giles asks, leaning forward. You look at him in disbelief. "Never mind," he says to the mummy.

"Yes, it is a threat!" Ethan cries out. "It's a mummy! It may be eating ice cream now, but soon it will be prowling the streets of Sunnydale, strangling people with one hand. It's what mummies do."

"Except mummies that steal gems and priceless daggers."

"Well, it won't even let me have those, will it?" Ethan says in exasperation.

"I'm sitting on them," the mummy says. "It's the only way I can keep him paying the rent on this place. This TV thing is great!"

You glare at Ethan through narrowed eyes. "Sunnydale beware."

"So let me get your story straight," Giles says. "You want us to believe that this"—he gestures pointedly at the chocolate-covered mummy—"terrifying specimen of evil is going to destroy Sunnydale. But it's clear you're only after the gem and the dagger, which he will not relinquish."

Ethan shakes his head indignantly. "No, Ripper. That's not it at all. I genuinely want to protect the people of Sunnydale. The relics have nothing to do with it."

"Oh, please," Giles mutters in disgust. He gestures you and Angel over, and you have a conference in whispers. "Whether or not it seems harmless," Giles starts, "that's still the Night Terror in there, and we have no way of knowing how long it'll stay in the mummy's body. Who knows who it will possess next? It needs to be stopped."

To put it mildly. You flash back to the terror of the creature pressing down on your chest, trying to possess your body.

"So what should we do?"

"Obviously, we can't let Ethan have the relics. We

need to banish the Night Terror, force it out of the mummy's body, and destroy it for good."

You glance at the TV. The Stargate team wanders through ancient ruins. It looks like an interesting episode.

"Hey! We could bore it out of the body," you offer.

Giles looks intrigued. "With some kind of tunneling device?"

"No, not that kind of bore. Make it watch really bad TV. Don't let it have ice cream. It's not like it can really go out for a night on the town in that body. Eventually the Night Terror will realize it has to leave the body. I'll stay here and keep guard while you anonymously return the gem and the dagger to the owners."

"That might make the Night Terror leave this body, but then we'd need to research a banishing spell to permanently block it. I have some ideas. . . . I've read about some German protection spells that might work."

"Sounds good."

"Then we can return the mummy to the Sunnydale Museum."

"Really?" You look over at the creature. "But Giles, it's sort of ruined. It's got chocolate ice cream trickling through its bandages. Dorito stains on its chest."

"It doesn't matter. It's still a priceless Nineteenth Dynasty mummy."

"Okay, Giles."

Giles then eyes the chocolate ice cream longingly. Maybe he gets peckish when he stays up too long.

Ethan tries to creep closer to interfere, and Angel stills him with a firm hand to the shoulder.

Ethan steps up anyway, shrugging Angel's hand away. "I know of a ritual to banish the Night Terror. I . . . liberated some supplies for it earlier tonight from the magic shop."

You and Giles regard him coolly.

SLAYER CHOICE:
Do you decide to . . .

\ attempt Ethan's spell? *If yes, turn to page 147.*

\ try to bore the Night Terror out of the mummy? *If yes, turn to page 274.*

You grip the Medallion of Morpheus tightly in your hand and speak the incantation clearly. It grows warm, glowing with a gold light, and the world swirls around you. Clouds whip by, scarlet and violet. Your body becomes light, lifting up from the ground and then tumbling, end over end, into a vortex of clouds. Your speed increases until you soar at such a great velocity that your hair streams behind you, and the wind in your eyes causes them to tear.

Then you land hard, tumbling in a somersault and flopping to a halt on an expanse of grass. You blink into the bright sun overhead, bringing an arm up to shield your eyes. You're on your street! Lying under your neighbor's tree!

You get to your feet, brushing blades of grass off your clothes, and start off toward your house two doors down. You reach a patch of shade at the edge of your property just as your front door opens. Angel steps out onto the porch, talking with your parents.

You stop abruptly. Angel in the sunlight? Your dad in Sunnydale? Are you still in the dream world?

Angel takes your mom's hand gently, and you see she's fighting back tears. "Thank you for stopping by," she tells him.

"If there's ever anything you need . . . ," he says, his voice trailing off.

She nods. "Thank you. We will call."

He squeezes her hand and lets go, starting down your front walk. Your parents close the door.

Stunned, you don't move. Then finally, as Angel turns to walk away, you say, "Angel?"

He spins around, face haunted. "Buffy?"

You step onto your lawn, into the sunlight.

He clasps one hand to his chest, then falls to his knees, staring at you.

You rush forward to steady him.

"I don't understand . . . ," he whispers as you kneel next to him. "How can you be alive?"

"How can you be out in the sunlight?"

Confusion wrinkles his brow. "How do you know about that?"

"About your being a vampire?"

His eyes widen. "I never told you that. And how can you be here? I . . . watched you die."

Now you're really confused. "I think you better explain this to me. Please. From the beginning, as if I don't know anything. Because I may be dreaming."

"I think I'm the one dreaming." He falls back, sitting down on the grass. "Your parents . . . we've got to tell them. How can this be?"

"Explain."

"You were killed. The Bronze burned down. You wouldn't leave . . . kept trying to get people out. A beam fell on you. You burned to death." He grabs your arm. "Buffy, I watched as the flames engulfed you. I heard your screams. I couldn't do anything. . . . I tried to put it out, so did Willow. We were both burned." He looks down. "I saw your bones, Buffy. We all did."

Burned alive in a fire? "Okay . . . now how can you be out in the sunlight?"

"I'm mortal now."

Your heart practically stops beating, then begins racing so fast you think you're having heart palpitations. "What?"

"But I never told you I'd been a vampire. Shortly after I met you, I learned of a ritual that can restore mortality to a vampire, banishing the demon inside. I performed it before you could find out I was a vampire. So how could you know that?"

You stare down at the grass, trying to figure this out. You're either still dreaming or the Medallion of Morpheus didn't quite take you to the right home. "This is what I know. My body was taken over by this demon called the Night Terror, and it stranded my soul in the dream world. I was trapped in my dreams. I met Giles's dream body, and he gave me the Medallion of Morpheus and told me to use it to travel home. There were two incantations, but he wasn't sure about either. Maybe I used the wrong one. Maybe I ended up in the wrong dimension."

Angel glances around. "Where's the medallion now?"

You check your hands, search your pockets, and realize you don't have it. Getting to your feet, you jog to the neighbor's yard and search the place under the tree. It's gone. "I guess it didn't make the trip with me." *Thanks for mentioning that, Giles, Mr. Just Try the Other Incantation If the First One Doesn't Work.*

"Your parents," Angel says, standing up. "We've got to tell them. They've been devastated, Buffy. This is amazing."

"Wait . . ." You take his hand. "Why is my dad here? For the funeral?"

Angel furrows his brow. "No . . . your funeral was weeks ago. Your dad lives here."

"They're not divorced?"

"No. They've always been together."

He pulls you to the door. You are reluctant, not because you don't want to see them, but because it's clear you're not in the home you left. It's so similar, but there are obviously some major differences.

When your mom answers the door, she blinks, puts her hand on her chest, blinks again, then moves forward in slow motion and hugs you. She feels like your mom. Smells like her. Sounds like her. If this is another dimension, it's eerily similar. "I don't understand . . . ," she says.

Your dad enters the room, sees you, and grabs the stair railing for support. "Buffy?"

"Hi, Daddy."

"What is—," he begins.

"I'll explain later," you tell them, unable to think of a believable excuse on such short notice. You can't just let them know you're the slayer now. It would take too long and be an even bigger shock to them. "Do you have a Giles in this place?"

"Of course," Angel says.

"Take me to him."

On the way, you tell your parents you need to see Giles alone. Reluctantly, they drop you and Angel off. Your Watcher lives in the same place. He looks the same. It's spooky. He has heard of the Medallion of Morpheus, and explains that it can transport the user to a variety of different dimensions. None of the incantations associated with it translate exactly as "home dimension," but instead, literally as the dimension where you would *feel* most at home. He then adds that his dream version was probably a bit out of sorts and didn't have all the facts straight, as the medallion does not travel with the user.

You have them call Willow and Xander. When your friends show up, they sit down on Giles's couch, stunned. Willow cries.

You sit down too, taking it all in.

You're in another dimension. It has a need for a Slayer in Sunnydale, since your counterpart recently expired. Your parents are still together. Angel is mortal. And there's no obvious way back. You guess you'll stay, you say, snuggling up next to Angel on the couch.

Giles says he'll search for another way to get you back. You know he'll figure it out soon. You think of your own dimension, of the Night Terror walking around in your body. You hate the thought of leaving your friends and your mom unprotected. But at least you know for certain that that dimension is not Slayerless— it has Kendra. And you think of your parents here, grieving for you. They don't have to now. It's almost too big to think about.

But at least for a few days, you'll just be with them, and spend time with Angel. You know that Giles must find a way to return you home. All you can do is enjoy what little time you have here in this strange parallel dimension, and hope everything works out.

THE END

You start toward Willow's. You can't believe this. Angel gone evil? Then not evil?

Angel killed someone. Your true love is a murderous vampire.

You move through the quiet streets of Sunnydale, your heart heavy and feeling like it's stuffed with too much sad blood. You need to get your head straight about Angel. Your emotions cloud your judgment. Maybe Willow will have some ideas. You could get the others and tie him up maybe, until Giles figures out what's wrong.

You reach Willow's block and see the mini-mart on the corner, its bright lights a beacon on the dark street.

Your stomach growls. When was the last time you ate anything truly substantial? You know that you should probably get something with protein, but one thing will make this talk with Willow easier.

Ice cream. You can sit on her bed, plowing through carton after carton, and figure this thing out while simultaneously drowning your sorrows in chocolatey gooey goodness.

SLAYER ACTION:
Turn to page 144.

Carefully, Giles replaces the Orb of Trakoa, nestling it in a velvety scarf. "I'll say the proper incantation to bring both of us home."

"Can't I just wake up after you leave?" you ask. You'd much rather use the tried-and-true method of simply waking up than trust surreal dream-Giles's translation of ancient Phoenician, though you're sure it's probably perfectly safe.

Probably.

"Very well," he says. "But if for some reason you can't return, this scroll and the medallion will remain here after I depart. You can always use it after me."

"Sure, Giles. I'll get right on that ancient Phoenician."

"Oh, Buffy," he laments, pulling out a small pad of paper and a pencil. On it he writes a phonetic equivalent of the home dimension incantation. "Now you can't possibly muddle it up." He rips off the sheet and hands it to you.

You look at the hurriedly scrawled writing. "Thanks. But I think I'll try waking up first."

"Suit yourself." He holds the pendant out, wrapping the chain around his fingers, and recites the incantation. The bronze pendant begins to glow, burning from the inside, and Giles grips it tighter. A vortex whirls out from the pendant, sweeping Giles up in it, and he swirls around and around, growing smaller and smaller. Clouds whip by in the whirlwind, growing gold, then red, then gray, and then with a deafening crack that leaves your ears ringing, the vortex collapses in on itself, winking Giles out of view. The pendant falls to the marble floor with a metallic clink.

You look around. Definitely no Giles. You hope it worked.

Now to wake yourself up.

You think of Angel, of wanting to be sure Giles made it home, of shoe sales you're missing, and you awake with a start, teetering precariously in the tree branches.

Forcing your pounding heart to slow as you catch yourself from falling, you take a deep breath. You made it!

Now you just have to be sure that Giles made it too.

It's light out now, the sun already bathing Sunnydale in its bright glow.

Cautiously you climb out of the tree, careful not to draw attention, especially from any gun-toting Englishmen. At the last branch, you leap down onto the grass below. You decide to look first at Giles's place.

Walking in that direction, you hear the unmistakable clatter, cough, and moan of Giles's Citroën. Moving behind a tree, you watch it sputter by, Giles behind the wheel. He looks tired and worried, but not homicidal.

Oh well, you think, *I've got to face him sometime.*

You step out onto the sidewalk and wave. "Giles!"

He spots you, pulling to the curb.

"Buffy!"

"Is it you?"

"Yes! The pendant worked!"

That's pretty specific.

"Climb in! Willow found a German protection spell against the *alpdruck*. We should be able to block its ability to take over hosts."

You're still not entirely sure it's him.

"Bay City Rollers?" you ask.

"Excuse me?"

"Bay City Rollers?" you insist.

"What real music is all about?"

"Okay." You open the rusty door and climb in, the springs in the seat squeaking and the old vinyl hissing.

"You mean to tell me you weren't sure it was me?" Giles asks, incredulous. "Surely you could tell before. Isn't that what tipped you off?"

"Actually, no. It was the whole you shooting at me thing."

"My *what*?"

"Yeah, with an old rusty revolver."

"Not my beloved dueling pistol from 1886!" he practically shouts.

"Yes, that's probably the one."

"But that was in no shape to be fired! It's probably ruined!"

"Glad you're so worried about me, Giles. Yes, I'm fine from being shot at."

"Oh, yes. Of course I'm glad you're all right, Buffy," Giles mumbles as an afterthought. He pulls away from the curb and heads toward Willow's house.

"So this protection spell will work?"

"I don't see why not. The ingredients are exceedingly simple."

"Well, I'm glad something is, for a change. I'll be glad when life and sleeping go back to normal." After a moment of picturing your normal life—dusting vamps, punching out demons, busting up nests of the undead—you decide to rephrase. "I'll be glad when I can go back to really biffing my enemies. I've had enough of this intangible stuff."

You arrive at Willow's just as her parents leave for work. Willow waves good-bye to them, then ushers you in. In her living room, Giles performs the *alpdruck* banishing spell, and instantly you feel better.

Tonight you'll sleep in your own bed, and you'll wake up tomorrow knowing your friends are really who they say they are.

THE END

Keeping to the shadows, you trail silently after Angel, who appears unaware of your presence. He climbs down into a manhole and you follow, retracing the familiar path back to his place. How many times you've walked this route, butterflies in your stomach at the thought of seeing Angel, that pleasant excitement burning in your stomach. And now, here you are, following him after witnessing a brutal murder.

At his door he pauses, leaning his head against the metal and closing his eyes. Finally he opens the door and disappears inside. You creep to the door and press your ear against it. Only silence greets you.

Then, after a few moments go by, you quietly let yourself in.

Inside, Angel lies sleeping on his bed, still fully clothed in his blood-soaked shirt and black pants, one arm hanging off the side. He looks so peaceful there, the terribly violent look now gone, his face angelic once again. You walk to him and gently take his hand.

His eyes flutter in his head and he opens them, focusing on you. "Buffy?"

"Yes."

"Is this still a dream?"

You shake your head.

"How do you know?"

"Because it hurts too much."

Angel blinks quickly, then sits up abruptly, pinching his face, rubbing his arms. "It's not a dream!" he nearly shouts. He seizes you in his arms, cradling you against his chest.

"Angel, tell me what's going on with you!" you demand, pushing him away.

His dark eyes study you. "It really is you, isn't it?"

"Yes," you assure him. "Now explain."

He leans back on one hand, not taking his eyes off you. "I've been trapped, Buffy. For days on end."

"What do you mean?"

"I was trapped in my dreams. I couldn't wake up." He puts one hand on his chest, as if reassuring himself that he really is there. "This *thing* traded places with me. It was imprisoned somehow inside its own dreams, and it exchanged places with me. My soul, my consciousness, went to the dream world, and its soul took over my body."

"And you were fighting over it?"

Angel shakes his head. "No—not at all. That's the scary part. I couldn't do anything about it. Sometimes I could see through the veil of dreams to my actual body, and I'd try to rejoin with it. But I wasn't able to."

"But it seemed like two personalities were struggling over your body just now."

"I wasn't one of them," Angel said, looking spooked.

"One was so . . . evil, so cold, Angel. The other personality seemed vulnerable, unsure."

"Evil?" Angel asks, raising an eyebrow. "This *thing* is called the Night Terror. He wants to steal a body to live in permanently. It may have been fighting it out with Angelus."

You think of the woman lying dead in the alley. "That makes sense."

"So what happened? Why are you back now?"

Angel shakes his head. "I don't know. I just suddenly woke up in my body. It's like the Night Terror just . . . gave it up."

"Why would it do that? Why does it need a body so much?"

"I exchanged a little bit of its consciousness when we switched places. I got the image that it was a prisoner, and that the intangible world of dreams was its prison. It longs to be corporeal."

"So why would it give up your body, then?"

Angel shrugs. "I don't know. It wouldn't."

"We need to figure out what happened, and fast. That thing will probably come back for seconds, and we can't risk that."

Angel can see the grave expression in your eyes, because he asks, "Buffy, what did it do?"

You look away, knowing how much Angel is already haunted by his past.

"Did the Night Terror kill someone?"

You meet his eyes. "I'm not sure. If you're right that Angelus might have been warring for dominance, it could have been that. But someone was killed."

"Oh, no," Angel breathes, putting his head in his hands.

"It's not your fault, Angel. But we need to figure this out. We need Giles."

Angel nods.

"And I think we should both stay up until we figure this thing out. If we don't fall asleep, it can't take us over." Your eyes burn with exhaustion, and all your teeth have taken up the latest in fall woolen fashion. You'd like to go home and check on your mom. With her late hours at the gallery lately, you've hardly seen her, and when you have, she's looked exhausted. "Maybe I should check on my mom first. She hasn't been sleeping too well lately." You could also use a change of clothes. After that fight with Angel, your clothes are more dirty rips than actual functional garments.

SLAYER CH⊕ICE:

Do you decide to . . .

❙ check on your mom before heading over to Giles? *If yes, turn to page 161.*

❙ ignore the mounting fuzz on your teeth and go straight to Giles's apartment? *If yes, turn to page 163.*

At Giles's apartment, you pound on his door. It's very late but you just don't care. "Giles!"

You think of Angel out there, possibly killing someone else right now while you waste time knocking on your Watcher's door. "Giles!" you shout again.

"Just a minute," you hear him grumble on the other side of the door, disengaging locks. As soon as the door opens a crack, you push your way inside, turning to see a sleepy Giles in his robe.

"Giles! Something bad has happened."

Closing the door after you, he relocks it and turns, squinting at you. He doesn't even have his glasses on. "What is it?"

"It's Angel . . . he killed someone," you finish with great difficulty.

Giles's mouth opens in dismay, his forehead creasing with concern. "Just now?"

"Yes, just now. In an alley. I saw it, Giles. He was evil."

"I don't understand . . ." Giles moves to his desk, where he finds his glasses and puts them on. "With Angel's soul in place, it should overpower the vampire in him."

"That's the weird part," you go on. "It was like watching two personalities fighting over his body."

"Angel and the vampire?"

"Maybe . . . though even when he was behaving more like Angel, it still wasn't quite right. He's out of sorts. In pain." After a moment you add, "Giles, I don't like this. Something is seriously wrong."

"Obviously, Buffy, if he's killed someone."

"It's more than that, Giles. It's not just that he's reverted to being a vampire."

"He already was a vampire."

"Okay, an evil vampire. Not a blood-bank-raiding vampire."

"Well, we do know from the Watcher journals that as Angelus, before Angel had his soul, he was one of the most vicious vampires to ever plague humanity. He delighted in torturing his victims, in playing with them before he made the final kill. He murdered their families while they watched. The sheer insidiousness of his devised tortures were legendary among—"

"Okay, Giles. I get the picture," you cut in, holding up your hands for mercy. You hate to think of Angel like that, even if the sweet soul you know now wasn't even present in the body back then. "We need to figure out what's wrong with him. I don't want to just stake him."

"What do you propose, then?" Giles asks.

"Capturing him."

"Is that wise, Buffy?"

"Wise or not, Giles, it's what we're going to do."

You move to the phone. "Let's get the others, some shackles and heavy chains, and go check the places he's likely to be."

Giles nods. After a few phone calls, a quick raiding of Giles's weapon cabinets for chains and a crossbow, you, Xander, Willow, and Giles begin the hunt through the streets of Sunnydale.

You check Angel's place, the area around the Bronze, then finally near the site of Angel's kill. Maybe he's returned to feast again.

SLAYER ACTION:
Turn to page 284.

You reach the mini-mart a few minutes later, ready to buy every carton of ice cream in the place. Of course, you realize gloomily, you only have $3.50. Great. On the newsstand in front of the counter, you see the latest edition of the Sunnydale newspaper.

PRICELESS RELICS STOLEN IN CRIME SPREE! raves the headline. Relics? Stolen relics always end up rearing their ugly heads in your life. You peer closer at the text beneath. Among the missing items are an entire Egyptian mummy stolen from the Sunnydale Museum and an ancient Egyptian gem stolen from a private collector's estate. A rather frazzled gardener at the estate saw the culprit and described him as "horrible," "bandaged," and "downright stinky." And only this morning, a Sumerian dagger was stolen from the archaeology department of UC Sunnydale. A grad student witnessed the theft and described the thief as "nightmarish," "terrifying," and "dating roughly to the Nineteenth Egyptian Dynasty under Ramses II."

Weird. Definitely Giles-worthy. You'll have to tell him about this tomorrow, though he'll probably already know about it by then.

You walk to the frozen section and glance over all the ice cream labels. Something with chocolate. With chocolate swirls. And chocolate chunks. And chocolate brownie bits.

You're so drowning in woe that you don't even see the strange figure staggering up until you catch the glimpse of its reflection in the freezer door. By then it's on top of you, and you feel a searing hot pain rip into your back. A hand flies up, clamping down on your neck, instantly crushing your windpipe.

You feel the knife rip into your back muscles, puncturing your left lung as your eyes stream with tears of pain. The arm grabbing you is ancient and moldy, wrapped in tattered bandages. You give a kick and spin, the blade painfully ripping through your side on its way out.

As you hold your throat, struggling in vain to breathe, you see the thing standing before you—an Egyptian mummy, coming toward you again with a rusted knife dripping in blood. Your blood.

As your head grows light and dizzy with lack of oxygen and your vision narrows to a dark tunnel, you hear cackling. You glance to the end of the freezer aisle and see Ethan Rayne, laughing with delight at your dilemma.

"Kill her," he commands the mummy, who continues to lumber forward.

You feel hot blood streaming down your back and legs, and still can't get a breath. "Come on, Slayer healing abilities," you urge, but even then you suddenly find yourself on the floor, your vision now completely black.

Lungs burning in your chest, crushed throat a bright center of pain, you feel yourself slipping away into darkness.

Death is stealing over you.

You feel the mummy's knife dive into your back

one last time, knowing in some strange slow-motion clarity that this time it will pierce your heart.

As the last spark of life leaves your body, you curse Ethan Rayne, then think of Angel, Xander, Giles, and finally Willow. Tears leave your unseeing eyes as you slip away.

THE END

Against your better judgment, you agree to go with Ethan's spell. He lays out the ingredients on the plastic table by the window. The mummy listens as Ethan chants, lights candles, and flips through a decaying leather book. It doesn't look too disturbed. Ethan's voice rises in volume, and as he chants, he grows bigger and bigger, his hands now twice as big as before, his head the size of your whole body. Alarm buzzes inside you. What is he doing?

Then you realize it's not Ethan that's getting bigger, but you and the others growing smaller. You can barely see over the top of the bed now. Now you can see under the bed without stooping over. The pile carpet becomes a dense jungle, something you'd need a machete to navigate through.

"Damn you, Ethan!" Giles squeaks.

"Far out," the mummy says, and you see its huge head leaning over the side of the bed. A melted drop of ice cream falls and explodes on the carpet like an antipersonnel mine. The blast of air from it knocks you and the others off balance.

"I'm going to kill you!" you shout at Ethan.

He cups a hand over his ear. "What's that? Oh, I'm afraid not. You see, I have the Gem of Ehktat, and know perfectly well when I'm going to die. And it's not by your hand."

"Change us back this instant!" Giles shouts.

"Sorry, Ripper, old man. But I can't have you hanging around, always mucking up my plans. This should slow you down a bit."

The mummy shifts its position on the bed and staggers to its feet. "I need another carton of Super-Fudge-a-Riffically-Cherry," it mumbles, and staggers toward the small motel refrigerator. Unfortunately, you stand directly in its path. Waving your arms, you cry out to attract its attention, but its bandaged, reeking foot crashes down toward you like a descending zeppelin in wartime. You try to push Giles out of the way, but the carpet, sticky with ice cream, won't let you through. It's like running in chest-high snow. The world darkens as the mummy's foot descends.

"Didn't see that coming," you hear Ethan say.

The last thing you think is, "At least he didn't say, 'I made short work of you, Slayer.'"

THE END

W hile Angel stands there immobile, eyes closed, you turn and dash off in the direction of Giles's place. If you can get enough manpower to shackle and chain him, you might be able to bind him until you figure out what's wrong. You could even lock him up in the metal cage in the library. That would likely hold him. Unless he got really pissed off.

Lungs burning with the effort, you don't stop running until you reach the patio outside Giles's apartment. A painful stitch has formed in your side, making each breath hurt. Then, leaning over, you gasp until you can breathe regularly again, and then knock on the door.

Giles answers almost immediately, a mug of tea in one hand. "Buffy," he says, opening the door wider. "You're hurt. Come in."

You look at him with weary eyes. "Thanks, Giles." Your voice sounds scratchy, your throat gone dry. Your nose throbs, but you don't think it's broken.

"Looks like it was quite a fight. I'll get you some ice and water," he offers solicitously, and moves into his kitchen. A moment later he returns with a glass of water, which you drink down appreciatively, the cool water soothing your throat. You notice a lump of emotion lurking there, too. He hands you an ice pack, which you place on your nose.

"What happened?" Giles says, his brow furrowed with concern. He sits down on the edge of his desk while you claim a barstool next to his counter.

"It's Angel," you say between gasps. The stitch in

your side finally starts to ease up. "I don't know what's wrong with him, but he's gone completely buggo."

"Buggo?" Giles asks, raising an eyebrow.

"Evil," you clarify.

"Evil?"

"Giles, I need your help, not a parrot."

Giles frowns at your sarcasm. "Where is he now?"

"In an alley near the Bronze. He was sort of in a trance when I left. We need shackles and chains." You stand up and move to the phone. "I'm going to call Xander and Willow. When I fought him in the alley earlier, he was amazingly tough. We're going to need all the manpower we can get."

Giles nods, moving to a large trunk next to his TV. He pulls out a length of heavy chain complete with shackles. For a second you wonder why he has these so conveniently stored, but then, thinking of your own trunk full of holy water, crossbows, and stakes, you decide you don't need to ask. Giles pauses, regarding you over his shoulder. "When you say evil, you mean . . ."

"Like feeding on people evil."

"I see," Giles says, frowning even more now. And you thought your sarcasm was the chief frown-causer for Giles. You'll have to try harder. "This is not good."

"Tell me about it. Getting into fistfights in some seedy alley with my boyfriend? Not my idea of a hot date."

"Hot date. Yes, of course." Giles grimaces.

"Sorry." You don't want to think of Giles and Jennie Calendar dating, and Giles doesn't seem to want to hear the lurid details of your love life, either. It works out well.

You pick up the receiver and start dialing.

Twenty minutes later, Willow and Xander show up and you all start for the alley. As you close Giles's door behind you, you think better of it and go back in for a crossbow. You hope desperately that you won't have to use it against Angel.

SLAYER ACTION:
Turn to page 284.

After several long minutes, Angel finally stirs. Shaking his head as if shaking off a bad memory, Angel brings one hand to his face and touches it. Then he touches his arms, his chest. "I'm back!" he says. Snapping his gaze to you, he says, "Buffy!" and rushes toward you, smiling.

You back away, ready to strike him if he gets close enough. He does and you do, landing a powerful blow to his nose. He stops, bringing his hands to his face. "Ow! What was that for?"

"Uh . . . maybe for attacking me?" You feel bewildered.

"Buffy, listen, I don't know what's been going on down here, but I've been trapped for days now in another dimension."

"What?" you ask, incredulous.

"Remember those nightmares we were having?"

You nod.

"They were caused by this thing people call the Night Terror. It's some kind of demon that is trapped in the dream world and wants to get out. It took over my body."

You're not buying it. Yet. "Go on," you say, still maintaining a cautious distance.

"When it took over my body, we exchanged consciousnesses, just for a second. I *knew* things about it. It wanted my body, Buffy."

"Oh?" you say, lifting an eyebrow. "For what?" You *try* to sound innocent. Really. But it doesn't work.

"Not like that," he says quickly. "It wanted to steal

my body to live in this world. It had chosen me specifically." After a moment of contemplation, seeing the
look of reluctance on your face he adds, "Buffy, you
don't know how good it is to see you. I've been trapped
in my dreams, trapped in a strange dream dimension
for days. For a long time, I didn't even realize I *was*
dreaming. Nothing made sense."

He looks at you, pain in his eyes. "It was a living
nightmare. . . . all my past crimes . . ." His voice trails
off, and he averts his gaze.

"Are you telling me that this demon took over your
body, sending your soul, your mind, to the dream
world?"

"Yes," he says.

"So it wasn't you who said all those terrible things,
who . . ." You look over at the body of the woman,
lying sprawled some distance away.

"Oh, God—," Angel says, swallowing hard. "That
thing . . . killed her?"

You nod.

"In my body?"

"Yes."

"Will she—"

"No. There was no exchange of blood," you assure
him, letting Angel know the woman won't become a
vampire herself.

"So you were fighting to gain control this whole
time? That was you fighting the Night Terror?"

Angel looks confused. "No. I only came back just
now. Suddenly I was just here." He thinks a moment.

"The demon wouldn't have been alone in my body," he says slowly, watching your face. "He would have been fighting Angelus. The minute Angelus sensed my soul wasn't coming back any time soon, he must have taken over. But he didn't have free reign, because the Night Terror was in there too."

You nod, beginning to understand the mood swings you'd witnessed, the back-and-forth from aggressive to passive.

"But why did the Night Terror leave your body?"

Angel shrugs. "I don't know. Maybe Angelus drove it out."

"Like it did with Eygon?" you ask, referring to the time Angel saved the Scoobies' collective bacon by letting a demon take over his body. The vampire inside him had fought Eygon and won, destroying him forever.

You study Angel's face for a long time. The kindness and emotion have returned to his brown eyes. This is the Angel for whom you've come to feel so powerfully.

"We need to get to Giles's place. Figure out a way to keep this thing from coming back."

SLAYER ACTION:
Turn to page 155.

Still not completely trusting Angel, you keep your eyes on him.

"What about . . ." His voice trails off, and he gestures toward the dead woman.

"The police will find her," you tell him, feeling a bit cold for saying that. But it's true. She's in the city's official domain now. She is a murder victim, and it is for the Sunnydale PD to puzzle over now. Your work is done.

Feeling regret fill your heart at the sight of her, you turn away and start off toward Giles's apartment. Angel falls in beside you.

You steal a look at him, and instead of seeing his usual brooding self, you see the hint of a rare smile on his face.

"Yes?"

"I'm sorry," he fumbles. "It's just so good to be back!"

You only hope it stays that way.

"I don't like your evil twin very much," you admit.

"Angelus or the crude Night Terror imitation of me?"

"Both."

You walk on, the silence hanging awkwardly between you, your distrust of him feeling heavy in your heart.

"You couldn't tell it wasn't me?" He looks hurt.

"Oh, yes. I definitely knew you were different. Instead of brooding and distant, you were brooding, distant, and mean."

"I'm sorry. I hope my body didn't say anything too offensive in my absence."

"I'll heal," you say.

Angel looks over at you, then stops. "I'm glad you're okay," he says, then pulls you to him.

At first you stiffen, still uncertain if he can be trusted. But he feels like Angel. Talks like him. Smells like him. You wrap your arms around him, too. "And I'm glad you're back."

You resume your walk toward Giles's place. Soon you're knocking on his door.

He opens it, holding a glass of scotch in one hand and a guitar in the other.

"Oh, Buffy . . . I wasn't expecting you."

"Can we come in?"

"Of course, of course," he says quickly, opening the door wider.

You and Angel enter.

"What are you doing, Giles?" you ask, gesturing at the guitar.

"Oh, just . . . nothing," he says, putting it down on his desk along with the scotch. Now what can I do for you?"

"The Night Terror."

"*The* Night Terror? What have you learned?" He sits down on the edge of his desk, eyeing you with concern.

"It took over Angel. It's been controlling his body for days now."

Giles widens his eyes at Angel.

"I'm back, though."

"He was trapped in the dream dimension," you explain.

"Really? How intriguing!"

"It was . . . not fun," Angel finishes. "I tried to get back into my body but couldn't. I kept hanging there above it. I thought maybe I'd be able to take it back once the Night Terror fell asleep. But it didn't. It forced itself to stay awake. After a few days of my absence, Angelus must have sensed the soul was gone and tried to take over."

"Why did the Night Terror pick you?" Giles asks.

"From the little information I exchanged with it during the body switch, I learned that the reason had something to do with the powers of my body. When the Night Terror takes over the bodies of regular people, the bodies break down over time, eventually ending up in comas. Then it has to go back to the dream dimension, where it is a prisoner once again."

"But the supernatural strength and immortality of your body would prevent it from breaking down . . . ," Giles says, following the thread.

"Exactly."

"Then why you? Why not any vampire?" Giles queries.

"The Night Terror has to exchange places with a soul."

"Ah," Giles says, nodding in understanding. "And vampires don't have souls."

"Except for you," you remark to Angel. Your

thoughts turn toward Simone, and the chaos of the fashion show. That's why Simone looked so haggard, so exhausted. Her body was breaking down. "But it came after me, too!"

Giles nodded, taking off his glasses. "I suspect it thought your body might not break down either. You have supernatural healing capabilities, after all. Either of you would have done quite well for it, I imagine."

You sit down on the chair by the desk. "So when I forced myself to stay awake so it couldn't attack me . . ."

"You made the choice for it, and it came to me instead," Angel finished.

"I'm sorry, Angel—if I'd known—"

Angel touches your shoulder to comfort you. "I'm glad it was me. You wouldn't like it there. Nothing made sense."

"Oh?" Giles asks, intrigued.

Angel continues. "I mean, for days I was followed around by a tiny blue cobra in an orange sombrero. It kept telling me to 'open the mustard jar.' Incessantly."

You cock one eyebrow at Angel, wondering if he's all there.

"And then there was the gas pump that kept trying to box me, and the grocery store clerk who was part camel, part the state of Texas."

"That is truly strange, Angel," Giles said. "Are your dreams often so . . . convoluted?"

"Not always," Angel says, not willing to expand. You see pain in his haunted eyes, the memories of murders relived.

Thinking of the woman in the alley, you say to Giles, "We need to keep this thing from coming back."

"That shouldn't be too difficult," he says, standing up from the desk. Replacing his spectacles on his nose, he rummages through a scattered pile of notes and books on his desk. "Ah, yes. Here it is. I uncovered a German protection spell against the *alpdruck*." He peers at you both over the top of his glasses. "This will not only keep it from possessing you, but make it unable to take over any sleeping person at all."

While Giles gathers the supplies from his cupboards and kitchen, you turn to Angel and take his hands, just enjoying meeting his eyes in this silent moment.

Returning to the living room, Giles gets out a bucket of multicolored chalk.

"Going to draw a mural outside on the sidewalk?" you ask. "I love those!"

Instead of answering, Giles narrows his eyes at you, his lips tight. Then he rolls up one rug and begins sketching a large circular symbol on the wooden floor. With a different color, he adds complex symbols in four quadrants.

"Are you going to use the powder blue one?" you ask. "That's a nice color."

Again Giles merely regards you coolly, then gets out the powder blue piece of chalk and draws the image of a horned beast in the center of the circle. With the purple chalk, he draws elaborate wings and a tail.

Angel nods in appreciation. "Good likeness."

After lighting candles placed over the four symbols, Giles instructs you to join hands with him outside the circle. Then, in German, he chants four lines over and over again. The flames sway and flicker, and an eerie howl starts as the merest hint of sound before mounting into a shrieking wail of lament. A sucking sound enters the apartment as wind scatters papers and pens. In the gale, you see a writhing green-brown shape with a lashing tail, struggling in the air over the chalk image of itself. Then, spiraling down, it enters the symbol and the candles wink out.

"It's banished," Giles says, releasing your hand.

Grinning, you turn to Angel, grasping both of his hands. "You're safe! I'm glad to have you back," you tell him, standing on your toes to kiss him.

"So am I," Angel replies, pulling you closer and kissing you deeply.

THE END

Exhausted, you go home, glad to have Angel back, and desiring sleep. You must stay up, though. It's two thirty a.m. by the time you get home.

To your surprise, your mom is up, lights on in the house. You are so busted. You peer around the side and see that the kitchen light is on. Maybe she just couldn't sleep. She might not know you were gone. You climb up the tree outside your window, hop onto the slanted roof, and slide inside your window.

After changing into your pajamas, you emerge into the hallway and make your way down to the kitchen, bracing yourself for a lecture. It would be so much easier if your mom knew you were the Slayer. But then you know she'd worry way more than she does now.

You find your mom sitting at the kitchen table, sipping hot chocolate.

"Oh, Buffy," she says. "Couldn't sleep?"

Whew. Buffy of the Not Busted.

"No. You?"

"No. Guess I'm worrying about everything tonight. You ever have those nights?"

More than you could imagine, you think. "You mean where you toss and turn, mind relentlessly going over classes and boy trouble and friend trouble and . . ." Your voice trails off.

"I see you do." She picks up an empty mug. "Hot chocolate?"

"Sure, thanks." You're hoping it won't lull you to sleep.

She heats up some milk and adds the chocolate

powder. The smell permeates the room. Mmmmmm. Rich chocolate.

Together you sip your drinks, talking of school, the gallery, Xander, Willow. After a few minutes, your stomach starts to complain about the hot chocolate. It rumbles and then erupts in pain, causing you to double over. A fire rises up into your throat, and you can feel all the muscles in your body contracting. You slide off the kitchen stool and crash to the floor, rolling up into a fetal position.

Your mom walks around the center counter and stares down at you. "Oh, is the poison upsetting your stomach, sweetheart?" she asks, then kneels down to meet your eyes. Your stomach contracts, pain spreading throughout your body. "Slayer," she growls in that same voice you heard Simone use in the mall. "Sorry to have to do this. Well, not really, actually. But I need to take Angel's body. I won't stay imprisoned in the dream world forever. And I won't have you staking the body that can provide my escape. I hope you understand."

And then your mom slumps to the ground unconscious, and in the brief moment before death you know that the Night Terror even now is on its way to possess Angel. Your body curls tighter into a ball and darkness fills your vision. You know that the *mare* will prove no match for Angelus, and that once again the evil vampire will feed and celebrate and devastate innocent lives.

As the last breath leaves your body, you hope Kendra or some future Slayer has it in her to stop Angelus.

THE END

You and Angel hurry to Giles's apartment, moving through the shadows of a rather quiet Sunnydale. You encounter only one other vampire on the way—a sleazoid hanging out on the swings in a playground, as if waiting for some vulnerable six-year-old who's going to have a sudden urge to play on the swings at two thirty in the morning. But you also know that some teenagers use this playground as a rendezvous spot to hang out after the coffee houses close. You dust him quickly.

You want to get to the bottom of Angel's problem and fast. You never want to see him like that again. You could have slain him. Or the other way around.

At Giles's, you knock and knock, and are about to give up when the door finally squeaks open. Giles's exhausted face appears in the crack. "Buffy?" he says groggily.

"Sorry to wake you, Giles. But something seriously bad is happening, and we need to figure it out."

He squints at his watch. "At . . . two thirty in the morning?"

"Especially at two thirty in the morning," you insist. "And I don't think any of us should go to sleep until we've figured this out."

Giles grunts in exhaustion and then opens the door all the way. "Very well. Come in."

You enter and immediately notice the two wineglasses on his desk, the twin plates that held what look like some sort of chocolate residue. Two forks.

"Are we . . . interrupting?" you ask, raising an eyebrow when you see Giles looking rather grumpy in his red robe and slippers. You don't even want to *think* about what he could be doing.

"No, no," Giles says quickly, seeing that you've noticed the glasses. "Jenny, uh, Miss Calendar, was here earlier. But she's home now." For a moment it hits you that Giles is an actual *person* who gets crushes on people, and who listens to music, and who even—you suppress a shudder—*dates* people. It's hard for you to imagine, but suddenly, seeing the two wineglasses and Giles in his robe, you can picture how the whole night went down. And then immediately wish you hadn't.

"So, bad things happening?" Giles prompts, clearly uncomfortable.

"Yes," you say quickly, glad for the distraction. Then, after a moment's hesitation, you turn to Angel. "You tell him."

Angel, not big on the whole using-words thing, looks a bit self-conscious and then embarks on his story.

"The last few days . . . ," he starts, then trails off. "I haven't been in my body. This *thing* took it over, traded places with me."

Giles furrows his brow in interest and then sits down on the edge of his desk. "Go on."

"It's like we traded souls. I was trapped in the dream world while this thing, people there call it the Night Terror, walked around in my body."

"People . . . there?"

"In the dream world," Angel explains. "There were other people there whose bodies had been stolen."

"It can take over multiple bodies?" you say in alarm, imagining battling a whole slew of possessed bodies.

"No. Only one at a time. But once it takes over a body, it hangs on to it until the body starts to break down. Eventually the astral cord breaks, and the person's soul becomes permanently trapped in the dream world."

"The bodies break down? Why?" Giles asks.

Angel shakes his head. "I wasn't too clear on that—for a moment our consciousnesses were linked, but it was only briefly. From what I could tell, the human body can't contain the energy of the Night Terror for very long before the body stops functioning, eventually landing in a coma." With a haunted expression, Angel adds, "But my body would have been different. It wouldn't have broken down because of its special healing abilities."

"What does this Night Terror want?" Giles asks.

"Permanent escape from the dream dimension." Angel looks at you, then at Giles. "And I don't blame it either. Four days there and I was about to commit dream hara-kiri."

You raise your eyebrows. "That bad?"

Angel nods. "Yes."

"So it needs a body to live in permanently, but human bodies break down," you sum up.

"Exactly," Angel says.

Giles crosses his arms. "But why not take any vampire's body? Why specifically yours?"

"From what I understood—things didn't make a *whole* lot of sense there—the Night Terror needs to exchange places with another soul or he can't possess the body. Someone has to take his place in the dream world."

You nod, understanding. "And since other vampires don't have a soul, he picked you."

"Yes," Giles says. "Angel presents a rather unique opportunity. An immortal body and a soul to displace. That would be quite tempting."

You think Angel's body is quite tempting too, but you keep that to yourself. "Plus there's the whole leaping over buildings in a single bound and bending solid steel girders thing."

Angel glances sideways at you. "I'm a vampire, not Superman."

"Yeah, I guess you're right. Besides, there's that whole not being able to see yourself in the mirror thing, too. How would the Night Terror fix its hair? Or know if it had spinach stuck between its teeth or . . ."

You get a stern look from Giles.

Bowing your head, you mumble, "Right. Off Topic Buffy."

After a moment of contemplative silence, Giles says, "But this doesn't make sense. Why would the Night Terror just give that up? Why did it leave your body?"

Angel shrugs. "I don't know."

"Was there another exchange of consciousness when it left?" Giles asks.

Angel nods. "Again, just a vague impression of its thoughts."

Pensively Giles slides a notebook over and uncaps a pen. "And what were they?"

Angel regards you with an intense gaze. "Pure, unadulterated terror."

"Of what?" you ask, thinking this could be the first clue to stopping it.

"Of you," Angel finishes. "It believed you were going to stake this body. It didn't know how to defeat you."

"So that's it? It gave up?" You think of its chilling words in the mall corridor after the fashion show. *"I'm coming for you next."* But it couldn't. You had stayed awake and thwarted it. So it went for a body it could live in. For eternity. Angel. Your beloved. This thing was going to be deader than leg warmers and parachute pants when you are done with it. No one messes with your boyfriend.

"I don't think we should be too hasty in believing the threat is over," Giles suggests. "If this thing is as desperate for escape as Angel says, then it won't stop now that it's found the perfect host. We need to be vigilant." Giles stands up. "Buffy, I need you to go over to Willow's and tell her what's happened. She's found some information on the Net that could prove useful."

You nod. "What are you going to do?"

Giles gestures at the mound of books on his desk. "Some more reading. If I can find some reference to the origin of the Night Terror, we might be able to discern its weaknesses and find a way to stop it."

You turn to leave.

"And Angel," Giles adds, "stay awake."

"I will," Angel says. "I've had enough of dreams."

You leave with Angel and begin the walk over to Willow's. As you pass by the magical supply store where Willow and Giles have bought herbs and candles in the past for different rituals, you hear the faint tinkling of glass breaking. You both stop, listening as a door opens with a creak. You sneak around the side of the building and see a man disappear through the back door of the magic store. You catch only a glimpse of him, but you can tell that he's not a vamp, just a regular human. Stopping burglars isn't your scene—that's a job for the cops. And you need to get to Willow's as soon as possible to figure this thing out. Still, you feel bad just walking away from a crime in progress.

SLAYER CHOICE:

Do you decide to . . .

❧ stop the burglar? *If yes, turn to page 169.*

❧ call the cops with an anonymous tip and then continue on to Willow's? *If yes, turn to page 172.*

Not sure how long it will take the cops to get there, and also curious about why someone would choose to break into a magic shop, you creep to the back entrance, signaling for Angel to move around to the front in case the perp tries to exit that way. From outside the jimmied door, you hear someone shuffling through boxes, then a crash and a curse in a decidedly familiar English accent.

You slide inside deftly, the burglar unaware of your presence. Inside, the shop is completely dark, with large shapes—shelves, you think—silhouetted against the streetlights filtering in through the curtained windows. You allow your eyes to grow accustomed to the dark and then discern the furtive shape of your quarry. From here you make out the familiar shape and weaselly movements of your old, annoying enemy.

Sliding up quickly behind him, you grab him around the throat, and he manages to squeak out a frightened, small, "Eeeep!" before you clamp off his air supply.

"Ethan Rayne," you growl. "I thought you were supposed to leave town."

He gently, desperately prods at your gripping fingers, pleading and turning rather purplish. You let go.

He runs his hand over his tortured throat, breathing in gasps of air. The bright lights suddenly flick on, and illumination bathes everything in a glare. Angel stands next to the light switch, leaning against the wall. "Oh, boy," Ethan says nervously.

"I hope you don't think," he says to Angel, "that whole thing with Eygon—I really am grateful, old chum, for you getting rid of that nuisance." He regards you pleadingly. "It really was nothing personal."

"Nothing personal?" you say, feeling snarkiness wash over you like mascara streaming free in a swimming pool. "Tattooing the mark of a demon on my back so that it would claim my soul was nothing personal?"

"Not really, no," he mutters.

"Well, you'd better start explaining why you're still here, or I'm going to start squeezing again." You reach for his throat, and he backs away.

"I just needed some supplies, that's all," he says, holding up his hands in a supplicating gesture.

"For what?" you demand. Every time this guy needs supplies, chaos careens after him like crowds swarming over Nordstrom's the day after Thanksgiving.

"Just a little side project I had going . . ." His voice trails off as he glances around for an escape route.

Angel moves forward, blocking his retreat, sandwiching Ethan between the two of you.

"Now, there's no reason for this to get ugly," he says hopefully.

"Oh, now, I'd say there's a whole lot of reason for this to get a whole lot of ugly. What side project?" you demand.

"Nothing, nothing," he says. "It didn't work out in any case. I was just getting a few little odds and ends to clear up a small matter before I left town. Truly."

"I think he should come with us," you say to Angel.

Angel nods, grabbing Ethan by the back of his neck. "Hey," you say, "I want to do that part."

Angel relents and you grab the Englishman's neck, forcing him toward the back door.

"There's really no need for this. Honestly. I mean, you two haven't even seen a mummy running around . . . have you?" he ends hopefully.

You stop. "Mummy? As in ancient Incan?"

"No," he says. "As in Egyptian, Nineteenth Dynasty?" He winces as he anticipates you punching him. You decide not to.

"No," you say. "Should we have?" You squeeze his neck a little harder.

"No, no," Ethan says quickly. "That was the thing that didn't work out—the walking around. I was just picking up some supplies to protect myself from the Curse of Ramses II for even trying to reawaken it. Honestly. Really."

Maybe you're crazy, but you sort of believe him. The pitiful, desperate look in his eyes seems truthful. Still, you think you should at least check all this out before you just blithely release Ethan Rayne into the night, or at least bring him by Giles's place.

SLAYER CHOICE:
Do you decide to . . .

❘ take Ethan to Giles's apartment and question him? *If yes, turn to page 184.*

❘ make Ethan take you to whatever hovel he's been cowering in to prove there's no mummy roaming about? *If yes, turn to page 63.*

You stop at a pay phone and call in an anonymous tip to the cops. Let them take care of it. You and Angel continue on to Willow's house, walking hand in hand. You rarely do this, and it feels right, having come so close to losing him.

When you get to Willow's house, ready to throw pebbles at her window to wake her, you're surprised to see the downstairs lights on. Her front door opens as you approach the house, and Giles and Willow appear in the doorway.

Why is Giles here? You just left his house.

"Well, just call me as soon as you see her," Giles says to Willow.

"I will." Willow shuts the door after him.

You glance at the street, and see Giles's Citroën parked at one end.

As Giles strides hurriedly down Willow's front walk, you head him off. "Giles, what's up?"

He glances over at you, startled. "Oh, Buffy. I didn't see you there." He falls silent, staring first at you, then Angel.

"What's happened?"

Giles remains silent for a few moments, then finally says, "Quite a lot," but doesn't elaborate.

"You . . . forgot to tell me something?" you prompt.

"Indeed."

He's acting very strange. Giles of the many words is now Giles of the few. Practically vying with Boo

Radley in the talkative department. Plus, he keeps staring at Angel. "Angel, Willow needs to tell you about what she found on the Internet."

"Shouldn't I hear too?" you ask.

"In a minute," Giles almost snaps. Then to Angel: "Will you go see her?"

Caught off guard, Angel says, "Sure," and starts toward the front door. He crosses the length of lawn and knocks softly on the door. Willow answers.

You can pick up snippets of their conversation as you wait for Giles to spill. "Angel," you hear Willow say with surprise. "Have you seen Buffy? Giles was looking for her, and he's really acting weird."

At this, Giles snaps his head to the door, glaring at Willow, and, as if sensing his stare, she peers out on the lawn and sees that he's still there.

"Whoops," she says.

"So there wasn't anything you needed to tell us?" you hear Angel ask.

Giles moves suddenly, whipping out a revolver from under his jacket. It looks ancient, rusted, as if he's had it lying around neglected in a box for years. Although you've seen him with stakes, spears, quarterstaffs, crossbows, axes, and halberds, to see him standing there with a gun is positively chilling.

He aims the gun at you. "Angel's body is mine, Slayer," he says in the same low, booming voice Simone had used with you in the mall corridor. "You're not going to destroy the only chance I have at escape." He draws the hammer back, and your heart races, your mouth gone dry.

SLAYER CHOICE:

Do you decide to . . .

❘ wrestle Giles to the ground and try to take the gun? *If yes, turn to page 84.*

❘ make a run for it to regroup and think of a plan? *If yes, turn to page 175.*

You dive and roll just as a thundering crack rings out. The back of a patio chair explodes into a rain of wrought iron, and you hear the bullet ricochet.

"Slayer," Giles says in the same low, booming voice Simone used in the mall that day. "You're not going to stake the body I need to escape from my prison! Angel will be mine!" Not even looking back, you weave and run toward the street, with Angel following close behind.

"It's the Night Terror," Angel calls to you. "It's got Giles."

"I noticed."

You glance back just as the revolver fires again, and Angel grunts in pain.

"Angel!" you call, slowing.

"Keep going!" he yells.

You see Ethan Rayne now, down the block, hiding in the shadows and beckoning you. You can't believe you're following this guy.

Another shot rings out, and Angel grunts again. You realize he's shielding you from the gunfire.

"Don't do that!" you shout back at Angel as you run on.

"Bullets can't kill me," he says through teeth clenched in pain. "And Giles is a good shot."

When you near Ethan, he starts running again, falling in beside you. "I've seen this before," he said breathlessly. "Ironically, it's why I was in the magic shop."

Another crack from the revolver sends branches

and twigs down on you from the tree above.

You get farther and farther away from Giles. Ethan can run surprisingly fast, but then you suspect that he spends a lot of time running from things.

You no longer hear the revolver fire, and when you chance a look back, you see the street empty behind you. You guess Giles went back for his Citroën.

After a few more blocks, you start cutting through yards, staying away from the streets. The residential part of Sunnydale falls behind you, and you enter the commercial district, filing by stores and bars. It's harder now to avoid parking lots and stay away from the roads, and you grow increasingly nervous. Vamps you can slay. Demons you can fight. Guns you'd rather not deal with. Especially when it's Giles waving one at you.

At last you reach a run-down motel that makes the Bates Motel look like the Paris Ritz.

Ethan fishes out a set of keys and opens the door to number 15. You notice it's attached by only one hinge. Ethan pops his head in, flips on the light, then after a moment turns back and says, "Okay. Come in."

Cautiously you enter the motel room, and immediately the stench of stale cigarettes, insect killer, body odor, and the faint, sour reek of decay assault your nostrils.

"Oh, God," Angel says behind you, wrinkling his nose. "Sometimes a vampire sense of smell is a bad, bad thing."

Ethan licks his lips nervously, checks the parking

lot, and shuts the door. "I know. It's a dive. But I needed a place that wouldn't ask questions."

"It smells like someone died in here and they just rolled the body under the bed," you say, trying in vain to cover your nose with the end of your sleeve.

Ethan kneels down and lifts one corner of the bedskirt. A corpse lies under the bed. One hand covered in tattered, brown bandages sticks out into the room.

He grabs the body's arm and gives a powerful tug, dragging out the corpse.

"A mummy?" Angel asks.

"Nineteenth Dynasty under Ramses II," Ethan adds.

You frown. "Why do you have a mummy under your bed?"

"It's a long story," Ethan says. "I'll tell you later. But the important thing is that I restored its soul and more or less reanimated it to do my bidding."

"I knew it!" you shout.

"But after it stole a couple things for me, it started waking up in the middle of the night, unable to move, seized by utter panic. After a few nights of this, it no longer acted like itself. It was as if something had possessed it. It wouldn't obey my commands, and it even tried to kill me."

You can't help but smile. "At least it has common sense."

Angel maintains his usual level of solemnity. "The Night Terror?"

"Precisely. I did a little research into night terrors,

and came to that same conclusion. So then I tied the mummy up, hoping the Night Terror would grow bored and leave the body."

"And did it work?" you ask.

"Yes."

"And then it went straight into Angel."

"I don't know about that part," Ethan says. "But once the mummy's soul returned from the dream world, I undid my original soul restoration so the Night Terror couldn't take over the body again. I do know of a banishing spell for the Night Terror. I was going to perform it tonight before I was so rudely interrupted at the magic shop. I wanted to be sure the Night Terror doesn't come back. Maybe take me this time." He looks sadly at the mummy. "Though my mummy's ruined now. It just lies there. Dead."

"Mummies do that sometimes," you offer. "So will this spell banish the Night Terror completely?"

"I believe so," Ethan says.

"Then let's do it."

"Very well." Ethan stands and starts fishing herbs, candles, and a bronze talisman out of his pockets and placing them on the chipped plastic table. "There's just one thing that occurred to me . . . ," Ethan says to you.

"What?"

"If the Night Terror is in possession of Giles now, he'll know where to find us. He was here before, in the mummy. So time is of the essence."

At the end of his sentence, you hear the familiar

sputtering of Giles's Citroën in the distance.

"Hurry!" you shout at Ethan.

Angel slides the chain home on the door, then starts piling furniture in front of it. You're sure that one hinge will make all the difference too.

"You could help," Ethan mutters to you.

You look away from the door. "Tell me what to do."

Following Ethan's instructions, you light candles in the order he tells you. He places the talisman in the center of the candles and spreads sea salt on the table. Then he starts chanting.

Giles's car pulls up outside, and you hear the car door slam.

"Slayer!" he shouts from the other side of the door.

Ethan continues to chant.

Giles pounds on the cheap wooden door, which begins to splinter under his weight. Angel braces the door with his body as it shudders violently.

The front window explodes as a crack resounds from the revolver.

"Hurry," you urge Ethan.

Giles appears at the window, ripping down the stained curtains and aiming the revolver at you. Angel tackles you just as the gun fires. The bullet barely misses, whizzing past your ear.

"Oh dear," Ethan says, diving down. He crawls under the bed, continuing to chant.

Giles clambers in through the window, and Angel stands up, clashing with him. Ethan's words gain in volume, and you look up from the floor as Angel struggles with Giles for control of the gun. You leap up, grabbing a chair and smashing Giles across the back with it. The gun goes off, raining plaster down over you.

You punch Giles in the solar plexus, robbing him of air, and he grunts but continues to hold fast to the gun.

Ethan stops chanting.

The talisman on the table glows brightly, emitting a powerful beam of light directed at Giles. It engulfs his body, and you see a horrible dark figure rise up out of Giles's chest, all wings, horns, and bristling brown-gray skin. The beam focuses its brightness on the struggling demon, pulling it completely out of Giles's body.

Giles slumps to the floor, and Angel grabs the pistol from his now loose grip.

The Night Terror fills the room with its size, a hideous creature with three rows of pointed teeth and silvery eyes that gleam with malevolence. The beacon of light pulls the Night Terror toward the talisman, forcing the demon to shrink, growing smaller and smaller until it's the same size as the talisman.

Then with a final bright wink, the beacon draws the Night Terror inside the talisman. The pendant raises up and clatters to the floor, no longer glowing.

Ethan crawls out from under the bed and grabs it, turning it over in his hand. "It worked!" He tries to hand you the talisman.

You are not *about* to touch that thing. "Just put it on the floor."

"Very well," he says, placing it in the carpet.

Giles groans and comes to, and you kneel next to him.

"Buffy?" he glances around. "What on earth am I doing here? Did I get knocked on the head again?"

"Not exactly. But it's okay now, Giles."

Giles spots Ethan. "Oh, I very much doubt that."

"Hello, Rupert," Ethan says lamely, still lying on the floor next to the mummy.

"And why is there an Egyptian mummy on the floor, and where in the world am I?"

"You're in the Ride 'Em High Hotel," Angel informs him.

"Oh, for God's sake," Giles says, getting to his feet. "On second thought, I don't even want to know."

He brushes himself off, and you steady him.

"So it's gone?" you ask Ethan, pointing to the talisman.

"Yes."

You sort of want to thank him, but you just can't bring yourself to do it.

"Come on, Giles," you say, taking your Watcher's arm. "We'll explain on the way. Think that mummy could fit in the truck of your car?"

Giles's eyes widen.

"We need to return it to the Sunnydale Museum, and then take Ethan to the airport because he's leaving and never coming back." You glare at Ethan. "Right?"

He sits up sullenly. "Right."

While Ethan and Angel carefully load the mummy

into Giles's car, you reluctantly pick up the talisman. Giles will know what to do with it.

On the way to the museum, you're going to explain Ethan's ritual to Giles. And as soon as your Watcher confirms that the Night Terror is truly banished, you are going to sleep for three days straight.

THE END

After several knocks, you begin to think Giles isn't home. But then the door opens a crack, and your sleepy Watcher peers out. "Buffy?" he says, surprised, and then, "Oh, gods. Ethan Rayne. What is it now?"

"I need your help."

Giles crosses his arms. "Oh, yes? Need me to laugh delightedly while a demon uses you as dental floss?"

"Let's be serious, Ripper."

"Oh, I assure you I am quite serious."

Ethan sighs nervously, glancing around at you all. Then he turns back to Giles. "There's a great threat that's come to Sunnydale, and only you can stop it."

SLAYER ACTION:
Turn to page 120.

YYou force Ethan to march toward Giles's apartment. When you get there, you knock, maintaining a painful grip on the back of his neck so he doesn't misbehave.

Giles opens the door, looking half asleep in his thick red robe. "And I thought this day had gone badly enough," he mutters, seeing Ethan.

"Rupert," Ethan says genially.

"Give me a good reason I shouldn't just kill you right now," Giles says.

"You know, I asked him the same thing," you say. "He couldn't think of a very good answer."

"Rupert," Ethan coos. "Your Slayer can't kill a human."

"I hardly think you qualify," Giles retorts.

"He was robbing the magic shop," you explain. "Babbling on about some mummy he didn't resurrect."

"Oh?" Giles says. Then he leans forward. "Buffy, could you come inside for a second?"

"And leave him out here unattended?" you ask incredulously.

"Angel can watch him."

"Yes, please don't worry about me," Ethan says. "I'll be fine out here. Angel and I are old chums."

"No, Angel should go home and rest. You look exhausted," Giles tells him.

"Giles, are you crazy?" you say. "Remember the whole night terrors thing? None of us should be sleeping. And besides, we have to decide what to do with Mr. Chaos here."

"Night terrors?" Ethan asks, raising his eyebrows.

"Like, waking up terrified, something in the room night terrors?"

Surprise takes over your face. Then suspicion. Then anger. "Did you have something to do with this?"

"No! No!" Ethan responds quickly. "It's just that . . . that's a strange coincidence."

You grab his collar roughly, pulling him to you. He lets out a long *eeeeeep* sound. "What is?" you demand.

"Buffy!" Giles practically yells. "Never mind that now. Come in here!"

You cock your head toward Giles in disbelief. He's *yelling* at you? Giles's face contorts in fury, and he booms, "I don't have the time for this!"

"The time for what?" you ask, confused.

Then he steps out onto the patio and produces an antique pistol from the pocket of his robe. He thrusts it forward, aiming dead at you.

In your surprise, Ethan breaks away from your grip and dashes toward the street. "Buffy!" he yells back. "Don't fight him! Follow me!"

You watch as Giles pulls back the hammer, aiming the revolver at your head.

SLAYER CHOICE:
Do you decide to . . .

❘ wrestle the gun from Giles? *If yes, turn to page 84.*

❘ follow Ethan? *If yes, turn to page 175.*

"What about the other disembodied spirits?" you ask the Great Transcendental Ned.

He clasps his hands together eagerly. "I'm so glad you asked. They've already started construction on the dreamcatcher. But they need one critical ingredient to continue." He looks around nervously and adds, "And may I just say that I'm overjoyed we have a Slayer to get it?"

You take a step back. "Why? Is it being held by a nest of vamps?"

He shakes his head. "No. Something far worse. I can't . . . I can't talk about it. But please follow me."

He leads you down several streets until you come to a rusted, run-down shack. "This is my dream storehouse. Inside, you'll find a cardboard box full of beads. It's in the far left corner."

"Can't you just go in with me?"

His hands fly up to his face. "No, no, no. I can't. There's something in there. Something horrible. It's like when you're a kid . . . the thing under your bed, in your closet . . . but far, far worse."

"A bogeyman?" you ask, studying the rusted shack. You see no sign of movement.

"Yes. I like to think of myself as very spiritually together and aligned. But I've never been able to face it. If you could slay it for me, we could get that box of beads."

"Okay," you agree. You just want to get home.

You step over the barbed-wire fence surrounding the shack and enter through one of the rusted sliding metal doors. Darkness lies so thick inside that you can make out only the dim shapes of objects in the room. Instantly you hear the rough breathing of some creature in the shadows. You feel along the wall for the light switch. Find it. Flip it on.

Light floods into the room, the shadows shrinking away. In the center of the room, seething and drooling, stands a framed needlepoint placard reading HOME IS WHERE THE HEART IS. The top of the frame splits open, revealing a maw full of glistening fangs. You draw closer, and the words transform into THE EARLY BIRD GETS THE WORM. It flings itself through the air, clipping your shoulder as you dive out of the way. Then, hovering several feet above your head, it changes again to read, A JOURNEY OF A THOUSAND MILES STARTS WITH ONE STEP.

You spot a baseball bat sticking out of a cardboard box and make a dive for it. Your hands grasp the cool smooth wood just as the chomping placard makes another pass at your head. It now reads FINISH YOUR STRING BEANS.

You ready the bat, and as the frame swoops down on you, you hit it hard, shattering glass and wood. The placard falls to the ground, unmoving. The mouth vanishes into the now normal-looking, if mangled, frame. It's no longer animated. Just to be sure, though, you smash it with your boot, hard, until you're confident it's not getting up again.

You drop the bat. Then, turning, you spot the box of beads in the corner and retrieve it. Outside, you scrape your boot on the barbed-wire fence.

The Great Transcendental Ned looks at you in wonder. "You . . . killed it?"

"Yes . . . but . . . it wasn't what I expected."

"Horrific, wasn't it?"

You don't want to downplay his bogeyman. He's obviously terrified of it.

He lowers his head mournfully. "When I was six, my father returned to Planet X, leaving my mother here. She pined for him from that moment on, and she completely stopped talking. She took up needlepoint, obsessively stitching into the wee hours every night. The only time she communicated with me was through needlepoint placards she'd frame and hang on the wall."

You grimace. "Brutal. Is she . . . okay now?"

He breathes in deeply, steeling himself, and lifting his chin. "No. She has taken up macramé now. She likes to make little Planet X men and then set them on fire or build gibbets for them."

"Wow." You're just glad you didn't have to fight an army of those. "Let's go to the dreamcatcher."

"Okay." He leads on, and eventually you come to a park with more than forty people laboring on a tremendous dreamcatcher. They lift it up, propping it against a tree. The Great Transcendental Ned clears his throat, and they all face him. "The Slayer has brought us the Bead of Dooderfunder!" He reaches inside the box, pulls out a single violet bead, and ties it with sinew to the center of the dreamcatcher. "It's ready!" he cries out, raising his hands in celebration.

The other people cheer, jumping up and down.

They gather around you, hugging you and clapping you on the back. You see that while some of them wear contemporary clothes, many of them have clothes from the sixties and seventies. One middle-aged man approaches you and says, "Thank you. I've been trying to get home for twenty years. My body is in a coma. Now I'll finally wake up."

Twenty years. You can't even imagine that. It's longer than you've even been alive.

The Great Transcendental Ned clears his throat again, and silence falls over the crowd. "Now all of you listen for my voice. As you enter the void, you will each see a gleaming cord of silver. These are your astral cords. Grab onto the cord and reel yourselves in. You will wake up in your bodies." He walks to you and grasps your hands. "Buffy, the Night Terror is currently in your body. You must wait to grab your cord until the creature gets caught in the dreamcatcher. Then follow my voice."

You nod your understanding, and he winks out of view.

Immediately you hear singing filling the air around you, beautiful, lyrical singing. The sky shimmers and becomes awash in streaking silver cords. Each person around you sighs and floats up into the night, grasping a different cord. When only one cord remains, gently waving and spiraling in the air, a violent boom shatters the silent night. A vortex opens before you, wind pouring out of it. Then a hideous black shape emerges, wings flapping against the maelstrom, teeth flexing and snapping, tail lashing. The whirlwind spits the creature out with turbulent force, sending it straight into the dreamcatcher. It tangles there, stuck in the sinew, writhing and cursing. "Damn you, Slayer!" it growls.

You can't help but smile. It worked!

Turning your head back up to the sky, you see the last waving astral cord. It calls to you, singing. Leaping up, you sail high into the air and grasp the end. A wind kicks up, spiraling you outward and downward, and you hold fast onto the silver cord as you speed through a dark void. Then you wake up, eyes wide in the soft glow of light from your bedside table. Angel sits next to you. And standing over him is the Great Transcendental Ned. He looks exhausted in real life, dark circles under his eyes, his turban off and brown hair tousled.

"You're back," Angel says softly, hugging you. He pulls away and gives his hand to the psychic. "Thank you."

"It's my pleasure," he answers, giving a bow.

"I'll go tell the others you're back," Angel says. He stands up and leaves the room.

The Great Transcendental Ned goes to your side. "I don't know how to thank you," you say, your throat dry. "You saved me."

"I help where I can," he answers.

As Giles, Willow, and Xander pour into your room, you grasp the psychic's hand tightly, knowing you'll never feel the same way about Planet X again.

THE END

As you get ready to describe the Night Terror to this collection of demons, you certainly hope they aren't his best friends, or part of a society that will be proud of a member who lays waste to human bodies, leaving them hollow, soulless, and comatose.

The creatures cluster around you, and the heat of the dimension presses in on you until sweat trickles down the center of your back and beads on your forehead.

"I got trapped here because of this creature, who calls himself the Night Terror."

"Night Terror?" the elder asks, cocking one eyebrow. You see no recognition in his face.

"Actually, he looks like he belongs to the same race as you. He lives in the dimension we call the dream world, and he wants out. He can take over the bodies of sleeping people, switching souls with them and stranding them in the dimension of dreams. But he can't stay in a stolen body for long, because it breaks down over time."

They stare at you, their mouths agape. You've struck something in them—you see recognition now in their eyes.

"I think that's why he wanted my body. I'm the Slayer."

Blank expressions.

"A warrior destined to hunt vampires and other evil creatures. My body has supernatural strength and may be able to withstand hosting the Night Terror's soul." You pause, gauging their reactions. Expressions of concern now crease their mottled green-brown, bony faces. "But I don't even know what's been going on with my body—if the Night Terror has been able to hold on to my body this long without it collapsing into a coma. . . . I only know I'm not waking up, and I've been trapped in my dreams. Until I came here."

"F'arnak," the white-haired demon whispers.

"F'arnak," nods the elder, sighing.

"F'arnak?" you ask.

After a moment, the elder closes his open-hanging mouth and says solemnly, "Yes. Oh, my. I think we may be responsible for this Night Terror. We may have made him what he is."

"What do you mean?"

"Here," says the white-haired demon. "Take my hand. It can be told best this way, by linking directly with my mind." He holds out a clawed hand for you to take. You really don't want to hold hands with a demon. Not on your list of things to do this year. Or next year. Besides, are those pus-filled nodules in his palm? *Ewwwwwww.*

"I—uh—," you start, but he grasps your hand anyway. Instantly the sand-covered world around you vanishes, replaced by a graphic vision of the past.

In the sweltering dimension of Chrossos, the demon F'arnak races on breathlessly, knowing his pursuers draw steadily nearer. He rounds the corner of a stone building, looking for shadows—a recessed doorway, a shadowed stairwell—anywhere dark to hide in. Behind him, shouts echo off stone, calling his name. The heat sensors in his thick reptilian wings tell him his pursuers are almost upon him. He doesn't fear they'll hurt him— he knows they won't. It's against their beliefs. But what they will do is much, much worse. He must escape.

Up ahead, dark stairs lead down from the stone street to a shadowed doorway. Chancing a look back, F'arnak sees his pursuers round the corner. He has the smallest chance that they might not see him duck into the stairwell.

But if they have hunter hounds with them, straining at their leashes, saliva drooling from hooked fangs, even hiding will do him no good. Not daring to study his pursuers long enough to find out, he tears onward, closing in on the shadowed stairwell. Then the sudden eerie baying of hunter hounds erupts behind him, and he realizes hiding is hopeless.

F'arnak knows now that has done the unforgivable. He has taken a life, stolen the identity of a wealthy Aknar demon in order to become rich himself. And now the law has caught up with him, and hell awaits. He wishes they would kill him outright, that they would rend him apart and leave his flesh for the hunter hounds. But his people would never take a life. Instead, they will rip him apart in a different way, rending his soul from his body and trapping him forever in that surreal and torturous prison—the world of dreams, where he will no longer be able to hurt anyone. His soul, confined there, will never escape, while his unconscious body will languish in a prison, never to be reunited with its spirit again.

The baying of the hounds thunders behind him once more and a brilliant flash of light tears through the night. F'arnak feels a searing white heat envelope him, surrounding him in blinding intensity. An unbearably agonizing sensation fills his chest, the worst kind of grief he's ever felt, worse than the anguish of suffering in a meaningless life. It is his soul, clawing up and away from his very being, departing his body against his will. The light grabs at him and tears inside of him, gripping his spirit and pulling it outward.

As hot tears stream down his face, F'arnak feels his body crumple to the cold stone street. Violently, his soul rips free from his body. With fingers that cannot grasp and arms that hold no corporeal strength, his soul tries to hold on. But spiraling upward, his soul helplessly sucks away into the night, looking down at his fallen body. His pursuers reach his prone form and gather around it. The hounds lift their heads to the night sky, baying in triumph.

Another flash erupts in the streets below and suddenly F'arnak finds himself no longer looking down on his crumpled body, but now looking over an entirely new plane filled with strange, rising spires and storm clouds gathering in an orange sky.

The dream world.

His nightmare has become reality.

His soul is trapped, never to return to his body.

A swirling vortex appears, violently sucking away the images. When they vanish, the scene around you is replaced by reality—the sand dunes, the strange spired city enclosed in walls, the horde of winged demons standing patiently around you. Your body exhales explosively, and bright flashes erupt behind your eyes and then finally fade.

"Did you see?" asks the white-haired demon.

You try to breathe in deeply, strangely short of breath. "Yes."

"We apologize," says the elder. "And we will rectify the situation. We thought it compassionate to release his spirit into another dimension instead of killing him, but now we see that this only perpetuated his evil."

"The Turagon Jar," says White Hair.

The elder nods. "Yes."

"What is that?"

"It's a jar that we can summon a soul into. We will take him out of your body, passing him through the dream dimension back into this one. Here we will imprison his spirit in the jar."

"Wow!" you say. "Great!" You can't wait to get home. "When can we—," you start to say, when suddenly a bright light envelops you. You recognize it as the same brilliant flash that surrounded the Night Terror in the vision of the past.

You travel up, up into the sky, streaking lightning-fast through the dream dimension. You briefly see the dream Bronze, then dream Giles lecturing to a gaggle of lumbering zombies, past the dream Sunnydale Cemetery, which currently brims with a churning lava flow, then through a deep blue sky, past clouds, down through the atmosphere, past trees, and then, with a solid thump, you land on a hard surface. Surprisingly, it doesn't hurt too much.

You sit up, stunned, and find yourself in your own room in Sunnydale.

"Buffy!" you hear Xander call. "Everybody, Buffy's back!"

Giles and Willow rush into your room, and Willow throws her arms around you. You stand up on wobbly legs and take them in.

"Is this home?"

"Yes," Giles says. "You're back."

"We knew you weren't you," Willow says. "You didn't even want to shop or kiss Angel or anything! And you kept trying to leave town."

"The Night Terror . . . ," you breathe, thinking of how close it came to stealing your body forever.

"Your astral cord was broken, Buffy," Giles says, putting a paternal arm around you. You feel sandwiched between him and Willow. "We weren't sure we could get you back. And as a matter of fact, I'm not even sure how we did."

You think of the dimension of kind, winged demons, and their strange Giles-like way of speaking. "I had some help. And we don't have to worry about the Night Terror again. He's gone." You can't believe you're back! Everything makes sense now. Your table is a table, there's no mouse with a microphone in your closet, and best of all, you're not dressed like a complete dork.

"Oh, well, that's a relief," Giles states.

"Definitely," Willow chimes in. "Did you know that the Night Terror version of you didn't even want to play Six Degrees of Kevin Bacon?"

"No!" you say in mock horror, relieved to be back home in logic land, surrounded by the people who love you and know you best.

THE END

Outside the school, you climb into Giles's Citroën, the familiar scent of old car filling your nose. Giles gets in next to you, and, clattering and sputtering, the car jostles to life, shuddering in its usual geriatric way. You lumber off toward his house, telling him everything that has happened that night, from Angel coming in through your window and acting strange, to following him and witnessing the murder, to fighting him in the dingy alley, and the strange conversation and following trancelike state.

"It does indeed sound like two creatures are vying for control of Angel's body."

"But Angel isn't one of them," you say, trying to understand.

"No. From what I can tell, the Night Terror demon and the vampiric demon Angelus are the two inside the body."

"Then where is Angel?" you ask.

"He may well be trapped in the world of dreams."

"What?"

Giles turns a corner and shifts the car into a higher gear, picking up speed. "From the few accounts I managed to find in which a *mare* proved unsuccessful in permanently taking over a body, two of them described the souls of the bodies returning, driving out the *mare*. They described the sensation of being trapped in their dreams."

"So what are dreams, then?" you ask, curious at the mention of this dream dimension.

Giles turns onto his street, slowing the car. "There

are some who believe that dreams are just the sub-conscious part of the brain, working out problems while the conscious brain sleeps." He pulls up in front of his apartment building and switches off the motor. The engine sputters, continuing to run momentarily even after he removes the key. Nice. "But there are others," he says, turning to face you, "other cultures, who believe that when we dream we journey to another plane of existence. The people we meet are beings on this other plane, some of them other dreamers, some spirit guides, and some malevolent beings like these *mare*."

You turn in your seat, regarding Giles. "So you think this *mare* entered Angel's body while he was sleeping, sending Angel's soul to the dream world and then taking over Angel's body for itself?"

"Precisely."

"Is there some way to contact Angel, then? Through my dreams? Could I help Angel get back into his body?"

Giles opens his door and climbs out, thinking. He moves toward his front door. "It's possible. Although the fact that Angelus has manifested, vying for control, does not bode well."

"What do you mean?" you ask, climbing out your-self and shutting the Citroën's door behind you.

"According to my research, a person's spirit is connected to his or her body through an astral cord. If the spirit is gone for too long—say, not just normal dreaming but being trapped for days on end in the dream plane—the astral cord can weaken and break, making it impossible to return to the body."

You both reach the apartment door and Giles unlocks it. "The fact that Angelus doesn't manifest every time Angel dreams leads me to believe that something must have changed. It's likely that Angel has been trapped for some time now, and that his astral cord has begun to weaken or even break. Angelus might have sensed that weakness and seized advantage of it, taking the body over himself."

"Trapped for some time?" you ask, following Giles through his front door. "But he only seemed different when he came to my house tonight."

"But that's only when Angelus came to the fore. It's possible the Night Terror has had possession of Angel's body for far longer, and was only imitating him."

"How could it do that?" you ask, thinking of how Angel really seemed like himself.

Giles shakes his head. "I'm not sure. It may be that the Night Terror can watch our dreams, or perhaps there is some exchange of consciousness when the possession occurs." He starts gathering up the notes on his desk, collecting three thick leatherbound volumes and several thinner paperbacks on dreams and astral projection that look brand-new.

"Giles," you breathe in mock disbelief, "are those really your books? But they're not two hundred years old." You point at them. "I won't get my usual healthy dose of mildew and sneezing fits reading those. I think breathing the layers of dust and mold on the ancient books is a whole dietary supplement for Willow."

Giles rolls his eyes, gathering up the old volumes and piling the new ones in your arms with more force than he really needs to. Grunting, you take the books. "Let's go," he says. "We should get back to the library."

You follow him out of the door, trying to think of a way you could reach Angel. Since the Night Terror is in possession of Angel's body, you could safely go to sleep and find Angel in your dreams. You remember seeing a show on the Discovery Channel about lucid dreaming—controlling the actions and events of your dreams. You wonder if you could use lucid dreaming to communicate with Angel and lead him back to his body.

Reaching Giles's car, arms laden with books, you feel so tired you know you wouldn't have a problem falling asleep.

Making good time, you return to the high school just a few minutes later. Using the side entrance, you and Giles slip silently inside. You take in the scene, relieved. Angel, or rather the thing inside Angel, still paces in the small confines of the cage, dragging the chains back and forth. Xander stands a few feet away, closely watching him. Willow sits at the big gathering table, reading volumes on sleep disorders, protection spells, and enchantments. When you enter, she looks up anxiously. "What did you learn?"

Giles fills her in on your speculations.

"Hey! Then I might have something here," she says excitedly.

"Really? What?" Giles moves quickly to her side and peers over her shoulder.

"We might be able to use one of these spells to reconnect Angel with his body."

A crashing fist against the cage commands your attention. "Don't bring that damn do-gooder back here! I can defeat this thing myself."

"Ah, yes," Giles says condescendingly, "and leave you to walk the streets of Sunnydale? To continue your reign of terror?"

"Wait," you interrupt. "If Angelus does drive out the Night Terror, would Angel's soul just automatically return?"

Giles considers this a moment. "If the astral cord isn't broken, I believe so."

"And if it is?" Willow asks.

"Then we would be stuck with Angelus."

You all turn and regard the scowling vamp in the cage. It's so strange to see hatred and evil in those eyes. You want Angel back now.

You turn to Willow. "But if that happened, could we still use the spell to reunite Angel with his body?"

"I'm not sure," she says, studying the pages. "I think these spells are specifically for victims of a *mare*. Once the *mare* is gone, Angel would just be a typical vampire . . ."

". . . with a demon in possession of the body instead of the native soul," Giles finishes.

"I say we just stake him," Xander says, glowering at the vampire.

You scowl at him. "That's why you're not in charge."

You think again about your idea to contact Angel in your dreams. It's sounding better and better to you. You could even try both methods if one didn't work.

SLAYER CHOICE:

Do you decide to . . .

\ go to sleep first and attempt to communicate with Angel and lead him back to his body? *If yes, turn to page 204.*

\ attempt the incantation first to rejoin Angel's soul with his body? *If yes, turn to page 206.*

"**I** have an idea, guys," you say.

"Oh, yes?" Giles asks, intrigued, as they all turn to look at you. You gesture for them to huddle close to you, where the Night Terror can't hear. They gather, and you whisper.

"From what Giles told us, Angel is trapped in the dream world. I'm going to find him."

"What about Mr. Whosits over here?" Xander asks, jabbing his thumb surreptitiously at the Night Terror. "Can't he take over your body then?"

"As long as he's in that body," you say in a low whisper, drawing nearer to them, "I should be able to go to sleep and remain unhindered. Right, Giles?"

Giles nods. "Where do we do this?"

"Here. I'll go into Giles's office, pretend I'm doing extra research, but I'll actually go to sleep."

Willow creases her brow. "Do you think you can do this, Buffy? How will you find him?"

"I've dreamed about him before," you tell her. "I should be able to again. Assuming Giles is right and that when you meet people in your dreams they are actually the dream body of that person." You blush a little, thinking of those previous dreams involving Angel's dream body. "I'll try to lead him back to his body. That should work, right, Giles?"

Giles nods. "It should drive the Night Terror out, and Angel's soul will be able to repress Angelus."

"Great. Let's do it."

Xander sidles up closer to you. "Do you need help falling asleep? I could give you a shoulder massage, or, hey, give you a nice soft shoulder to sleep on." After a brief pause, he adds, "Not that I'm that soft. Figuratively soft. It's actually quite firm. Muscular." He prods his shoulder, displaying its muscles. Willow socks him in the arm. "Ow!"

You ignore him and walk into Giles's office, saying, "Those books are in here?"

Giles picks up the charade and answers, "Yes, I've made a stack of them for you to go through."

You close the office door behind you and then look down at Giles's desk, littered with papers, notebooks, and discarded issues of the *Journal of Sleep Disorders*. You push them aside, clearing off a small place, then remove your jacket. Folding it into a pillow, you place it on the desk and then curl up on the hard wood, letting your exhaustion sink in.

For a moment you don't think you'll be able to sleep here in this public place with the wood digging into your hip, but then your eyes grow heavier and heavier, and sleep claims you.

SLAYER ACTION:
Turn to page 57.

After gathering up most of the ingredients for the incantation, Giles is finally ready. It's nearly four a.m., and you are so tired you're practically falling asleep standing up. He needs only one more item—a funerary sconce raided from the tomb of a Jesuit priest. Willow helps Giles set up the spell, while you guard the Night Terror and Xander grabs the sconce from the Sunnydale Cemetery. Even though Giles gives Xander very specific directions to the mausoleum of a Jesuit priest, you still worry that somehow you're going to end up with a tiki lamp. But you put your faith in Xander, arm him with a cross, and send him on his way, wondering if you should go yourself.

Your mouth feels like it's filled with cotton, and your head pounds. You can't wait for this to be over so you can finally get some sleep. Just the thought of sleep fills you with excitement, and you realize how pathetic that is—to be excited just to sleep.

The moments drag by as you wait for Xander's return. Giles and Willow finish the enchantment setup, and just as you begin to think Xander has been dragged away into a den of peckish vampires, he comes through the side door carrying a cumbersome stone sconce with blackened, charred remains in its core.

"You forgot to mention the whole stone part," Xander says. "I didn't exactly have a chisel."

Giles studies the sconce ruefully. "You're sure this came from the tomb with the omega symbol above it?"

Xander nods. "Positive."

"Very good, then," Giles says, taking the heavy gray sconce from Xander's hands.

"At least, I'm pretty sure. You know, in the dark, an omega symbol can look a lot like a doughnut with two little feet. But I'm pretty sure I got the right one."

Giles raises an eyebrow. "You actually saw a crypt with a doughnut with two little feet on it?"

"Yeah. I saw it the other night. And the really weird part was that there was a mummy there, kicking back against the doorway, eating a Twinkie."

"Are you sure about that?" Giles asks, incredulous.

"Yeah! I was expecting him to attack me, one-handed, you know, mummy-style. The old drag-and-slump, I-move-slower-than-the-DMV-yet-still-manage-to-strangle-you mode of attack." He shrugs. "But it didn't. It just sort of looked at me, then continued to eat the Twinkie. It had a package of Ding Dongs under one arm."

"Now I know you're making this up," Giles accuses him, turning his back to prepare the sconce for the spell.

"I'm not!" Xander snaps his fingers, just thinking of something. "Wasn't there something about a mummy stolen from the Sunnydale Museum recently?"

Giles nods. "Yes, but I hardly think a mummy walked out of there so that it could eat Hostess cakes in a cemetery."

"But I ask you," Xander pressed, "where else would a mummy eat Twinkies?"

"Okay," you cut in. "Enough! Can we get down to business here?"

"Yes, please let's," says Giles. Everyone falls silent, and after a moment Giles and Willow finish the preparations, Willow setting up candles in the four cardinal points of the library.

You douse the overhead lights, Xander lights the candles in the east, west, north, and south, and Giles begins the incantation, reading in Latin. Willow stands, sprinkling anointing oil in a pattern in the center of the floor, then shaking some on the Night Terror through the cage's mesh. Instantly the creature screams, falling to his knees as Giles continues the spell, now calling out loudly in Latin. The candles waver, the creature cries out, collapsing completely to the ground, and all the candles go out as one, inviting darkness into the room.

"Damn you!" you hear the creature scream, then silence. A wind kicks up in the room, and you can hear a heart beating, louder and louder, and then voices in the ether around you, whispering and taunting, rising up in a chorus. Then Angel's voice appears among those whispers. His voice grows louder than the others, a whisper into a low moan, a moan into a shout. "Buffy!" he yells, disembodied, the voice floating in the air around you.

"Angel!" you whisper urgently.

Giles shushes you. "He must find his body," he adds quietly.

As you strain to see in the dark, able to make out only dim shadows, you hear a rustling in the cage, then a moan. "Buffy?" you hear Angel say. Then: "Buffy!"

You hear him struggle to his feet, the cage rattling against his unsteady weight.

"Turn on the lights," Giles instructs Xander. Painfully, light floods into the room. You squint against the dazzling brilliance, turning your face toward the cage. Angel's deep brown eyes meet yours, kind and loving.

"I'm back!" he says, touching his face, looking at his hands. He laces his fingers through the wire, locking his gaze on you. "Buffy, I'm back. I didn't think I'd ever see you again. I wondered if you'd figure out it wasn't me in this body."

"We did," you say, moving to the cage.

"That *thing*," Angel breathes, then looking to Giles. "We've got to find a way to keep it from coming back. It wanted me, wanted my body in particular."

"It wasn't alone in that," you tell him, instantly regretting how it came out.

"You mean—," Angel starts.

"Angelus," Giles finishes for him. "The Night Terror and Angelus vied for dominance."

Fear washes over Angel's face. "Oh, God, Buffy . . . I didn't—"

"It wasn't you, Angel," you tell him.

"But—" He can read your face, knows instantly that someone is dead. "He killed someone?"

You nod.

Angel bites his lower lip and glances away, his eyes haunted with the agony of countless murders of the past.

"It wasn't you," you say again. Turning to Giles,

you ask, "Is there a way to keep the Night Terror from coming back?"

"It won't give up this easily," Giles says, moving to his stack of books. "We'll have to do a protection spell now that Angel is back." He begins to flip through the pages neighboring the enchantment he just finished.

You move to the cage door and unlock it, wanting to be in Angel's arms once again. As the door opens, Angel moves to you quickly, enveloping you. You breathe in the familiar scent of him, feeling your face against the skin of his neck. "I missed you."

"I missed you, too, Buffy," he whispers in your ear.

You produce the manacle key and unlock the chains. With a metallic clink, they fall to the floor.

And then Angel shoves you aside, casting you into the cage where you crash painfully into a metal filing cabinet, cracking your head on one corner. He grabs the cage key from your stunned fingers. Then, in a single movement, he slams the cage door shut between you, locking you inside.

Before Willow has even turned around, before Giles has a chance to grab the crossbow lying on the table, Angelus springs between them, violently snapping Willow's neck with a single movement and then sending Giles sprawling across the floor with a crushing blow to the face.

Xander runs to the cage, fumbles with the lock, and then realizes he doesn't have a key. "Tsk, tsk," Angelus scolds, holding the key up where Xander can see it. On the floor, Giles groans and Angelus walks to him, slamming his boot down hard into Giles's gut. Crying out in pain, he twists on the floor, grabbing ineffectually at Angelus's leg.

"Angel!" you cry. "Why are you doing this?"

"Why am I doing this?" he mocks, beginning to stride over to where Xander stands, terrified, at the cage door.

"Xander," you urge, "run. Get out of here. Now!"

"But Buffy," your friend protests. "I can't just leave you here!"

"You can and you will," you order. "Now."

Xander turns and looks at Willow's body, his eyes wide and full of grief. "But Will . . ."

"I know. And the same thing will happen to you!" Behind him, you see Angel looming up, eyes gloating and burning with hatred. "Run, damn it!"

With a terrified glance over his shoulder, Xander dodges out of the way and darts through the swinging double doors of the library.

"Angel!" you plead. "If you're in there some-where . . ."

"Angel," he snorts back, stopping at the cage to stare in. "You think I would let that sniveling weakling back into this body? The incantation didn't work. But I drove out the Night Terror. I can only imagine what he has in store for you the next time you fall asleep. I don't think he'll be wanting this body anymore. But a body with Slayer strength? Now that's the next best thing."

He pauses a moment, staring in at you. "I guess we'll just have to disappoint him. I'd let you out," he says, backing away, "but after our little scuffle in the alley, I don't think I have the time to invest in a lengthy fight." He continues to back away. On the ground, Giles stirs, and Angelus grabs the crossbow off the table. In one heartless motion, he swings it around and shoots a bolt into Giles's chest. Instantly your Watcher stops struggling, lying still, his vacant eyes staring up at the ceiling.

You rattle the cage violently, trying to force the door open. But already Angelus is reloading another bolt into the crossbow and walking back over to you. Your frantic eyes search the cage for something you can use as a weapon or a shield. But all you find are two pencils and the filing cabinet. If Angelus got close enough, you could stake him with the pencils.

But already he is raising the crossbow, taking careful aim at your heart.

"I think it rather ironic, don't you," he asks, "for a Slayer to be killed through the heart?"

As his finger caresses the trigger, you dive behind the file cabinet. The bolt hits the metal with a twang and ricochets off, clattering against the wall and falling. You dive down and grab the wooden arrow, gripping it like a knife.

"Fight me, damn you!" you curse at Angelus, desperate to get out of the cage.

"I just don't have the time," he says, reloading the crossbow and striding confidently up to the cage. He holds the bow only inches away, and you don't know how you'll escape it if he fires from that close.

For one brief, crazy second, you imagine soldier

Xander bursting through the doors with an arsenal of flamethrowers and rocket launchers, but he doesn't come. The next few seconds feel like endless days as Angelus extends the weapon and fires. With a searing pain the bolt enters your chest, piercing your heart. A shooting agony penetrates your body and you are barely able to cry out as your body falls to the cold tile floor, life pumping out of your heart so quickly you are aware only of a vague, dizzying darkness before death comes, sweeping you away into nothingness.

THE END

You dive and roll just as a resounding crack rings out, destroying the peaceful night. Giles curses, cocks the hammer back again, and fires a second time as you dive and roll again, almost at the street now. As you hear the click of the hammer again, you leap behind a tree, and a bullet strikes the sidewalk one foot from your shoe. Then you break into a run, bounding into the neighbor's yard, getting the house between you and the gun.

You think of your friends, but Willow can stay inside and lock the door. You're not that worried about leaving Angel. He'll likely pursue Giles, and you know that being a vampire, he can survive a gunshot wound. The gun booms again, splintering one corner of the house as you dive behind it. You keep running, hurtling over a hedge, sprinting across the lawn of the next house, then the next and the next. In no time you've outdistanced him.

As you run, you try to think of a safe place. You can't go home. You don't want crazy Giles to shoot your mom. Public places will be bad, because he's clearly desperate and may not hesitate to shoot a few bystanders.

This thing has now taken over Giles. Did it leap from Angel's body straight to Giles? When it left Angel's body, it must have been furious. You can see why it was forced out; you would have staked Angel, as much as that would devastate you, and it needs Angel's body to permanently escape the dimension.

As you sprint out into the expanse of grass in a

small park, you start to slow down, aching from lack of sleep and exhaustion. You have to find a place to rest. You spot a huge old oak at the edge of the park and stop. Swinging up onto the trunk, you climb high into the leaves and sit down on a thick branch. Chest heaving, you struggle to breathe. You could really use a bottle of water, too. Fresh, cool water.

Piecing everything together in your mind, you try to figure out your next move. So the Night Terror needs Angel's body. But when it displaces Angel's soul, and the body's connection to that soul grows weak with Angel's prolonged absence, evil Angelus is able to rise more and more to the surface. The Night Terror vies for dominance, but cannot contain Angelus all the time. You imagine that when Angel's astral cord is severed, Angelus will sense the soul's permanent departure and take over completely. The Night Terror will be trapped in yet another body it can't use.

Briefly you wonder if you can explain this to the Night Terror, explain Angelus's long and vicious past, and how he is too powerful for the *mare* to dominate. But then you remember the gun, your ears still ringing from the shots, and know that reasoning is as out of the question as catching a performance of *Murder, She Wrote* on Ice.

Okay, what then?

You hope Willow shut the door. You hope she and Angel are safe.

What you really need is for Giles to come back to his body. He hasn't been out of it for that long, because the Night Terror just left Angel's body, not more than an hour ago. So how do you communicate with Giles's soul in the dream world?

Then it hits you. You dream yourself. Find him in the dream dimension and help him return to his body. He may not even realize he can't go back yet. And with the Night Terror in possession of his body, it won't be coming after yours any time soon.

This is the perfect opportunity to fight the NT and catch some zzzs, up here in a tree, braced between two branches.

Trying to get as comfortable as possible, you lean back against a particularly wide branch and close your eyes. Your body is exhausted from lack of sleep as it is, and you hope it won't be long before you doze off. You also hope you won't plummet to your death out of the tree.

You force your breathing to slow, your body to relax, and soon you find yourself drifting in that strange place between sleep and consciousness, where things make a whole different kind of sense. And then you doze off completely.

Moments later, with a jarring thump, you land harshly on your back at the base of the tree. Pain spreads through your body. You fell off the branch! Glancing nervously around for Giles, you get to your feet and start to climb again. But you find that you can just float up through the branches.

You launch off a few of them and reach the top of the tree in a matter of seconds. From here you can see

Sunnydale stretching out before you, including Giles's apartment. You spring from the top of the tree, sailing through the air with your arms stretched wide. You should be able to spot Giles easily, maybe even swoop down on him and steal the gun.

As you whip through the air, hair flying in strands around you, you pass a small family of owls, who hoot at you and give a small wave. You wave back, surprised to see they're wearing top hats. You always thought owls wore graduation caps. And none of them are chewing on Tootsie Roll Pops. Weird.

You pass the owls and continue on toward Giles's house, passing over Xander, who sits on a park bench kissing a gorgeous woman. And then it dawns on you. You're dreaming. You've successfully crossed over into the dream world. And now you really do need to find Giles. Not crazy gun-toting fake Giles, but the real soul of Giles.

You fly toward his house and touch down on his patio. But where his apartment was now stands a nightclub. Screeching sounds of an electric guitar assault your ears, all feedback and discordant notes. You walk inside the club, which is patronized entirely by fiftyish men in golfing outfits—plaid pants, high socks, outrageous hats at rakish angles—and mermaids. You instantly spot Giles onstage when his familiar voice says, "This next number is about the difficulties of lecturing to a gaggle of Kaklar demons in a bowling alley." He stands with electric guitar in hand and dives into a new discordant song, wailing out of tune to it.

You don't know whether this is your nightmare or his.

You jump up onstage in front of him. "Giles!"

"Oh, Buffy," he says, standing back from the microphone but continuing to "play" the guitar. "I don't know what's happening. I can play the guitar. I really can. And I can sing. But everything's coming out ghastly."

"I know, Giles," you say, leading him away from the microphone. He refuses to relinquish the guitar, so you unplug it and pull him offstage. "It's a nightmare. None of this is real."

"Then the mermaids?"

"Weird, I know," you say, watching as one tries to dip her tail into an oversize margarita glass. "But also part of the dream." You stop, turning him to face you. "This is really important, Giles. You've got to pay attention."

You pull him out the front door into the relatively peaceful night, pausing on his patio.

"The Night Terror has taken over your body. You need to return to it."

"Oh. That explains a lot. I tried to wake up more than once in there. But then I kept forgetting it was a dream."

"Do you know how to get back to your body?"

Giles shakes his head, pulling up a lawn chair and sitting down on it. "Once a *mare* takes over your body, I know of only one way to get it back."

"Okay. Spill."

"You have to wait for the *mare* to go to sleep, and

when it enters the dream world as a dreamer itself, you take back your body while it's away."

"Okay. That sounds simple. Let's do that."

"We can't. There's just one problem."

"There's always just one problem. At least."

"I assume I haven't been gone that long?"

"Two hours, tops," you tell him.

"As long as the astral cord to my body is intact, the *mare* will not risk going to sleep. But once the cord is severed, it will allow my body to sleep, because I'll no longer be able to find my body. My spirit will be permanently detached."

This is bad news. "There has to be another way, then."

Giles thinks a minute, then puts his head in his hands, slumping over his guitar. This is not a good sign.

You try to think of everything Giles and Willow described to you about night terrors and the *mare*, but nothing helpful occurs to you.

Then Giles's head snaps up. "My storehouse!"

"You have a storehouse?"

"Yes! In my dreams. My dream storehouse. It's filled with every amulet, talisman, spell book, incantation, magical orb, and charm I've ever seen or even read about. I'm sure there'd be something there that would help us!"

"Go, Giles! What are we waiting for?"

He leaps to his feet and strides off in the direction of Sunnydale Cemetery.

"Giles," you say. "Are you going to keep carrying that guitar?"

"Oh, right." He doubles back, placing it gingerly on the patio table.

In the strange way of dreams, you don't really walk anywhere, but instead suddenly emerge in front of a huge Greek-styled structure that looks remarkably like the Parthenon. It stands where Sunnydale Cemetery lies in the waking world.

"This is it," Giles says in awe. "My dream storehouse." He waves excitedly for you to follow. "Come, come."

As Giles enters between two columns, you climb the marble steps, impressed with Giles's dream architecture. You don't have anything cool like this in your dreams. You've got to remember this. You could turn your house into a sprawling mansion or make yourself stop having those going-to-the-grocery-store-naked dreams. You hate those.

You follow Giles between the two pillars and emerge into a vast room filled with gleaming treasure. Gold, silver, glowing orbs, and chalices . . . you take it all in with wonder.

"Isn't it amazing?" Giles asks.

You have to admit it is pretty darn nifty, like some kind of secret pirate cave loaded with booty. Xander would be running amok in here.

Then the sheer volume of treasure overwhelms you. "How do we know where to start?" Hopelessness creeps up on you, and you think of your prone body in the tree and imagine evil, possessed Giles pointing a crossbow up through the branches.

"I have a few leads already," Giles says, then straightens up and says loudly, "The Orb of Trakoa." With that, a blue, glowing sphere rises from amidst the treasure and drifts lazily through the air into Giles's waiting hand. Then he pronounces loudly, "The Pendant of Kamrusepas." A tinkling of metal accompanies the rising of a shiny bronze pendant strung on a chain. It snakes out from inside a golden chalice and drifts through the air to Giles's other waiting hand.

You join him at his side. "What do they do?"

"Once activated, the Orb of Trakoa can rejoin any lost soul to its original body. Even if that body is dust in the grave."

"Ewwwww. What, is the soul then trapped in its own dust?"

"No. If the person has died, the soul goes to wherever it normally would have gone upon death."

"Like heaven or hell or wherever we go?"

"Exactly."

"And the necklace thingy?"

Giles grimaces. "The . . . necklace thingy, as you so elegantly put it, is the Pendant of Kamrusepas, goddess of spells and healing. Capable of transporting the user between dimensions." He slips it into his shirt pocket and says, "The Kamrusepas Incantations!" With a brisk flapping of paper, a roll of parchment disentangles itself from under a golden knife and streaks through the air like a paper airplane, biffing Giles in the ear before it lands in his hand. "Using these incantations," he explains, "the user can travel to a variety of dimensions."

"And there's one in there for our dimension?" you ask, taking and unrolling the parchment as Giles winces.

"Careful! It's very old."

"Yeah, but it's the dream version of it. We could roll this up into a ball, set it on fire, and you'd just have to dream it up again."

"Yes, but, all the same, let's not." He gingerly takes the parchment back, pocketing the orb in his pants pocket and examining the incantations. You can't make heads or tails of it. Looks a little bit like Greek letters.

"It's written in an ancient dialect of Phoenician," he says.

"Any relation to Greek?"

Surprise widens Giles's eyes. "Why, yes. Many linguists believe that Phoenician evolved into Greek and Hebrew."

"Thought so," you say, as Giles continues to look on in wonder. "I've seen some of those symbols on frat houses." Then quickly you think of Giles talking to your mother and add nervously, "In movies, I mean. Not that I go to frat houses all the time or anything." *Yeah. That whole thing with Cordy and the giant reptile? Movies. Right.*

"Yes, of course. Why do I get my hopes up?"

"So. Home?" you ask.

Giles returns his gaze to the parchment, studying it. "There isn't an incantation specifically for our dimension, but there's one for the user's home dimension."

"That'll work. And the orb? How does that work?"

Excitedly, Giles pulls the orb from his pocket. "After saying the right chant over the orb, you only have to touch it for your spirit to instantly be returned to your body."

A great idea sweeps over you. "Can we use that thing on the Night Terror?"

Giles gives a slight grin. "I don't see why not. We'd just need to catch him in spirit form."

"What about the Pendant of Whosits?"

"Kamrusepas."

"Whatever. Can we use that on him?"

"I think the user has to say the incantations himself," Giles says with regret.

"Could we trick him somehow?"

"We could try."

"I like this storehouse, Giles."

SLAYER CHOICE:

Do you decide to . . .

\ use the Pendant of Kamrusepas? *If yes, turn to page 133.*

\ use the Orb of Trakoa? *If yes, turn to page 39.*

You follow the tiny griffin out of Giles's front door and into the street beyond. The sky above broils with clouds and the thundering of airborne engines.

"What is that?" you shout, covering your ears against the din.

"The invasion fleet!" the griffin shouts back. "We're too late."

"What invasion?" you call back. But the griffin dashes off into a hole. You see his wing beckoning desperately for you to join him, but there's no way you can fit in there. It's only four inches across.

A roar and boom fills the sky as you see wires descend from the clouds. Soon men in black zip downward, wearing gas masks and black uniforms. "Everyone into the evacuation vans!" the men yell through bullhorns. "No exceptions."

"You, miss!" one orders, seeing you. "Get into the vans."

You're not about to let these guys take you anywhere. You punch the first one in the face when he gets close enough, and knock the next one over.

"She's not cooperating," one bellows through his bullhorn. You snatch it out of his hand and fling it, kicking him in the face.

Then you take off down the street, evading the evacuation vans parked on one corner.

"Catch her!" voices sound behind her. "She needs to be reprogrammed."

You are *definitely* not going with these guys.

You run all the way to the edge of town, entering a

dense forest beyond. You'll find other rebels, other people to join and overthrow this invading force. You won't stop until you've freed everyone who's been taken already. These jerks have no idea what they're up against.

As you pick your way through the forest, looking for a place to hide, it never occurs to you that you're dreaming. Sometimes you feel like you left something behind . . . some other life. Something important. You have terrifying images of a creature with wings and multiple rows of teeth taking over your body, living out your life while you stay trapped here in this insane place of invaders, griffins, and nightmares. But then the feeling fades, and you're sure this is the *real* world. It must be. After all, you feel like you've been here forever.

THE END

You walk out of Giles's front door, into the hallway outside the chemistry lab at Sunnydale. Several students cast bowling balls at the pins at the end of the hall, and you hear them crashing over as you see Willow leaving through the lab doors.

"Will!" you call, getting her attention.

She looks up. "Hey, Buffy!"

You catch up to her. "Have you talked to Giles?"

"About the whole Night Terror thing?"

"Yeah. Weird, huh?"

"Being stuck in the dream world? Imagine how horrible that would be!"

You feel a chill and look down, embarrassed to see that you forgot to put on a shirt and are walking around in just your bra. "Can I borrow my jacket?" you ask Willow, who is suddenly holding your black leather coat.

"Sure," she says, handing it to you.

You slide it on as you exit out a pair of double doors at the end of the hall, emerging into Sunnydale Cemetery. "It's a good thing these things stay on so easily," you tell her, pointing to the rulers stuck to one sleeve of your jacket.

"It should make math a whole lot easier," Willow agrees.

"So, Will, Giles says there might be people who have become trapped permanently in the dream world."

"And you want to try to contact them?" Excitement wells up in her voice. "Oooh, ooooh! We could do a séance, or use a Ouija board, or, or . . ." Distractedly she pulls a piece of paper out of her pocket. "What's this?" She reads it, frowning. "Oh, no!"

"What is it, Will?"

"It's my class schedule," she says, voice rising in a panic. "There's an advanced trig class on here that I've never even been to, Buffy, and it's almost the end of the term!"

"Are you sure?" You look at the schedule, but to you it looks like random scribbles. You can't make sense of it.

"Oh, my God, Buffy! I've missed the midterm and never turned in any homework for it! I'm going to flunk!" Her eyes well up with tears. "I have to go talk to the teacher right now!" Turning, she runs off across the cemetery.

You watch her go, realizing that the sun has set and that you should be getting home for dinner.

As you walk past a mausoleum, you notice a tall man with long, flowing brown hair and a gleaming gold lamé turban. He's wearing a white suit with a Nehru collar and a gold lamé capelet. His boots, also of gold lamé, end in very pointy toes. In his palm he holds a small crystal ball, which he rolls from one hand to the other. His intense blue eyes fix on you.

"Hi," you say.

"Hello," he responds. "Nice night."

"Yeah," you say, looking up at the stars. They

sparkle vividly, way more than you remember seeing them recently. You can even see the enchanted white expanse of the Milky Way, stretching across the zenith of the sky. A few bats flit overhead, blocking out sections of stars as they pass.

"You been here long?" the man asks you.

"In the cemetery?"

He stares inscrutably.

"In Sunnydale?" you try again.

He continues to stare in silence, but stops juggling with the crystal ball.

The ground suddenly rumbles beneath your feet. You catch your balance and snap your gaze down, where you see cracks opening in the grass. "It's started!" you yell, remembering something about earthquakes that always coincides with film premieres and alfalfa festivals. As you jump over one fracture, fire roars from the fissure. You look over at the man to urge him to run, but he is gone.

As you dart out of the cemetery, you pass a thin, balding man wearing glasses and a neatly pressed suit. On top of a granite tombstone, he neatly lays out several square slices of cheese. "The cheese was not born yesterday," he informs you matter-of-factly.

No time to talk to him, you leap over fissure after fissure, barely make it out of the cemetery unscathed. You hope Willow made it out okay. Sulfur fills the air around you, vile-smelling and stinging your eyes. As you reach the sidewalk, you see the man standing at the corner, capelet billowing, hands beckoning you forward. There is something decidedly strange about him, and you're not sure what to think.

SLAYER CHOICE:

Do you decide to . . .

❙ find Willow and make sure she's all right, continuing on in your quest to contact spirits? *If yes, turn to page 232.*

❙ approach the stranger beckoning to you? *If yes, turn to page 239.*

Y ou look at your watch and see that it is fifteen minutes past Spain. Angel will probably be at home right now. You set off across town, pausing on the covered bridge to peer through one of the open windows at the water below. In the water you see a tiny kayak rowed by what looks to be a drunken four-inch cow with a crown. You wave to him, and he waves back, calling out, "Be sure to stop at the cider shop!"

You nod, smiling, and continue on your way.

Just as you pass by the massage and doughnut shop, a figure steps into the street in front of you. He's fortyish, wearing a white suit, a gold lamé turban, and gold boots with pointy toes.

"Buffy," he says. "I have an important message for you."

You don't recognize him, and you pause to study his face. His high cheekbones and long brown hair are striking, certainly, but you've never met him before. You would certainly have remembered a man wearing a gold lamé turban and capelet.

"What is it?" you ask.

"You've been here too long."

You've only been stopped on the corner for a second—not long at all.

"Here on the street?" you ask.

"No. In dreams."

You frown. "I don't know what you mean." A jewel-encrusted dragonfly lands on your shoulder, softly humming the theme from *The Greatest American Hero*.

"Come. Let me show you something." He turns and waves over his shoulder, beckoning you, and starts down the street.

Intrigued, you follow him, not sure what to expect.

SLAYER ACTION:
Turn to page 276.

You set off down the street, walking away from the strange man, who stops beckoning and silently watches you go. He doesn't move to follow you. Glancing back into the cemetery, you see that the fissures have already sealed shut.

The night is still and strange. No traffic sounds or night birds, or even the rustle of wind in the trees meet your ears. Halfway down the block, a bright flash brings your eyes up to the sky. A meteor streaks across the blackness, impacting harshly with the ground a few miles away. You see fire and smoke rise up around the impact site, and then the ground rumbles beneath you. Pitching you forward, the street buckles and rears, emitting an acrid stench into the air as a chasm yawns open before you. You land harshly on your hands, scraping them on the asphalt. Fire crackles within the fissure, and you hear the Master's laugh echoing up from the depths. Seconds later the pale, translucent skin of his bald pate rises up through the opening. His dark eyes come into view, locking on you and twinkling with malevolent delight.

The Master's dead, you tell yourself. *You aren't really him. This is a trick.*

Instantly the figure sinks. The fissure seals up, the laugh dying abruptly. Overhead, a thousand meteors now streak across the sky. Ash streams down in large clumps, coating your arms, legs, and body, collecting in your hair and eyelashes.

"Over here!" a woman's voice calls. You follow the voice to find a young woman gesturing for you to approach. Four people huddle under a building's awning as bits of fiery rock rain down from the heavens.

You run over there, squeezing in under the protective canopy as a particularly large piece strikes a car next to you with a sharp crack. You hope none strike the awning. It doesn't look sturdy. "Is this because of me?" you ask the woman, who you can now see is in her early twenties and is dressed in a tie-dyed T-shirt and faded bell-bottom jeans.

"No," she says.

On the horizon a hulking body rears up near the initial impact site, blotting out the fire from the meteorite strike. Savage spikes adorn its back, and it raises its reptilian head high, emitting a gleeful ululation of delight. Storming forward, it crushes cars in its wake, knocks over buildings, pounds bus-size holes into the street's asphalt. You brace yourself for the impact as it steps onto the street where you hide with the others.

But the closer it gets, the smaller it becomes, until it strides up to you no taller than a gecko. Bending down, you pick it up and put it in your jacket pocket. "It's where it belongs," you tell the woman.

"Listen," she says earnestly, and the others turn their attention toward her. You can see they are all young, some about your age, others no older than twenty-five. "Don't buy into it all."

"Buy into what?"

"What's your name?"

"Buffy," you tell her.

The others gasp, and for a moment she shuts her eyes in concentration, as if preparing what to say next.

"You're the Slayer."

"Hey!" you start to say, wondering how she knows. Like Simone. Simone. That name is very familiar. You're almost sure you know someone named Simone.

"He's been searching for a Slayer for a long time," she continues. "He needs one to live."

"Who?"

"The Night Terror." You think of that strange exchange of consciousness with the *mare*, of the Slayer who was killed in Roman-occupied Britain. "He's taken your body, and if you don't get back to it soon, your astral cord will break."

This is familiar too. "Giles told me that that may have happened to other people, that there could be disembodied souls unable to reach their comatose bodies."

"Look, I'm Meg, and this is—," she starts to say, gesturing to the others.

Just then a woman staggers by, wearing a threadbare flannel shirt, dirty jeans, and a black knit cap over oily dark hair. "Hey, you!" she yells at you, stopping in the middle of the street. "You some kind of dinosaur hunter?"

"Something like that," you answer.

"I got something for you." She places a small object on the street and then staggers away. You step out from under the overhang and realize it is no longer raining ash and burning rock.

"Don't!" the woman behind you whispers urgently.

You ignore her and walk out into the street to see what the woman left. It is the plastic lid to a coffee can, and in it are several cold spaghetti noodles. You reach down to pick the lid up but jerk your hand back when you see the noodles begin to squirm and writhe among one another. One of them slithers off the lid and burrows into the shadowed asphalt under a parked car. A moment later, something oily, slick, and gray emerges from the darkness there. You stagger backward as a creature emerges, bloating outward, gray and smooth like a slug, with a slug's tail but a donkey's head and front legs. It whinnies and stares at you with wide, terrified eyes.

"Don't buy into it," the woman says again, grasping your arm this time. You realize she crept up beside you while you were distracted.

"Don't buy into what?" you demand, watching the donkey slug slap its thick tail on the pavement.

"The dream!" She grasps your shoulders and turns you toward her. "You're dreaming, Buffy. You're trapped in the dream world. The Night Terror is walking around in your body as we speak. If you don't find a way back soon, your astral cord will break."

"Like the disembodied spirits?"

"We are the disembodied spirits. At least, we're four of them. And soon, you'll be one of us." The others come out from under the shadowed overhang and gather around you. "We are all victims of the Night Terror," Meg continues. "Our bodies lie in comas around the world. And some of us have been trapped here for so long that our bodies have since turned to dust."

You shake your head.

"But I drove it off tonight! I beat it when it came to take me over!" But even as you say the words, you know they don't feel right. You think of your house merging with Giles's place, and watch as the donkey slug slithers down a manhole with a loud, guttural bray. You are in the dream world. And it feels so real. "But I can't be trapped!" you say indignantly, then look at the faces of the four people around you, gaunt, worried, and lost.

Meg looks at you. "You have friends. We've seen your dreams. Watched you, ever since the Night Terror first noticed you. You're different. We know that. You could stop him from stranding anyone else here."

You look around at the meteor-streaked sky, at the slime trail left by the donkey slug, and say, "I don't know what to do. How do I get home?"

"You've got to contact your friends. Convince them they need to find help. They're used to dealing with the supernatural. They'll listen."

You nod. It's a good plan. Maybe Giles knows of a spell, or Willow some kind of sleep technique, or maybe they can put their minds together and come up with a different plan. "How do I find them?"

"Contact them through their dreams. You're all linked, so their dream bodies shouldn't be too far away from your own dreamscape. Just explore a little and you'll find them. Go to places where they'd each be. You may have to find them one at a time if they're not dreaming about each other."

You turn away, ready to leave.

"And Buffy!" Meg says.

"Yes?" You meet her eyes.

"People in dreams often aren't the same as they are in waking life. You may be tempted to find your best friend or a mentor. But they may not be so easy to reach. Sometimes the more emotionally involved they are with you, the harder it is for them to be objective and understand your message."

You nod in understanding, thinking that she must have been here a long time to know so much. "Have you tried to contact your friends and family?"

She lowers her head. "Many times." Then, after a pause, she adds, "They didn't understand. And now it's too late."

"Your body is dead?" You dread the answer.

"It's on life support. It's shutting down. Even now my family is trying to decide if they should pull the plug. I've seen their nightmares."

"How long have you been gone?"

"Ten years."

Your mouth falls open involuntarily. "You've been stuck here for ten years?" You can't imagine that. To be separated from your family, your loved ones, your life. To have it stolen like that, while you look on from this surreal dimension, watching your loved ones grieve for you, is a new idea of hell.

"Yes," she says. "Please, you must contact your friends and find a way to stop him."

"I will," you say, determination swelling within you. There's no way you're going to be stuck here like this or let it happen to other people. You turn away, thinking. But who should you seek out first?

SLAYER CHOICE:

Do you decide to . . .

\ find Willow first? *If yes, turn to page 240.*

\ find Giles first? *If yes, turn to page 246.*

\ seek out Xander first? *If yes, turn to page 251.*

\ try to find Cordelia? *If yes, turn to page 257.*

\ find Angel first? *If yes, turn to page 262.*

You approach the man cautiously. He waves you closer with one ring-laden hand. Are those real gems? Sapphires, rubies, emeralds—the stones are huge. You stop a few feet away from him.

"Come," he says. "I want to show you something." He turns and walks down the street, a wind kicking up dry leaves around his feet. You follow reluctantly, intrigued yet still not sure what to make of this stranger.

SLAYER ACTION:
Turn to page 276.

Y ou decide to find Willow. The library or her house are good bets, and you're closer to the library, so you check there first.

As you walk through the main doors, you discover they've changed into a revolving glass door. You step inside, push it around, and emerge into the library. Behind you, the door whooshes to a stop. At the main table, surrounded by four-foot-high stacks of books on all sides, you find Willow. Her mother leans over her and says, "I came here to get books, not talk to you. Do I even know you?"

"I'm Willow. Your daughter," you hear your friend answer softly.

Her mother shakes her head, then turns to leave. "No, no. I'm certain I don't have one."

She passes you on the way out and says, "Off to present a paper at the university! Important stuff!" She exits with a busy *swoosh* of the door.

"Will!" you say, rushing forward. "Am I glad to see you!" Your heart feels light just at the sight of her. Maybe you'll get out of here now.

With eyes rimmed in red, Willow gazes back at you, nose pink from crying.

"What is it? Your mom?"

"Buffy, three of my finals are in five minutes, and I haven't studied at all! I don't know what's wrong with me. I even missed the other three this morning. I slept through my alarm and didn't get to school until one o'clock. And then when I finally got here, I realized I'd forgotten to put on a shirt, and so I had to go back, and now it's five o'clock, and I think school is over, except that there are these finals I have to take that I haven't even studied for, and they're all in chaos mathematics, and I didn't even take that class this semester." She pauses for breath, and you go to her side, placing a reassuring hand on her back.

"Will, this is a dream. Finals aren't for a few months yet. You're safe."

"What?" She looks up at you, confused. "But I looked at my schedule, and they're today."

"No. They're not."

You hear the revolving door move and look over the stacks of books to see Xander enter. "Hey all. Looking for Will."

"She's here, behind the books."

"Great!" He approaches, peering between two stacks. "Willow! I've been looking for you everywhere!"

"You have?" she says hopefully.

"Yes! I met the most amazing girl. She's twice as smart as you, and man, is she a looker! I was actually so desperate I was considering dating you, but now I don't have to!"

The door shushes again and in walks Oz, the cute guitarist who likes Willow.

"Hey," he says.

"Hey," you answer.

"Have you seen Willow Rosenberg?"

"Behind the books," you tell him. "But there's a line."

"No problem."

As Xander turns away, Oz takes his place.

"Hi," he says. "I just wanted to say that there's no way I'd ever go out with you. I can see how you've been staring at me in the halls, and I just thought I'd let you know that."

You can hear Willow's painful swallow even from where you stand. "Oh."

You want to smack Dream Xander and Dream Oz through the revolving door, but you resist. This is just Willow's nightmare, and you thought you had it bad. At least in your nightmares you can kick the Master's ass all over again.

"Willow," you tell her. "They're not real either. You're dreaming this. Oz really does like you. Just ignore them. I have something really important to say."

"Okay," she says, looking smaller and smaller behind the stacks of books. Nightmare Oz and Xander do the Snoopy dance and exit.

Willow frowns. "Aw . . . that was cute. But I guess Xander's off to do the Snoopy dance for his new flirty-flirty girl."

You touch her shoulder. "Willow, listen. I'm trapped here in the dream world, and I need your help. That thing, the Night Terror, is walking around in my body. It's not me in there. I need you to wake up and get me out of here."

She grins, pivoting in her chair to face the books. "I may already have something, Buffy! I was just reading in here about protections against *alps* and *mares*. I found an old German banishing spell."

"Can you wake up and cast it?" She opens a book to a marked page. You see diagrams of how to make a kite. "Is that the right book?"

"I think so," she says, "though it looks different now. I don't remember the kite part. Just the mittens."

Your heart sinks. This isn't going to work. Hello illogical dream world. You feel like you'll never get through to your friends.

"I can do the spell with Giles."

"Can you remember to do it when you wake up?"

"Sure," she says, nodding confidently.

"Can you do that now?"

She frowns. "I guess so . . . but what about the finals?"

"They're a dream, Will. No finals. No mean Xander. No mean Oz. Just trapped Buffy."

"Okay. I'll wake up now, then."

Instantly she vanishes. You're left alone in Sunnydale High Library next to the looming stacks of books. That was fast. You wonder if it worked.

But before you even get to complete your thought, the library shimmies and dances around you, the books warping in and out of focus. You feel a strange rushing sensation as the world goes black, as if you're speeding through a wind tunnel.

And then with a harsh thump you land on the floor of your room. Groggily, you push yourself up on one elbow. You see your wonderful bed, your delightful bedside table, your lovely rug. Willow sits in one corner in a chair. "Willow?" you breathe.

"I'm here, Buffy! It worked."

"It did?" You get to your knees and then sit back on the carpet, taking in the whole room. It's full of your friends. Giles sits in a chair by the window, Xander on the edge of the bed, and Angel cross-legged on the floor a few feet away. "Angel . . ." You slide over to him, laying your head on his shoulder.

"It was actually Willow and I who saved you," Giles says. "Though Angel did contribute some glowering, and a bit of sulking, if I'm not mistaken."

You smile and get to your feet, and then hug Giles. "Thank you!" Willow and Xander stand and hug you too. "But how did you do it so fast?"

Willow raises her eyebrows. "Fast?"

"You only just left the dream world a second ago."

"Buffy, we've been up for two days straight preparing the spell," she says.

"Two days?" You can't believe it. Time passes so differently in the dream world.

"I thought I was going to have to take up slaying vampires if you didn't come back soon," Xander says.

You can picture that. Actually, you can picture Xander getting very killed.

"And the Night Terror?" you ask.

"Banished," Giles says. "We won't be troubled by him again."

"Thank you," you say. "It's so good to be back!"

You hug your friends again, blessed to have such amazing companions.

THE END

You head toward Sunnydale High, figuring that Giles is likely to be at the library. But when you reach it, it's locked up; the entire school is dark and actually looks abandoned, with broken windows and smashed bottles littering the grounds. The light-up sign out front has been shattered, the letters of SCHOOL DANCE TONIGHT lying scattered on the deserted parking lot. Dead leaves skitter down the street.

You decide to try Giles's house, but as you start out in that direction, you encounter a bowling alley looming up before you. You can hear big band music drifting through its open double front doors. Curious, you reach the entrance. Inside, you don't hear the typical crash of bowling pins or the thundering of balls coughed out by the ball retrieval systems. Instead, you hear a familiar voice rising above the music.

You walk inside, instantly spotting Giles in the center of a lane. Before him stands a table with a complete setting for high tea. Several china tea cups and saucers, a teapot, and a silver multitiered serving tray full of snacks rest on a lavender tablecloth. Giles doesn't spot you, but instead continues lecturing to a cluster of Kaklar demons. You recognize them because of their long ears, hooked noses, and thick mucusy ropes of phlegm that they wear stylishly tossed over their shoulders like scarves. Each demon holds a delicate china teacup filled with tea.

Some of them are sticking cucumber sandwiches up their noses.

"The entire point of a formal tea service," Giles is saying to them, "is to chat with your friends while enjoying a light meal." He gestures at the teapot, cups, and multitiered silver serving tray. "Common savories include egg salad sandwiches with the crusts cut off and small muffins. For sweets, you might have Devonshire cream, small scones and pies—"

He is cut off abruptly as one of the Kaklar sneezes thunderously, spraying the nearest rack of bowling balls with viscous strands of mucus.

"As I was instructing earlier," Giles continues, trying to ignore the outburst, "spread the Devonshire cream over the scone, creating a smooth layer, then add a small dollop of marmalade."

A second Kaklar explodes into a sneezing fit, ropes of phlegm emerging from his nose like thick green-yellow silly string. A scone flies out of the crowd and hits Giles in the forehead.

"Giles?" you say, pushing through the Kaklars. You pick one particularly gelatinous strand off your jacket.

Giles spots you as you emerge from the sea of gray-green glistening skin. "Oh, Buffy, thank God you're here. I've been trying to deliver a lecture to these Kaklar demons, and they aren't listening to a word I'm saying." He raises his eyebrows in concern, looking rather distressed. "What's the point of trying to teach civility to cretins? Besides, I can barely talk over Tommy Dorsey there in the corner." He gestures at a complete big band set up in one of the seating areas. You hadn't spotted them before. The conductor waves back, grinning. Giles gestures down to his own legs, and you see he's wearing brown pajamas with little built-in fuzzy feet and a large pocket over his stomach. "And I'm wearing kangaroo Underroos," he continues. "I don't even know how I got here."

"It's a dream, Giles," you tell him. "You're just dreaming. And I need your help."

"Oh? Yes?" He leads you away from the Kaklars, narrowly missing another high-velocity sneeze.

When at a safe distance, you say, "Giles, I'm trapped in the dream world. I need to find a way back to my body."

"Ah! Really! How intriguing. What you need is the Medallion of Morpheus. It allows you to travel between dimensions. If you say the proper incantation while holding it, you can return to our waking world."

"Sounds perfect!" you say. "Where do I find it?"

"Oh, there's one at my storehouse."

"Your storehouse?" You've never heard Giles mention this before.

"Yes, since you've pointed out I'm dreaming. It's my dream storehouse. Full of every medallion, pendant, orb, and magical object I've ever seen or even read about."

"How come we've never used this before?" You think of all the jams you could have gotten out of with a little bit of magical doohickey assistance.

"Because I don't have it in the waking world. I only have it in my dreams." He pulls you outside the bowling alley and adds confidentially, in a whisper, "And there's almost no mucus in there at all. Seriously," he says, leading you away from the bowling alley, "I can be there in two shakes of a lamb's tail, or one each of each kind of snake."

You're beginning to worry for Giles's mental cohesiveness while dreaming. You raise one eyebrow and nod, humoring him. "Gotcha."

He looks around over each shoulder, checking for eavesdroppers. "Meet me at my flat in five minutes. I'll bring the medallion. But we'd better split up now. There are grasshoppers *everywhere*, and you can't trust those little buggers."

"Sure thing, Giles," you say, not quite sure what you're agreeing to.

"Buffy!" he nearly shouts, desperately. "You understand about the neutron flow, right?"

You nod emphatically. "Of course, Giles. And I understand about the Teflon, too. And the cupcakes."

His eyes fill with wonder. "You do?"

"Yes."

"Five minutes," he repeats, and starts to walk away. Suddenly he whirls around, races toward you, and grabs your arm. "Don't let the grasshoppers see you! Especially the moody ones."

"Okay there, Giles," you agree.

SLAYER CHOICE:

Do you decide to . . .

\ meet Giles at his place in five minutes and hope he brings the medallion? *If yes, turn to page 270.*

\ find Willow, afraid that Giles is totally crackers when dreaming? *If yes, turn to page 240.*

\ find Angel, hoping that maybe he can understand you? *If yes, turn to page 262.*

You walk toward Xander's house, taking a route that will lead you past the Bronze, thinking he might be in there. As you near the nightclub, you hear the throbbing bass of a dance song pulsing through its walls.

You enter the alley next to the Bronze's entrance and see Santa Claus packing up a sack full of presents, even though you know the Santa Claus is really Teddy Roosevelt, and it's not even December. You walk by him and nod. You can't believe this is the dream dimension. Everything feels so *real*. Quickly you duck inside the Bronze, hoping to run into Xander.

Luck is with you tonight, and you see him sitting in the shadows on a couch in the far corner. You stride over there, then realize he's talking with a woman— no, *kissing* a woman. Xander. You hold back, unsure, not wanting to interrupt.

He holds her close, passionately kissing her. She's an extremely attractive woman with long, wavy brown hair and skin the color of a café latte. She eyes him wantonly with her dark, smoky eyes and kisses him back, wrapping one leg around his. You can't believe it. Well, go Xander. You don't want to interrupt this for him, even if it is a dream. The boy's got to get a break somewhere. You hang back near the bar, thinking of ordering a dream mocha. Would it taste better than ever?

Xander's math teacher walks by and you smile at her. She gently grasps your arm as she passes. "It's the lemmings," she whispers insistently in your ear. "It's always the lemmings."

"Don't I know it?" you agree with her. She nods and walks off, and then you realize she's not his math teacher at all, but rather a large beetle with bristling legs. You watch her skitter away.

Turning your attention back to Xander, waiting for a good time to interrupt, you try not to stare. They're seriously kissing now. You look around for something to occupy your attention, but you can't help but notice the woman's sudden strange behavior. She leans her head back, arcing her neck so far backward that her throat juts out painfully. You see then that a zipper runs across the width of her neck, from one collarbone, up across the base of the neck, and ending on the second collarbone. While Xander looks on, his eyes wide and mouth agape, she slowly unzips her neck and her head flops backward, as if swinging uselessly on a hinge, onto her back. Something shiny, hard, and yellow emerges from the opening in her throat. At first you don't know what to make of it, and then you realize it's a large piece of rectangular candy.

Xander leans away, horrified, and then tentatively reaches toward the candy.

"Xander!" you shout, emerging from the shadows.

He throws his hands up in resignation. "What's wrong with me, Buff? First a praying mantis, then an Incan mummy girl, now a . . . a . . ." Words fail him as he gestures at the woman with the large piece of candy protruding from her throat.

"Pez dispenser girl?"

"Exactly!" he agrees, exasperated. He buries his face in his hands.

"The good news is, this isn't real," you reassure him.

His hands part and he looks up. "What?"

"It's a dream. You're dreaming this."

"What, I'm going crazy now too?"

You shake your head. "No. This is a dream. And I'm in it with you."

"Well, is it my dream, or yours?" Xander asks, standing up from the couch.

"What difference does it make?"

"Lots," Xander answers. "Because in my dream, you're all sweaty from combat and I've just saved your life in the nick of time. And then comes the whole grateful smoochies part." He walks closer, holding his arms out.

You push his arms out of the way. "Xander, try to focus. You need to listen very carefully to what I'm going to tell you."

"I can listen and kiss at the same time," he assures you.

You place a hand on his chest to keep him at bay. "I'm sure you can. But we're not going to do that now. Listen. I'm trapped in the dream world. The *mare*, who calls himself the Night Terror, has taken over my body. It's not me in there. Do you understand? I'm trapped here. You've got to wake up and tell Giles and the others about this, and then find a way to get me back to my body."

"Your body looks just fine from here," Xander says, cocking one eyebrow. "But I may need to move in for a closer look."

"Xander!" you practically shout, stopping him dead.

His face looks temporarily stunned.

"If you don't get me out of here, my body will become permanently separated from my spirit, and there will be no more Buffy. No more Slayer. I don't even want to think about what this would do for the Slayer line." You hadn't even thought about that until this moment. If you don't die in a traditional way, if the Night Terror successfully steals your body, and your soul is here, in this state of limbo, will another Slayer be triggered, or will the Slayer line remain in limbo? *Of course, if something bad happens to Kendra, the line would go on,* you think, then immediately push those thoughts out of your mind. This isn't helping. You need to focus, which is incredibly difficult in this strange dimension of dreams. On top of that, it feels so real that you keep forgetting you actually *are* dreaming, and have to constantly remind yourself that you are.

"Please," you tell Xander earnestly. "Wake up and tell the others that I'm trapped in the dream world. And remember that it's not me walking around in my body."

"But you look so good walking around in your body," Xander tells you, reaching for one of your hands.

You silently thank the gods that Xander isn't this

forward in waking life. "What are you, some kind of
sleazy lounge act when you sleep?" you ask.

"Do you want me to sing you my rendition of 'Da
Ya Think I'm Sexy?'" he asks in a smarmy tone.

"No," you say quickly.

Just then a shrieking voice pierces through the
music and loud conversation of the Bronze. "Alexander
Harris!" it shrieks again. "Where the hell are you?"

"Mom?" Xander whimpers, his face flushing red.

"What are you doing here? I told you to stay home
tonight and wash your Uncle Rory's velour robe. The
one with urine stains and beer on it, remember? He
threw up on it again."

His mom staggers into view, wearing a billowing
muumuu and gripping a bottle of cheap blended
scotch. As she nears, you can smell the stench of
alcohol on her breath, pluming around her as she
yells. When she reaches Xander, she pulls another
bottle out from the folds of her dress and presses it
into Xander's hand. The label reads 100 PROOF
UNAVOIDABLE ALCOHOLISM.

"But, Mom," he resists, trying to hand the bottle
back.

"You'll drink it and you'll like it. If it's good
enough for your father, then it's good enough for
you."

"But I don't want to become . . ." Xander's voice
trails off as she shoves the bottle back at him. He
shakes his head, squeezing his eyes shut, and then he
begins to fade entirely. You can see the couch through

him, and the Pez dispenser woman, who now has the head of a rather drunk-looking gnu.

"Xander!" you shout as he and his mom fade into nothingness. "Tell the others! Please!"

And then he is gone.

The music in the Bronze abruptly changes from the usual excellence to complete aural torture. You wonder if it was his dream or yours that was providing the tunes. The band onstage starts performing "Macho Man." You make a hasty retreat, bursting through the front door into the alley beyond.

The huge, muscle-bound man at the door eyes you suspiciously, but he says nothing as you pass by him.

You don't know if contacting Xander has done any good at all, if he'll take what you said seriously, or if he'll even remember the dream when he wakes up. You think it might be good to contact your other friends, too.

SLAYER CHOICE:

Do you decide to . . .

\ find Willow next? *If yes, turn to page 240.*

\ find Giles next? *If yes, turn to page 246.*

\ seek out Cordelia? *If yes, turn to page 257.*

\ find Angel? *If yes, turn to page 262.*

Maybe Cordelia would be a good person to find. You think of Meg's advice, that the closer the person is to you, the less likely they are to understand your message. It doesn't take you long to figure out where she could be—the Bronze or the mall.

You are closer to the Bronze, so you check there first. Inside the club, you find that no band is playing. People are dancing to silence, waving this way and that in slow motion. In the center of the dance floor, you see Louis Armstrong on a horse. You think of asking him where Cordelia is but realize blissfully that he wouldn't know her. He's way too cool for that. Glancing around, you search for her. After checking the dance floor, tables, couches, and bar, you know she's not there.

Leaving the Bronze, you head for the Sunnydale Mall. It soon looms up before you, but it no longer looks like you remember. Instead the mall has become a towering Mayan pyramid made entirely of glass. You see two World War I Russian soldiers walking toward the entrance, and you fall into step behind them. As the automatic sliding glass doors *whoosh* open, a small stuffed dinosaur bursts from the opening, dashing between the feet of the soldiers. One of them cries out, and they chase it down in the parking lot, which is now full of huge conifer trees with snow collecting around their bases.

One of the soldiers grabs the plush dinosaur, and for a second you can't see it. But when the soldiers part, you see that where the dinosaur was now sits a package of what looks like cellophane-wrapped chicken.

A booming announcer's voice echoes across the parking lot. You don't see the source; the voice is disembodied. "Yes," the announcer thunders, "even in the Cretaceous Period, processed meat was available."

You nod, turning back toward the mall. Makes sense to you. You glide through the sliding doors, emerging in Cordelia's favorite boutique. Immediately you spot her, or rather hear her shouting voice.

"Are you saying it was declined?" she yells at a rather upset-looking clerk behind the counter.

"It was refused," the clerk explains.

"Well, run it again!" Cordelia demands.

"But I just ran it three times!"

Cordelia exhales in disgust and digs in her purse. Producing another credit card, she says, "Then try this one." As usual, Cordy looks impeccable, dressed in a tightly fitted red dress and black sling-back heels.

The clerk takes it and runs it through the machine. You approach Cordelia.

"This one is being declined too," the clerk says, cringing.

"This cannot be happening!" Cordelia vents. "You obviously don't know how to do your job. Where is your manager? I demand to see your manager!"

You sidle up next to her. "Hi, Cordelia."

She looks at you, rolling her eyes. "Can you believe that? None of my credit cards are working." She hooks a thumb at the clerk. "Obviously this loser should be working at the Doublemeat Palace making fries, not working behind the counter at the Visage du Chien Boutique."

"Excuse me, miss," the clerk counters, "but I *do* know what I'm doing, and I'm telling you that your cards aren't working." The clerk looks to be about twenty-two years old and near tears at Cordy's sharp words.

"This is *such* BS," Cordy storms. "I'm taking my business elsewhere. And I'm going to talk to your manager and see that you don't work in this boutique again."

"Cord," you cut in. "Maybe the cards are maxed out?"

She puts a hand on her hip. "Maxed out? These cards have practically no limit. Their machine is obviously broken. Or this girl's intellect is broken, being the size of a pea."

Taking the rejected cards from the clerk, you lead Cordelia out of the boutique. "Cordelia, I need you to listen to me."

She looks up and down the mall corridor, spots another boutique, and strides toward it determinedly.

"Cordy, wait!" you tell her, walking quickly by her side. "I need you to give the others a message. I'm trapped—"

Suddenly Cordy is no longer wearing the slinky red dress and black heels. Instead, a billowing orange and brown polyester dress hangs loosely on her, complete with huge plaid purse, mousy brown straw hat, and knee-high green go-go boots.

"Oh, my God," Cordelia breathes, stopping abruptly. She spots a large potted plant and makes quickly for its dense foliage. But before she reaches it, Harmony and the other Cordettes emerge from a music store and lock eyes on her.

"Cordelia?" Harmony says, and immediately bursts into loud, rude laughter. The other Cordettes join in. "I can't believe I thought you were cool," she blurts out condescendingly. "What a joke! Girls, look at that outfit!"

"But, but . . ." Cordelia's voice trails off as she faces them, cheeks burning red.

Cordelia embarrassed? This definitely *is* the dream world.

"I didn't pick it out myself," she says, trying to defend herself.

"No, obviously the Salvation Army thrift shop did it for you!" Harmony gazes around at the other Cordettes smugly. "What did you pay for it? A buck fifty?"

Cordelia straightens up and juts out her chin. "There is nothing wrong with this outfit," she says, trying a different tack. "You just aren't up on the latest fashions."

"Hah!" Harmony laughs. "And here's hoping we never will be!"

"Yeah," says one Cordette.

"Totally," says another.

And then, as a unit, they march off.

"My life is over," Cordelia murmurs, stepping completely behind the plant.

You see her face between several large, flat leaves.

"Cordelia, you have to help me. I'm trapped in the dream world. You need to tell the others that I'm not in my body. It's the Night Terror in there. You've got to think of a way to get me out of here before my astral cord breaks."

Cordelia nods. "If you can just get me out of here!" she whispers. "I can't believe this! First my credit cards are declined, and now this!" She looks down disgustedly at her outfit. Her eyes widen and she takes on a dazed, horrified look. "Buffy, this is going to be all over the school. I'll never live this down. And I can't buy new clothes to wear home. I'm going to have to leave the mall dressed like this, and everyone will see me!" She slumps against the wall dejectedly.

"Cordy, can you remember what I told you when you wake up?"

She nods distractedly. You don't know if you've reached her or not. To play it safe, you should keep trying to contact people until someone definitely understands your message.

SLAYER CHOICE:

Do you decide to . . .

❘ find Willow next? *If yes, turn to page 240.*

❘ find Giles next? *If yes, turn to page 246.*

❘ find Angel? *If yes, turn to page 262.*

You decide you must find Angel. If anyone connects with you on a deep-down soul level, it's him. Suddenly wearing clogs and a yellow terry-cloth dress you owned in sixth grade yet somehow still fit into, you start toward his place.

You have gone no more than a block when you see the odd man from the cemetery again. He beckons you toward him, streetlights flashing off his lamé turban. His kind eyes welcome you, which makes you feel more than a little suspicious. Still, something in him intrigues you.

"Come," he calls. "I want to show you something." He walks away, gesturing for you to follow him down the street. Curious, you follow, keeping a safe distance.

SLAYER ACTION:
Turn to page 263.

Your guide, who has introduced himself as the Great Transcendental Ned, leads you down a tree-lined street, and as you walk, night falls, bathing Sunnydale in soft darkness. You pass a lemonade stand manned by two slavering demons with tusks protruding from their mouths. To make the lemonade, they drool into each cup and then add an entire lemon, unpeeled. "Four dollars and fifty-two cents!" one calls in such a low voice that it reverberates inside your chest, like standing too close to a revving Harley. *What a strange time of night to sell lemonade,* you think.

You wave a "No, thanks," and then wonder if you should kill them. Still, they don't seem to be particularly evil, unless someone unwittingly buys their lemonade. You look back at them over your shoulder after you pass, but they are no longer demons. One of them is your mom, with a red kerchief tied over her hair, and the other is a beagle. "I'll bet I can beat you to grandma's house," your mom calls, producing a small basket filled with food.

"It's a deal," you answer, doubling back to shake on the bet.

The Great Transcendental Ned places a firm hand on your shoulder, stopping you. "My psychic powers can help you. This is what I speak of," he says. "That's not physically your mother. Your loved ones aren't here. They are merely protrusions into the dream world. You witness their dreams. You walk through your own."

You pause, turning to study his face. He doesn't

smile, merely looks on with concern. He clasps his hands together, then sticks his foot out, drawing a triangle with his toe.

"What is that for?"

"The Meager Ones. It is they who have brought us forth into this great unknown, they who have ushered forth this age of unknowing, this place of all the tremendous truths we cannot know, who—"

"Never mind."

The psychic continues to look at you gravely. "If you're going to stop the Night Terror, then you must constantly be aware that this is a dream. If you become lost in these images, you will be stranded here forever."

His words sink in, and you get a sick feeling in your stomach. You can't believe you're really trapped in the dream world. It all seems perfectly normal, so convincing.

"Then what are you? Am I dreaming you?"

The psychic shakes his head. "No. I am journeying here purposefully, by astral projecting to this plane. I could see the stranded souls here in the dream world and wanted to help them. You are the Slayer, and I think we can stop the Night Terror together."

You stand silently, mulling this over. And hey, does everyone know you're the Slayer? You don't remember putting out a PSA, though Giles would beg to differ.

"Come, follow me." He continues down the street, and soon you stop in front of your house. But instead of the usual welcoming white-painted exterior, an ominous red-gold glow engulfs the house, pulsing and alive.

"What is that?" you ask, breathless.

"It is the Night Terror's emanation. He will not sleep, but the evil energy of his soul still affects the dream world. Right now he is in your house, walking around in your body. He looks like you, talks with your vocal chords, and attempts to imitate you. Those closest to you will see through this. Therefore he must find a safe place to go, where no one will know who you are."

You puzzle this over. "Well, can't I just wait until *he* goes to sleep, and then take my body back in the same way he possessed it?"

"No. He will not sleep until your astral cord is broken and you are no longer a threat."

"How long until that happens?"

"Very soon."

"Are you kidding me? But I feel like I've only been here a few minutes."

"Time passes differently in the dream world. But don't be afraid. This can be a good thing. Once your astral cord breaks, the Night Terror will allow your body to sleep, and he will enter the dream world once again, like any other dreamer. Then you can fight him and defeat him."

"How?" you demand a little too harshly, the panic of being trapped forever in this surreal dimension finally, truly hitting you.

"By building a dreamcatcher."

Your eyebrows raise. "A dreamcatcher? One of those weblike thingies you put over your bed?"

"That's one way to describe them," he answers. "But this will be a big dreamcatcher. And built here in the dream dimension. Bad dreams get caught in them, and good ones pass through. The web will entangle him, opening the possibility for you to return to your body."

"The possibility? Not the certainty?"

"Your astral cord will be severed by then. I see now that it is already very weak, barely detectable. I imagine it will break within the hour. Once that happens, you cannot enter your body merely by finding and returning to it. The way is lost to you. But I can sing you back into your body."

"Sing?" You are starting to feel like a parrot.

"Yes. I discovered the technique while astral projecting in Australia. I found a small boy whose astral body had been stranded on the astral plane. I sought out his comatose body in the waking world. I was able to retrace the path back to his physical body and then chant and sing for him. He followed my voice back to his body and reentered it."

"And you can do this for me?"

He nods, placing his hands together. "Seeem seeem salabeeem."

"Wait a minute," you say suspiciously, "isn't that from *Jonny Quest*?"

"It is a far older magical phrase, predating *Jonny Quest*."

Your confidence is not soaring.

"I will go to your house and perform the ceremony that will reunite your astral body with your physical one. Then you will be restored."

"Wow." It's a lame thing to say, but you are oddly speechless. You've experienced your share of magic since you've been the Slayer, but it's strange to be at the receiving end of such an important ritual, especially one performed by a complete stranger. A really strange stranger. A strange stranger who may well be, well, from Planet X. Yet something in him speaks to you. His kind eyes, patient face, and frankness all make you think that you can put your trust in him.

"How do I build this huge dreamcatcher?"

"We will find wood and sinew and beads here, and you will weave it while I leave the dream world and prepare your house for the ritual."

"Wait," you suddenly say. "How are you going to get into my house? What about my mom? And do you need Giles?"

"I've already met Giles. I found him when I sensed your astral body was in danger, along with the others."

"Others?" Parrot time again.

"The disembodied spirits."

Right.

"I've already been in your house a few times with Giles. Your mother is very gracious. She makes good cookies."

Hey, you think, *she hardly ever makes* me *cookies.*

Then it hits you. *Already been in your house a few times.* "How long have I been gone?"

"Two weeks."

The news hits you like a blow to the gut. It feels like hardly any time has passed. Your mom must be so worried—but no, she wouldn't be. At least, not because she thought you were missing. The Night Terror was there, walking around in your body, imitating you. But there's no way he could totally pull it off, and she was likely worried about strange changes in behavior.

"How can the Night Terror imitate me for that long?" you ask.

"He watches our dreams. Knows our friends, our families. Learns our behaviors, the way we speak. Then he can move in and imitate us. Sometimes he is very convincing."

You think of the Slayer that the Night Terror got killed. If he does that with your body, you're going to be one pissed-off disembodied Slayer.

He places a hand on your shoulder, directing compassion-filled eyes at you. "Your astral cord has broken, my dear," he says gently.

"What?" you glance around, hoping to spot it.

"You will not be able to see it. I can detect such disturbances because I am highly trained by my master Kajunro-Mo-Glop, of the Lava Men. And I can tell you, it has been severed."

You don't feel any different. Except maybe even more reluctant about this guy.

"Lava Men?"

"They live in the interior of the Earth. They are infinite in their wisdom."

"Do they wear gold lamé too?" you ask.

"Ah," he says, nodding. "I see you are already familiar with them. Come. We must hurry. Soon the Night Terror's astral body will enter the dream world. I will take you to a place where you can get the supplies you need for the dreamcatcher. Then I will leave."

It sounds like quite a project, and one you'll have to pull off in a limited time, as much as time means in this dimension. You think of the other disembodied spirits. Maybe you could ask them to help. On the other hand, in the time you spend trying to find them, you might just as easily be able to finish the dreamcatcher yourself.

SLAYER CHOICE:

Do you decide to . . .

\ build the dreamcatcher by yourself? *If yes, turn to page 289.*

\ find the other disembodied spirits and enlist their help? *If yes, turn to page 186.*

To get to Giles's house, you take a shortcut through the sewer tunnels, which lead you first through battle-torn France during the French Revolution (boy, that film you thought you slept through during World History class certainly made an impression), then out into a dense jungle with gray vines that move and slither like snakes. As they wind around your ankles and you lash at them to keep them at bay, you begin to think that maybe it's a good thing people don't always remember their dreams. Are you really wearing blue sparkly jelly shoes?

After hacking through a section of particularly thick foliage, you see Giles's door. Just as you raise your hand to knock on it, the door sweeps open, revealing Giles in the door frame. Only it's not the Giles you know. He's at least twenty years younger and wears ripped blue jeans, a white T-shirt, and a worn black leather jacket.

"All my bloody clothes have gone missing," Giles says in a British accent wholly different from the formal one you're used to. "Can't find my best black T-shirt."

"I know the feeling."

"Anyway, love, this is what you're here for, eh?" He hands you a bronze medallion. "This little gizmo made quite the ruckus when I stole it off some traveling French students last year. They came back looking for it, none too pleased, right? But me and Ethan straightened them out." He pats down his pockets, frowns, and at last produces a lone crumpled cigarette from a pocket. He lights it, takes a long, nasty drag and mutters, "Bugger it. I'm out of fags." He picks a bit of tobacco off his tongue and leans against the door frame.

You've never seen Giles like this. He's so . . . irreverent. "Ripper?" you hazard, referring to the nickname he held during his wild youth.

"What's it to you?"

Definitely Ripper. Oh, boy.

But maybe he can still be helpful. You hold up the medallion. "Info?"

He snorts with derision. "Sure. Lots. Mainly, good luck getting the sodding thing to work. Tried it myself countless times. Anyway, there's some incantations that go with it. Bloody hard to pronounce, too. But you're welcome to them. The whole thing's a useless piece of junk if you ask me."

You study the medallion. One side has an image of the crescent moon, with an owl sitting in it. The other side sports an ancient, many-branched tree with a lyre and flute in its branches. You look up at Ripper.

He takes a final drag and throws the cigarette into the bushes. A moment later you hear crackling and glance over to the shrubbery catching on fire. "It's called the Medallion of Morpheus," he explains, pulling out a crumpled piece of paper from his back pocket. It's a menu he stole from a pub called "The Bloated Pig." He goes on. "I have two incantations that go with it. Each serves a different purpose—providing dimensional travel of varying sorts." He holds out the menu, revealing two separate lines inscribed on the back. "Don't know if I got this right. I tried to double-check it, but all my books have gone blank. Can't explain it."

"They'll fill back in later," you tell him. *Hopefully when you get back to normal.* Birds start evacuating from the bushes.

"At any rate, I can't quite remember which is which, and good luck getting the crock to work."

Reluctance consumes you. *Can't remember which is which?* "Are you sure about this?"

"No, not really. I was going to hock it and buy an amp, but bollocks, you can just keep it."

You take the crumpled menu from his hands, glancing down at the two lines.

"Had a bit of trouble with the translation. . . . it's in an obscure dialect of Etruscan. But I think I got the basic gist of it right. Should be as easy as stealing a car."

This is young *Giles*? "Basic *gist* of it? We're talking dimensional travel here, not automotive hijacking. If you got this wrong, I could end up in some hell dimension of polyester or place of the no fun."

"No need to be dramatic," Ripper says defensively. "Since you can't read proto-Etruscan, I wrote down the phonetic sounds of the phrases in the Latin alphabet." After a pause he added, "That's our alphabet."

"I know that," you say, exasperated, though you're not actually sure you knew that.

"They're not entirely certain how proto-Etruscan

was pronounced exactly, but I got the general idea."

This just gets better and better. Bad translation of an unpronounceable language. "They? Who they?"

"Linguists. Stuffed shirts. You know the type. It should be pretty close."

"Again, not inspiring the confidence."

"Well, I'll be amazed if you get it working at all." He closes your fingers around the medallion and then grabs your hands, thrusting them up in the air. "Just hold up the medallion, pick one of the phrases, and speak it. If that phrase doesn't work, just pick the other one and try it. If it works, you'll be home faster than you can say 'Bob's your uncle.'"

"Bob's not my uncle."

"It's a colloquialism."

"I know." He lets go and you study the medallion apprehensively. "I'm just not sure about this thing."

He sniffs indifferently. "What've you got to lose?"

"Okay," you breathe, knowing this is your best bet so far for a way home.

Now you just have to pick the right phrase.

SLAYER CHOICE:
Do you decide to . . .

❘ pick the phrase "furan-nak-ta-ha-farnak?" *If yes, go to page 279.*

❘ pick the phrase "ak-bah-mah-ha-nee?" *If yes, go to page 126.*

You call Xander and Willow for backup. When your friends arrive at the motel, Angel leaves, dragging out a resistant Ethan to return the stolen dagger and gem to their rightful owners. While you restrain the mummy, Giles and Xander tie it to the bed. Willow flips on the infomercials. You leave the mummy stranded there, returning only when the channels need to be changed to maintain the infomercial marathon. Miracle pancake makers. Improved hair removal systems. Improved hair regrowth systems. Unbelievably easy-to-use weight loss contraptions. Every time you come back, the mummy is in worse shape, groaning and tossing, cursing at you. You keep the torture coming. Weight loss pills. Weight gain pills. Miracle juice makers. Miracle coffeemakers. Plastic storage bins for plastic storage bins.

Meanwhile, Giles researches banishment spells for the *mare*.

When you return on the third day, after Giles finds a spell, the mummy's soul is back. The Night Terror has left the building. You think it may have been the miracle toaster/radio that did it in. At Angel's unyielding insistence, Ethan returns to the motel room and undoes the original spell that restored the mummy's soul, sending the spirit back to the Egyptian afterlife.

While Angel escorts Ethan out of town, Giles performs the banishment spell, ensuring that the Night Terror can no longer possess the bodies of sleepers. No matter where he is, whether in a new body or currently in the dream world, the spell will find him and disempower him forever. Giles pushes the bed to the wall, then draws in chalk on the carpet. After creating a large circle, he draws the image of a hulking, winged beast a lashing tail at the center. You hold hands around the circle while Giles chants in German. As the words enter the air, you see Giles's breath frosting. His words form visible gold symbols, painted in light itself, that drift through the room and enter all four walls. A crashing sound erupts overhead, and for a moment you think the ceiling is caving in. But it remains untouched. Lightning strikes, filling the room. A portal opens, sizzling with electricity, and an enormous figure emerges from the rift. Wings flapping in resistance, jaws clacking, the green-brown winged beast hooks its tail around a motel chair, smashing the small table. The portal closes overhead, leaving the creature behind. The beast's image in the center of the circle begins to glow as it sucks the creature ever nearer. With a blinding flash of light, it consumes the beast and then winks out. The *mare* is gone.

"It's banished," Giles says.

You help load the mummy into Giles's Citroën and return it to the museum. You just hope they have a miracle cleanser that can get ice cream out of millennia-old linen.

THE END

Several blocks later, you catch up with the stranger at the edge of a small neighborhood park. "See?" he asks, pointing into the shadows. You walk to his side and follow his gem-laden finger. Sunlight now streams down, and you can clearly see that he points to Angel, who sits on a bench in the sunlight, spots of brightness falling on his coat and face through the tree leaves above. Your heart feels light.

"Angel!" you call, approaching him.

He sees you and stands, a huge smile spreading across his face. Usually he is pretty good at masking his emotions, and his smile touches you. You reach him and slip your arms inside his coat, hugging him against you. He holds you for several long moments before the gold-turbaned stranger approaches you again and says, "See?"

You look at his face, at the suntanned cheeks and deep brown eyes. "What should I see?"

"Angel," he says.

You study Angel's face, dappled in light and shadow.

And then you realize. He's in the sunlight.

"When did this happen?" you gasp.

"It didn't," the stranger replies. "Do you see?"

You don't see. Or actually you do see what's before you—there is your love, in the sunlight.

Then Angel pulls away and looks down at you. "I have to bury them," he says.

"Who?"

Angel gestures off to the side, where you see a

man, a woman, and a little girl in eighteenth-century dress sprawled on the grass. Coagulating blood oozes out of each of their throats, which have been viciously torn out. "That's going to attract bears," you tell him.

He nods and leaves your side, bending mournfully over the bodies.

"Liam," the stranger says to Angel. "Tell her."

Angel squints at you in the sunlight. "I did this," he says. "But I did it a long time ago. It's not happening now. None of this is really happening now." He looks back at the dead bodies.

"Do you see now?" the stranger asks you.

You frown. Not really. When you look back at Angel, he's your seventh-grade English teacher. He straightens up and says, "It's always this way. They never listen," and walks away solemnly.

"Let me show you more," the stranger says, and begins walking again.

"Wait! Who are you?"

The man turns. "I am the Great Transcendental Ned. A powerful psychic. I am part X-ian."

"X-ian?" you ask.

"My mother was an Earth woman. But my father hailed from Planet X."

"Excuse me?"

"I sensed you were in trouble on the astral plane, and I have come to help."

"They've never even *discovered* Planet X, have they?" you ask, pretty sure that it's only a theory. You remember reading about it in earth science class, something about a mysterious planet yet to be found that might be disturbing the orbits of comets.

"No. But that's because they've been searching in the wrong dimension."

"Oh. I see." You start to look for escape routes.

"Please," he says, "you need to see. You are in grave danger." Then he strikes a pose, with one leg up and both arms straight out behind him.

After a moment, you ask, "What are you doing?"

"The Stance of the Many Coins on the Desert Floor," he replies, then calls out in a loud voice, "May the wafers come in unison!" Straightening up, he says, "The way is clear now. Come."

He continues to walk, beckoning you farther on.

You don't think you want anything to do with this guy.

"Please," he says over his shoulder. "You're in great danger. You must follow me."

You watch him from a distance. Your Slayer sense is tingling about this guy. You just don't know if it's tingling because he's one lima bean short of a bowl of succotash, or because he actually might be sincere.

SLAYER CHOICE:

Do you decide to . . .

\ follow the Transcendental Ned? *If yes, turn to page 263.*

\ explore your surroundings on your own? *If yes, turn to page 232.*

Walking out onto Giles's patio, you hold the medallion before you and pronounce the words as clearly as possible—Xander once showed you *Army of Darkness*, and you don't want to make an incantation flub-up like that.

Instantly the medallion grows warm in your hand. You grip it tightly as the world starts to swirl around you, the sky spinning from blue to deep purple and then to darkest red. Billowing gold clouds lower down around you, clustering ever closer until all you can see is a vague golden aura. Then with a crack that sends your hands flying protectively to your ears, the sky careens outward, revealing a vast plain of dark gray sand stretching to the horizon beneath a scarlet red sky. Strange purple clouds float near the horizon, and black turrets of rock jut out of the plain at odd angles. Jumbles of orange lichen-covered boulders lie piled up at their bases.

You stumble as you try to take a step forward and realize you're standing on top of a very steep sand dune.

From this vantage point, you see a strange city in the distance, surrounded by a great wall rising from the desert floor. Made of what looks like adobe and adorned with countless towers, spires, staircases leading to nowhere, and multitiered pyramids like Sumerian ziggurats, the city leaves you stunned and bewildered.

This is not Sunnydale.

Where the hell did the medallion send you?

Oh, please, no, you think quickly. *I didn't mean that literally. Please not a hell dimension.*

You listen for any sign of voices or laughter, or even

engine noise of some kind, but hear only the wind's lonely sigh as it wanders aimlessly across the vast dunes.

Already your ankle boots are filled with sand. You look down at your outfit and see that it is actually real—something you'd not only wear, but actually own—your blue jeans and red top with the dramatic, drapey collar.

Turning around completely, you find that the only sign of civilization is the city beyond.

You look back down at the list, still clutched tightly in your hand, and consider reading the next incantation. This is definitely the wrong place.

And you then realize that the medallion is no longer in your hands. You still have the incantations, but the pendant is missing. Did you drop it?

Desperately you fall on your knees and dig around in the grit. You don't stop until your skin nearly bleeds, rubbed raw by the coarse sand. You're so intent on finding the medallion that you don't notice the four hulking demons arcing through the air until they're almost upon you.

You instantly recognize them as being of the same race as the Night Terror. With great beats of their leathery wings, they descend, mouths open, revealing the three rows of glistening teeth. In the distance you see more demons taking off from the countless towers and spires in the city, all headed toward you, until the sky is a swarm of gray-brown flapping reptilian wings, lashing tails, and gripping claws.

The first four land roughly in the sand next to you,

and you jump to your feet, raising your fists to fight.

Age grizzles the face of one of the four. Sprouting from his ponderous, bony head are immense horns, four times the size of the Night Terror's.

This demon regards you carefully, as if judging to see how it would best like to prepare you for a seven-course meal, in which you'll merely be an appetizer.

You start moving in the sand, keeping distance between you and the creatures. Another batch of them lands behind the first four, and all stare at you intently through narrowed, silvery, pupil-less eyes. You can barely move as your feet keep sinking, and you know fighting in this environment will be difficult.

Suddenly you miss Xander. He would say something loony right about now that would distract them long enough for you to get in a few surprise kicks and punches.

The old demon strides over to you, his rough, clawed feet sinking into the desert sand.

You brace yourself, looking around for a weapon. Nothing but sand. The rock spires are too far away to hide in. You'd never outrun these beasts with wings. You must stand your ground. Steal a weapon off one of them.

The old demon stops in front of you.

"So sorry if we've disturbed you, my dear," he says, attempting a smile that has the same calming effect on you as leaning into the mouth of a starving crocodile.

"You . . . speak English?" you ask. They even *sound* English. Giles would be proud.

"Oh, not at first. Which is why we paused. But I

read the language centers of your brain and pieced it together from there."

You take a step back, a little put off.

"I saw several different dialects in there, so I chose the dialect of the one you refer to as Giles."

No wonder Giles would be proud.

"Welcome to the Chrossos dimension. Might we inquire," adds one of the original four, sporting long, flowing white hair cascading between his horns, "how you came to be here?"

You continue to stand still, stunned. "I, uh, was trapped in another dimension. The dream dimension. Giles gave me a medallion so I could travel back to my own world. Only," you look around at them, "I don't think I made it."

"Medallion? The lost Medallion of Morpheus?"

You nod. "That's the one. But if it was lost before, I hate to tell you, it's lost again."

"Oh, it isn't lost, merely where you left it last. The medallion does not transport with the user."

Nice. You make a mental note to completely kick Giles's ass the next time you see him. If you ever do see him again.

"So what should I do? How do I get back?" You swallow the panic rising inside you.

"What dimension are you from?" the elder demon asks.

You furrow your brow. "I'm not really sure I know. . . . It's not exactly something we learn in school. It has Earth in it. And Sunnydale. And Mt. Everest. Oh, and there's James Spader and café lattes"—man, you'd give anything for one of those right now—"and Velcro." You're really excited now, standing on the tips of your toes and gesturing. "And accordions and clean clothes."

"Ah," says the elder, and all the other demons clustered around murmur with a collective rasping and mumbling.

"Sounds like the dimension we call 'Don't call us, we'll call you.'"

You stand there blinking. "Nice name. Can you send me back there?"

The elder nods. "I believe so. But first, tell us how you came to be trapped in the dream dimension."

You pause. Should you tell them? They're obviously the same race as the Night Terror, and he's the reason you were trapped. What if they become offended and refuse to help you? On the other hand, maybe they'll be sympathetic and know a way to stop him for good.

It's a hard call to make in an alien dimension with sand in your socks.

SLAYER CHOICE:

Do you decide to . . .

❘ describe the Night Terror? *If yes, turn to page 191.*

❘ make up a reason, leaving the Night Terror out of it? *If yes, turn to page 299.*

When you get to the alley, Angel is nowhere in sight. You find blood congealing in the spot where he attacked the woman, but the body is gone. Briefly you hope that she wasn't dead after all and an ambulance has carried her away. But you know that's pointless thinking. You watched her blood stop pulsing—her heart no longer working.

Angel must have dragged the body off to feed on it, you realize with disgust. Quietly prowling through the alley, you listen for the faint sounds of vampire feeding, and at last you are rewarded. Down a neighboring dark street, you see the woman's feet sticking out from behind a Dumpster.

You creep over there, signaling for Giles and Willow to circle around the other way. You keep Xander by your side. Together you slink forward quietly. That is, until Xander accidentally kicks a soda can, and the clatter echoes in the confines of the alley.

Instantly Angel leaps up from behind the Dumpster, wiping blood off his mouth. "You're back," he croons, then looks at Xander and licks his lips. "And you've brought hors d'oeuvres. How thoughtful."

"Jeez, he *is* evil," Xander says in surprise, taking a step back. "Didn't I tell you? Didn't I warn you all? But does anyone ever listen to me?"

Angel doesn't see Giles in time. Your Watcher throws the chain out. You grab the other end and rush Angel, knocking him over as he tries to dive aside. You slap one manacle onto his wrist and manage to lock it while Giles struggles with the other. While Angel thrashes in the chains, Willow and Xander pile on top of him, allowing Giles to lock the other manacle. You force him to sit up, wrapping the chains around and around his arms. Angel lashes out, kicking you and then kneeing Willow painfully in the jaw. But together you manage to bind him.

"Oh, God," Willow squeaks when she sees the woman's dead body lying crumpled in the shadows. "Buffy!"

You don't know what to say. "I know," you manage lamely, not sure how to comfort your friend. Angel has done something horrible and there's no way around it. "We need to get him to the library, put him in the cage."

"I'll be damned if I let you put me in a cage," Angel growls. You can smell the blood reeking off him, and you train the crossbow on him in case he moves suddenly.

"You *are* damnèd," Giles snaps, then shoves Angel forward, forcing him to march.

Together you manage to sneak Angel into the school without drawing attention. Luckily it's nearly so late that no one is there except the night janitor. You lock Angel, chains and all, in the library's cage and set the crossbow down on the table. Your shoulders ache from lack of sleep.

"What's wrong with him?" Willow asks as Angel snarls and spits blood at you.

"I don't know." You turn to Giles. "Can this have something to do with the Night Terrors? Could one of those things have taken him over?"

Giles narrows his eyes on Angel, who paces in the cage, then stops and grips the wire mesh, smearing it with blood. "This body's been too cramped for too long," Angel says. "I'm sick of sharing it. If you can find a way for this damned thing to leave my body, I'll even help you."

You turn to Angel, surprised. "What's in your body?"

Angel regards you with yellow, ethereal eyes. "The Night Terror."

"So it does exist," Giles breathes. "A tangible demon seeking entrance into our world?"

"Well, I wouldn't exactly call it tangible," Angel sneers, "if it's in my head."

You approach the cage, trying to recognize something of the man you have come to love in this blood-smeared beast. "So you're in there, then, Angel? Fighting with the Night Terror?"

"Oh, honey. Didn't your Watcher tell you who I am?" He fixes you with a hungry gaze. "Did he warn you about me, little girl? Didn't he tell you of the people I've tormented, of the sweet tortures I've devised for innocent little lambs just like you?"

"I'm not so innocent," you warn him.

"No," he replies smoothly. "I suppose you wouldn't be."

Willow takes your arm. "Are you really listening to this?" She nods toward Angel. "He's trying to hurt you, Buffy." She walks you away from the cage. Xander continues to stand near Angel, as if afraid to stop watching him for even a moment. Now that you have captured Angel and the adrenaline has left your body, you realize how exhausted you are. Your back aches and your eyes burn.

Giles waves you over to the door of his office. "I need to go home, find some materials I've left there on night terrors. If he's telling the truth, and this creature has entered his body, we need to find out where Angel is."

Willow looks confused. "But . . ."

"That thing in the cage is not Angel," you tell her.

"No," Giles agrees, studying Angel, "I don't think it is." Gently he puts a hand on Willow's shoulder. "Willow, do you think you can stay here with Xander and keep an eye on our guest? Buffy, I need you to come with me to my house. Tell me more about what Angel said. You can describe everything you remember on the way."

"Giles, I don't think that's such a good idea," you say quickly, worried about your friends. Besides, the thought of sitting down in a car, the motor droning methodically around you, gently humming, makes you want to fall asleep right now.

"We'll only be gone a few minutes," Giles says. "They can take care of themselves."

Willow nods in agreement, reassuring you.

SLAYER CHOICE:

Do you decide to . . .

❚ stay in the library and guard Angel yourself while Giles gets the materials he needs? *If yes, turn to page 297.*

❚ go with Giles to his place to save time and trust your friends to guard Angel? *If yes, turn to page 198.*

The Great Transcendental Ned motions you forward, and again you find yourself wandering through the streets of Sunnydale. The streets, still oddly quiet, lie deserted. No foot traffic, no people walking dogs, no cars on the road. Why is your dream world so sparsely populated? Is it some reflection of the isolation you feel in your waking life? The streets there may be full of people, but you feel like you can't relate to any of them. Even among your dearest friends, you often feel like an outsider, with a tremendous responsibility weighing down on you.

You could populate your dreamscape with anyone, but instead emptiness comprises it. This is your dreamscape, you think, walking down the abandoned street, following the psychic.

Suddenly it all sinks in—the implications of being in the dream world. Does this mean you could do anything? Could you fly?

You stop walking, bend at the knees, and spring up into the air. You don't fly, though, not exactly, but instead bound through the air in a huge, slow-motion arc, like leaping on the moon. You sail over the head of the psychic and he looks up at you, grinning.

"I see you're catching on," he says. When you land, a gentle touchdown, you see that once again he is somehow in front of you, though you didn't see him run or jump as you did.

He looks over his shoulder, still grinning. "See if you can do that."

What, teleport? you wonder. How cool would that

be? You stop again and think about it, will it, squeeze your eyes shut, and picture being down the street, but you don't move.

So instead you leap back up into the air, launching really high this time, well above the treetops and rooftops. You see a full moon in the sky with illuminated white clouds nestled around it, and then you arc down, the moon becoming obscured behind the trees.

A whitewashed cottage comes into view, and behind it stands a rusted shack surrounded by a barbed wire fence strung along wooden posts. Two black guard dogs slink into view, growling ominously low in their throats.

The psychic holds up a hand, motioning for you to be still. You listen intently as he cranes his neck, peering around.

"We're here," he says. "But we need to be quick. There's a thing here . . . a creature. I haven't quite figured out what it is, but this is one of the only storehouses of supplies I've found so far in the dreamscape."

"A creature?"

He nods.

"What kind of creature?"

"It's beyond description. A beast. It knows me, and waits for me here, for it knows I will need to visit this place."

"You mean . . . you have a bogeyman?" You're taken aback. If this guy has a bogeyman, you don't want to meet it. He's weird enough by himself.

He nods, and you see sweat beading on his fore-head. "I suppose I do."

"Let me go in then. I'm used to dealing with bogeymen."

He looks at you, grave, his face gone ashen, and makes no move to argue. All gaiety drains from his face. "One day I will be able to face it," he says as you walk past him and hop over the barbed-wire fence as if you're jumping a hurdle.

You walk across an expanse of crumbling asphalt and push open a rusty sliding door that moans and squeals on ancient wheels. Wincing, you shove the protesting door aside, creating an opening big enough to squeeze through.

Inside, it is so dark you can barely make out several hulking shapes leaning against the walls and scattered around on the floor. You feel along the doorframe for a light switch and find it, flipping it on.

Light chases away the shadows, and you see the hulking shapes for what they are—a pile of juggling pins, a rack of sequined silver and purple lamé outfits that look straight out of a lounge act in Vegas, boxes full of light bulbs and comic books, and an old Model T.

"I didn't tell you what you'll need," the psychic says suddenly from behind you, making you jump.

You turn to face him, watching as he nervously scans the interior of the shed. "Grab that box in the far corner." He points to a large cardboard box, which you walk to. One flap lies open, and inside you can see thread made of sinew, branches, beads, some stones. You close the flap and hoist the box, carrying it back to the Great Transcendental Ned.

"Let's go," he says. "Today is not the day for me to face it."

Together you hurry away from the shed, hopping again over the barbed-wire fence.

"That place was kind of . . . rusty and abandoned," you say, not wanting to hurt his feelings, but curious all the same.

"Yes . . . I have neglected it because of my fear, and it has fallen into disrepair. Kajunro-Mo-Glop says this is not the way to Truth and Being of Light and Geometry, but I cannot help that just now. But this present journey isn't about me. We need to get you back."

A few blocks later, you stop in a grassy park next to a fountain, and the Great Transcendental Ned tells you how to lay out the branches and weave the thread between them to create a web. "When the Night Terror enters the astral plane, he will be drawn to the dreamcatcher. Stay here, next to it, and when he becomes entangled, be still and wait for my image and voice. I will be using a great meteor. Grab onto its fiery tail, and it will draw you back into your body."

You're having serious doubts again. "Did Kajunro-Mo-Glop come up with that?"

"No. It is the work of Huni-ya-ba-tooey, the Sacred Lagomorph of the Between Time."

You're sorry you asked. You don't know if your dream's making this guy totally surreal, or if he's pulling it off all by himself. "But how will I know—"

"You will recognize it," he reassures you.

You don't feel very reassured. "You're leaving, then?" You'd never admit it, but you feel a little nervous setting this up without his input. You hope you'll get it right. You guess you've gotten rather used to someone hovering around, making sure you're not making any mistakes. But if all goes well, soon you will be united with Giles, who certainly fills that role well.

As you pull branches out of the box, you look back to find no trace of the psychic. He's vanished.

It sure would be cool to learn how to do that.

You start weaving the branches together as he showed you, and soon the dreamcatcher takes form, looking more and more weblike. You prop it up against the fountain as you complete it, making it easier to weave the sinew around the back of it.

At last you are finished, and you step back to look at the final product. Pretty impressive, you must admit. It stands nearly six feet tall and as wide, with many long strands of sinew strung between each other.

Now all you have to do is wait for the Night Terror to fall asleep and begin to dream.

You can almost taste the café mocha you're going to sip when you get back. Hell, you're even excited to do your Western Civ homework.

You sit down on the dream grass and leisurely take in the dream world around you. You're tempted to try flying again, or maybe teleporting, but you don't want to leave the dreamcatcher. A huge, beautiful, green dragonfly alights in the grass next to you, its wings glistening in the moonlight.

You're studying the dragonfly so intently that when a loud *thwang* shatters the quiet, you start violently. Following the noise, you find the Night Terror, all seven feet, wings, and horns of him, stuck fast in the dreamcatcher. His narrowed silvery eyes fix on you and he opens his mouth, sharp teeth glistening in the moonlight. "Slayer," he growls. "What have you done?"

It worked! You can't believe it. Just like the Great Transcendental Ned said it would!

"So you're what bad dreams are made of," you say, walking over to the struggling creature.

"This will do you no good," he snaps. "Your astral cord is broken. You're trapped here forever."

"You obviously haven't heard of the Lava Men."

He cocks one eyebrow in genuine confusion.

And then you hear it. A tremendous roar and crackling, coming out of the darkness. Then the Great Transcendental Ned's voice singing, "Hear the call of the lava. See the meteor. Return. Return."

You move toward the sound of his voice, tuning out the anguished cries of the Night Terror behind you. "You'll never get away with this! You'll never get back!"

The farther you walk, the farther away the singing sounds. You keep following it, until you step out into a black void, walking on nothingness. Then you see the great meteor, streaking across the darkness toward you. A gleaming tail stretches out behind it, and as it passes, you grab onto the fiery trail. At an intense velocity you career into the blackness, closing your eyes tight against the brightness of the meteor. Then the light diffuses as the feeling of speed diminishes. Still you cling to the meteor's tail. You slow then, your feet touching down on something soft. You're standing. You open your eyes, bright fiery gold meeting your gaze.

It's lamé.

You're holding on to the Great Transcendental Ned's capelet.

Willow stands next to you, with Giles on the other side, holding on to your arms.

You feel a bit odd.

You're in your room.

"You made it!" Willow cried out, throwing her arms around you. You release the psychic's capelet and hug her back.

"I did?"

"Yes," Giles chimes in.

Xander appears suddenly in your bedroom door, carrying a box of doughnuts.

"Buffy? Is it really you this time?"

"I think so," you say, still trying to adjust. So you made it back here. You're in your actual physical body again.

You look to the Great Transcendental Ned, who is smiling contentedly and shaking Giles's hand.

"What about the Night Terror?"

"He's bound for now. My colleagues and I at the General Occult and Taco Society will be able to think of a permanent solution."

"G.O.A.T.S.?" you ask.

He shakes his head. "No, even goats wouldn't eat him. We'll think of something humane. Maybe send him back to his own dimension."

"Planet X?"

"Oh, no," he says, shaking his head vigorously. "We wouldn't have him there. But you needn't worry about him anymore."

"Thank you, thank you," Giles says, shaking his hand again. "We're so glad to have her back."

You're so glad too. Finally! Everything makes sense. No demons selling lemonade here, just the usual carnal rampages and occasional cat spleens.

You hug Willow again, then Giles and Xander, ecstatic to be home once more.

THE END

With Xander standing near the cage, eyeing Angel carefully, and Willow sitting with a crossbow at a neighboring table, you finally allow yourself to rest. Pulling up a chair by the main table that has held so many Scooby meetings in the past, you sit down, your aching body grateful. How long has it been since you've slept? It feels like a week. Your eyes burn, and your back feels like it's fallen victim to some medieval torture rack.

Giles gathers his jacket and keys and leaves through the side door. You sit there, staring at the thing in the cage, wondering what has happened to Angel, and what sort of thing this Night Terror is. You want Angel back.

The thing in his body paces back and forth angrily, then finally leans against one wall.

"Sure you don't want just to stake him?" Xander offers. "I could watch."

"No, Xander," you say, knowing that even when Angel is in possession of his body, Xander is not a card-carrying member of the Angel Fan Club.

"We'll figure something out," Willow says hopefully, turning to give you a faint smile. You can see your friend is tired too. It is the middle of the night, after all.

Settling back in your chair, you watch Willow's back, her soft hair falling over her shoulders. Then you turn your gaze to Xander, who wears a white rugby shirt, with a solid green stripe across the back and chest, over tan corduroys. He sits down on the edge of one of the small study tables, still staring at Angel.

Then you stare back at the thing in your love's body, blinking the heaviness of sleep out of your eyes. You can't believe Angel is gone. . . . You wonder how to reach him, where he is. As you gaze at the creature in the cage, your eyes grow heavier and heavier, your head leaning forward more and more, and before you can even catch yourself, you nod off.

SLAYER ACTION:
Turn to page 57.

"Well," you begin, brain ticking away at believable excuses. Once again you wish Xander were there. No one can concoct a whopper of an excuse at a moment's notice like Xander, though no one ever believes him. Still, it's funny and distracting, and right about now, with a horde of demons staring at you expectantly, you could use funny and distracting.

The elder demon leans closer to hear you better.

"Well, you see, it was a funny thing, really. I was on my way to buy a sandwich—cucumbers, no sprouts—when I heard this really loud squeaking kind of noise coming from . . . my backpack. So I ditched it"—you imitate the motion—"and found a doohickey inside."

"Doohickey?" the elder demon asks.

"Yeah. You know, like a thinggummy or a whatsit. Anyway, I pulled this thing out, and it started to shake in my hands, so I threw it, and it skittered into the storm drain."

The white-haired demon's eyes grow wider and he creeps a little closer. A collective hush falls over the entire gaggle of winged creatures, the only sound the wind in the dunes.

"So I continued on my way, but suddenly the street buckled up, and this huge worm rose up, the size of "—you struggle for something big, then see the rock spires in the distance—"well, as big as those things!" you say, pointing to them. "And it started to shout."

There your imagination fizzles out with anticlimactic pzzzzz. *What would a giant worm shout?*

"What did it say?" prompts the elder demon.

"GET OUT OF MY DIRT!" you yell, so loudly and suddenly that several of the closer demons startle violently.

"Well, I see," says the elder demon.

"Indeed," says White Hair.

"So I grabbed hold of it and started to fight with it, and then *poof*! Here I suddenly was in this dimension." After a moment you add, "Because it was a dimension-traveling worm."

Again, silence sweeps over the demons. They simply stand, staring, until you can feel the weight of their gaze practically pushing down on you. You struggle to hold their gaze, sticking to your story.

They stand there for close to fifteen minutes. You begin to wonder if you've stunned them into some sort of sleep state or trance. The shimmering heat in this dimension really grows stifling.

Then just as suddenly, the elder gives out a great clearing of his throat and says, "Well, then, we'd better get you back as soon as possible, my dear girl." His thick rubbery lips quiver slightly as he turns, and his eyes are nearly misty with tears. "What an adventure," he says dreamily to himself as he strolls away, with you following. "What an adventure."

You climb down off the dune, your legs sinking in up to your knees. As soon as you hit level ground, all the demons turn toward you, enclosing you in a circle. You have a rather sinister feeling about it, but you try to give them the benefit of the doubt. They begin chanting, singing, and raising their hands skyward, and slowly an electrical charge builds between them, snaking blue-white energy squirming and cavorting in the air.

Your hair pricks on your head as the electrical field grows in intensity. It envelops you, flowing over your hands, arms, legs, then your entire body. You feel the air pulsing and alive with static, and you can taste the acrid flavor of it in your mouth.

A bright pulse shoots out above you, and you feel yourself going up, up, toward the sky, far above the rock spires now, through the clouds, above the clouds . . . now you can see the planet's two moons, blue-purple and ghostly above you.

Then another bright flash and you're falling. Air speeding past you, clouds, then a dizzying view of forests and snowy peaks far beneath you, with the sea approaching fast to the west of them.

Then another bright flash and you land hard, gushing into something soft and cool.

It rebounds, bouncing you back in the air, and finally you land with a solid thump on a carpeted floor. Groaning, you lift your head, seeing your own bed and room, the familiar nightstand and desk. You just bounced off your bed onto the floor.

"Buffy!" you hear Willow cry, and suddenly there are arms all around you, holding you, picking you up. "You're back!"

You shake your head gently, getting your bearings, and see Giles, Xander, and Willow before you.

"The Night Terror!" you say, remembering.

"Gone, forever, Buffy," Giles says. "I worked a banishing spell on it. But . . ." His voice trails off.

"What 'but,' Giles? I hate it when you 'but.' "

He takes his glasses off. Cleans them with his handkerchief. "We tried everything to get you back. Your astral cord had been broken. We knew we were banishing the Night Terror from taking over another victim, but we didn't think you'd ever be able to come back."

You think of the other dimension, of the strange and wonderful winged creatures there, and say, "I had a little help."

THE END

Holding your ruined nose, which is now freely streaming with blood, you turn to flee. But he's too quick. You only manage to run a few feet away before he lands a powerful kick to your back, knocking you painfully to the asphalt.

Catching your breath and getting a mouthful of blood, you turn to regard him as he stands over you, a gleeful look on his vampiric face. You reach inside your jacket and pull out the stake you carry there.

Leaping to your feet, you try to block out the throbbing pain in your neck and face, and bring your injured arm close to your body. If you could get a couple of good blows in, you could stun him enough to make your retreat.

SLAYER ACTION:
Turn to page 118.

ABOUT THE AUTHOR

Alice Henderson has been writing since her father gave her his old Underwood manual typewriter when she was six. From early on she wrote tales of the supernatural, spooking herself as she pounded away on the typewriter in her childhood turn-of-the-century house. She earned her BA in literature and language at Webster University. After working as a writing instructor in the College Writing Center at St. Louis Community College for several years, Alice pursued her lifelong fascination with folklore and mythology at the University of Oregon, earning her MA in folklore.

Her journey then brought her to San Francisco, that dreaming city on the bay, where she worked for Lucasfilm Ltd. There she began writing for video games, both manuals and strategy guides, including the manual for *Star Wars: Galactic Battlegrounds*. Her love of travel to wild places inspired her novel *Insatiable*, which takes place in the stunning backcountry of Glacier National Park. Please visit her at www.alicehenderson.com.